The Haunting Of Black Lake

T. C. BREEN

World Castle Publishing, LLC
Pensacola, Florida
Copyright © T. C. Breen 2022
Paperback ISBN: 9781958336076
eBook ISBN: 9781958336083
First Edition World Castle Publishing, LLC, June 6, 2022.
http://www.worldcastlepublishing.com

Licensing Notes
Cover: Karen Fuller
Editor: Maxine Bringenberg

CHAPTER 1

12 Years Ago

What was I thinking? he asked himself. *How did I get talked into this?*

Troy Kender tightened his grip on the handles of the snowmobile so hard it hurt, and his knuckles turned white. The cold winter air of Black Lake, Michigan, cut along his face, causing tears to well up in his eyes, as the driver, Mitch Hampway, took a hard right.

They had been out in the clearing at their secret spot in the woods. In the spring, it served as their private fishing hole, and in the winter, a place for the two to get away and do as they pleased. There was a creek and a small hill not too far away. It often served as a place for backyard snowboarding, but today they had felt a little more adventurous and taken the snowmobile out. Using the paths that had been made for years, they found themselves deep into the place.

They had been out there for almost an hour, and the few beers that had been slung back between the two of them had just begun to wear off. The liquid courage had gone with it, and the worry had just started to set in for Troy.

You're going to die out here, he concluded. *You're going to die, all because you couldn't just say no.*

The pair had been told time and time again to never race over the lake, period. You could never be too careful with a Midwestern winter. Especially a Michigan one. The seasons were unpredictable. An ice filled lake could thaw out in a matter of days if the weather changed just right...and it often did.

Usually, they listened. Troy's father had even gone to the precaution of showing them exactly how they should claw themselves out if they ever got stuck in a half-frozen lake.

"'Don't panic, and if the worst of the worst were to happen, you make sure one of you gets out...even if there's both of you. Do not go looking to be a hero. Anything else would lead to two funerals, which no matter the circumstances would always be worse than one.'" His father always had a funny way with words and advice. He gave the hard, uncoated truth. The boys listened. They never went onto a frozen lake. They never even tempted that fate — except this winter.

The season had been cold, freezing even, since late October. It had been a brutal winter that started early and had not let up a hair in almost three months, and January had only made it even colder. Troy had still said it wasn't a good idea, but here he was anyways.

He was the timid one, always worried and *always* wrong about the worst-case scenario. Because of this, he often found himself in a situation he did not feel all too comfortable with, but he would willingly go so long as his best friend was by his side.

Mitch had a way that could get Troy to do damn near anything. In fact, he was the only one who was able to do so for the carefully planned and nervous wreck of a sixteen-year-old. And on this very day, they had taken a six-pack of beer and a joint up into the woods and the part of the lake by Mitch's house.

"C'mon." Mitch had said. "We only have another year,

maybe two if were lucky, where we still get to do this kind of thing. Once you put that ring on Becky's finger — "

"Hey. Hey. Let's not get carried away," Troy had replied.

"Hey man, I'm just saying. Everyone knows what happens when you make it out of high school. It's the 'I want a house.' It's the 'I want a ring.' Then it's the 'And I want a baby.' You're a people pleaser, Troy. Everyone says so, even my mom and dad."

"I'm not sure why that's a bad thing," Troy answered.

"I'm not saying it's bad," Mitch defended, then took a hit of the marijuana cigarette. He coughed twice and finished. "I am just saying, people pleaser plus pretty girl makes a ball and chain real fast."

"Whatever you say," Troy said, laughing just a little. Mitch did seem to have a knack for calling the future, though, so he took his suggestion and grabbed the joint for himself before they headed off into the woods.

The pair of young boys had gone out with a pellet gun and had shot the empty cans until that had lost its luster. They sat around for a while, but as it started to get dark, Mitch had thought up a better idea.

It was the middle of January, and Mitch had said there was no way the lake's ice could be any less than eight inches deep. And although the lake was enormous, centering and curving through the town that took its name, it was mostly shallow.

At Mitch's property line, the lake was known to be about six feet deep. That was just taller than Mitch and only four inches taller than Troy. It was already unlikely the ice would even creak from their weight, but even if it did — *even if*, Mitch had said — as long as they did not get totally trapped under the ice, they would be fine.

So, in their drunk and high state, Troy had gone with him.

But now that the substances had lost their flare and Troy began the sobering come down, he was, admittedly, a bit scared...

but that was probably the weed, right? Paranoia was a bitch.

He also assumed he was subconsciously worried about Becky, his new girlfriend, and how she would flip if she knew what he was up to. But if she could party a little, why couldn't he?

And even though all of Mitch's talk about marriage and houses and babies was way too early to carry any weight, he did have *one* good point. They would not have times like this forever. You were only a teenager for so long, and you were only sixteen once...and Mitch had his heart set on the military.

When they graduated high school, Mitch would be gone for at least three years, and that was if he hated it. Sure, he would see him here or there and catch up around the holidays, but it was not going to be the same, and the clock was ticking for the pair of best friends. Moments like these were not going to be around much longer. So, with that in mind, Troy pushed the thoughts away, letting reassurance dance in.

Besides, like Mitch said, the ice is thick enough.

It was freezing, though. Troy had dressed in only a hoodie and some sweatpants. He wasn't one to wear a winter coat.

Mitch was dressed in jeans and a Carhartt jacket, prepared for this kind of thing. He had offered Troy an extra one that they had laying around at the house, along with a large hunting knife. It was for 'just in case something weird happens out in the woods,' or at least that's what he had said as he handed it to him.

Mitch was that kind of guy to come up with a bad idea but remedy it with an odd solution that only made sense with an elaborate backstory and a vivid imagination. That was his redneck remedy way of doing things. Drive over a hopefully frozen lake with a snowmobile, but offer a knife as the grand solution to any problem they may have.

"What exactly would we need a hunting knife for?" Troy questioned.

"Coyotes," Mitch had said, sort of in jest, sort of not. "Or if we happen to get stuck somewhere. I don't know, man, just take it."

Troy had declined the jacket. He had taken the knife, though, sticking it in his sweatshirt pocket. He was paying the price for that now. A jacket would be far more useful in the cold than a sheath knife.

Less dangerous too, Troy thought, as he pictured the snowmobile crashing and the knife stabbing him in the gut through the sheath, blood painting his gray hoodie.

"This is so fucking stupid," Troy muttered to himself as he felt the lurch of the snowmobile.

Mitch hit the gas again, almost causing Troy to fall off the back end of it. He forced himself to let go of his grip with one hand and tap the back of Mitch's shoulder, who only answered with a grin and another gun of the accelerator.

Troy shook his head.

Loosen up! He could almost hear the words come from Mitch's mouth. *Why are you always so uptight all the time?* Troy gritted his teeth and then sighed. As worried as he might be, his friend was probably right. It would do him well to loosen up. At least a little.

"Hey! Look!" Mitch yelled, his voice excited and enthusiastic. He was pointing straight ahead at a snowbank that was the perfect slope for a jump.

Troy looked and felt his heart begin to race. Jumps were not quite what he had in mind tonight, and knowing Mitch, this was going to turn into something he was not prepared for. This was the exact kind of thing he was just imagining would cause this sharp piece of steel to stab him right in the center of the stomach. He could see the news headlines now, "Boy Dies of Knife/Snowmobile Accident!"

But he had just finished telling himself that he needed to

loosen up...this was supposed to be fun, right? What were the odds of a sheathed knife stabbing him? Pretty low, he imagined.

He tightened the grip on the back handles and let his face break out into a smile.

They hit the snow ramp, and Troy felt his heart and throat drop right into his stomach as the snowmobile left the ground.

"Yeehaw!" Mitch screamed as they flew, and although Troy could still feel his stomach drop, the half case of beer threatening to make its way back up from where it sat, he felt exhilarated.

This reinforced the decision to come out here. He loved being around Mitch, after all. Everything was better when it was the two of them. He made Troy a better person, broke him out of his shell, and Troy felt a twinge of gratitude as the snowmobile landed back on the ground.

The snowmobile turned and came to a stop.

Troy instinctively checked to make sure his phone was still in the pocket of his sweatpants. He hated how some pairs, especially the ones he was wearing, seemed to have the shallowest pockets. He had already lost his phone twice that day due to it, and he knew if he lost it out here on the snowmobile, they would be out almost all night looking for the goddamn thing. That would be a buzzkill he would likely never hear the end of.

He was grateful to feel it still in his pocket, somehow.

"Did you see that shit?!" Mitch yelled. "We had to be ten feet in the air!"

Troy shook his head in reply.

"C'mon, that was awesome!"

"Yeah, that was something else," Troy replied, but he could not help the smile coming across his mouth. "I think I need a break, though; my hands are killing me from holding on."

"Really?"

"Yeah, just gimme like fifteen minutes," Troy said as he

unsaddled himself from the back seat and plopped himself into the snow. He wanted a break more for his nerves than his hands, but either way, he wanted a break. And he wasn't entirely lying. His hands *did* hurt.

"Suit yourself. I am going to hit it again. Make yourself useful and take a video for me."

Troy was the resident cameraman for the pair of boys and had just started making it more of a true hobby, which again was from the push of Mitch. He had told Troy for months that he always had the coolest pictures on his camera roll out of anyone in their friend group. He had said that Troy really was onto something.

In the summer before this year, Troy had saved every dollar he earned, went to the local shutter shop, and bought himself a Nikon. Now, with all the practice he was doing with it, there was no escaping his cameraman duties, even if it was just some snowmobile jump on his smartphone.

He did not mind, though. It was a lot less on the nerves to hit record than being on that goddamn snowmobile death trap.

Troy sat and watched from a distance as Mitch revved the snowmobile up and made his way back to the start of the stretch. He pulled out his phone and hit the record button, watching through the camera as Mitch neared the jump.

He was picking up speed, maybe going thirty miles an hour, far faster than he had when Troy was on the back of it. Troy stood in awe, still watching through his phone as he saw the snowmobile hit the ramp and fly. He was at least five feet higher this time around.

Mitch landed smoothly and without a hitch, bringing the vehicle and himself up to where Troy was now standing, skidding to a halt.

"Now that, that was a *fucking* jump! How high was I? I had to be at least twenty feet in the air!" Mitch yelled.

Troy smiled. "We'll call it fifteen."

"No way, way higher!"

"Twenty it is then."

"I think I got this thing up to thirty miles an hour. I wonder how fast it goes."

Troy sat there a second, weighing his options. He did not care much about going that high in the air on the back of a snowmobile. He was feeling a little worn out of adrenaline from his own jump with Mitch already, but he knew he was being baited.

"Tell you what, I'm good on jumps, but this is a good straightaway. Let us see how fast this thing can go," Troy said, making the compromise with himself more than Mitch.

No matter how fast they went, it wouldn't be anything compared to being ten feet in the air, hanging on to some open ride death machine by his fingers, which for the record, barely worked in this cold.

"No jump?" Mitch asked, a little disappointed.

"No jump."

"All right, all right. Hop on then, let us get this thing cruising!"

Troy slipped his phone back into his pocket and unclenched his fists from beneath the sleeve of his sweatshirt. He exhaled on them, which seemed to bring them back to life after the initial burn wore off. He did this two more times and hopped on.

Mitch steered the machine to the back end of the clearing, ten feet from where the trail of the Michigan woods started and revved the engine.

"Ready?" he yelled over the hum.

"Do or die!" Troy yelled back.

Mitch gunned the gas hard, flooring it. The snowmobile leaped forward and began to accelerate, kicking up the snow behind it from the force. Troy had no idea how fast they could get a snowmobile going, but he figured by the wind on his face and how fast they were crossing to the other edge of the lake, they had to be going close to forty miles an hour.

They were almost to the other end, at least eighty percent of the way there when they heard it. Troy's body froze in shock, and he could feel the blood leave his face, travel through his chest, and hit him in the gut before his brain had fully recognized the sound.

It was the first crack. It was hard to hear over the motor, but the second time there was no mistaking it.

"Oh, shit!" Mitch cried. "The ice! It's cracking!"

Troy went wide-eyed and silent, unable to speak as Mitch, the always levelheaded one, pushed the accelerator to the floor and hunched down. While Troy was in a frozen panic, Mitch was doing everything he could to outrun the quickly breaking ice.

Crack. Crack. Crack.

The sound of the ice cracking seemed to bring itself above the roar of the snowmobile in quick sharp bursts that echoed throughout the clearing of the lake. Troy swore he could even hear the rumble and splash of the water underneath them, like the waves of an ocean storm ready to swallow them whole.

Troy looked to his right and then to his left, sweeping the area. It was cracking everywhere, turning into little pieces all around him.

He heard Mitch scream as the snowmobile began to descend. Troy was thrown off balance as the cracks began to swallow the vehicle, like a mouth sucking in air. This was just like his nightmare worst-case scenario had been envisioned.

Troy felt little splashes of it along his face and his freezing hands. He felt his toes submerged under the water first, and then quickly his foot and his ankle as he continued to fall faster and faster into the lake.

The freezing water stung harshly as it traveled up his legs

and his waist. He banged his head hard against something—the snowmobile, or maybe it was the ice, he wasn't sure—and felt himself thrown hard to his left.

This is where I am going to die, Troy thought.

Then only moments later, he was completely submerged in the water. It was almost pitch black when Troy opened his eyes, the coldness of the water burning them so severely he closed them out of impulse. His head had a ringing pain from whatever he had hit it on.

Instinctively he grabbed at his head and gasped, his mouth filling full of water before he closed it, just in time to not choke himself to death.

It was so dark Troy could hardly see anything, only the glimpse and specks of light that came from the moon that peeked through the slabs of ice over top of them.

Do not panic. Do not panic. Do not panic. Troy chanted to himself.

Staying calm was imperative if he wanted to get to the surface, he remembered. Find where you broke through, get to the surface...then kick and pull with everything you got, like your life depended on it. Because it did.

Troy looked around, trying to feel for Mitch, but he had nothing. He turned around and was relieved to see he was there. They were together, which meant they had some time. He figured they probably had a minute's worth of air to find the surface.

Mitch was already swimming to the top, feeling for the gaping hole from where the snowmobile had broken through by the time Troy looked over. It did not take long for them to find it, the light from the sky shining through there far more clearly than anywhere else.

Mitch pointed to the spot and began to swim his way up, with Troy close behind. He was only a few feet away, and within a few seconds, he was almost there himself. He could almost taste the fresh air against his lungs that would bring the relieving feeling of pressure leaving his chest. He felt his hands wrap around the ice slab to pull himself up, and he fluttered his legs, kicking and pulling, almost getting his head to the surface when he felt it.

Something grabbed at his ankle and yanked him down.

Troy felt himself lose his grip on the ice patch and sink down about four inches back into the water. The rush downward began filling his nasal cavity with fluid, causing him to cough, expending almost all the air he had left in his lungs.

Troy looked down to see something, a hand of some sort, with big, long fingers, wrapped around his foot.

He kicked and kicked, partly to kick whatever thing had grabbed him and partly to bring himself back to the surface before his lungs would give in, which was any second now. His efforts so far were futile, though. Whatever had grabbed his leg had a firm hold on him.

Reaching into the pocket of his sweatshirt, he gripped his hand around the handle of the knife Mitch had given him. How it had stayed there amidst the chaos, he had no idea, but he had no time to ask questions.

With a short stroke, Troy pulled it from its sheath, its blade gliding through the water. With one forceful stroke downwards, he plunged the blade as hard as he could through the water into the black mass of a hand with its long claw-like fingers. Troy felt the pressure as he contacted the hand, and immediately it released its grip on him.

Troy's eyes burned greatly, and he could barely keep them open. The only thing he could make out was a cloudy substance within the water, almost blood-like but pitch-black. A pool of it was leaking from where the thing had been punctured.

He was released from whatever had a hold of him moments ago, but in the struggle, he had used valuable oxygen. Troy felt his vision begin to blur, the edges of it fading and closing in on him. He was losing consciousness. He had only a third of his vision left by the time he had grabbed hold of the ice. He grabbed for it, locking his fingers around it, and kicked his head through the water's surface.

He splashed his way out and took a huge, sharp breath of fresh air that burned his throat on the way down, harsher than any whiskey he had ever taken from his father's cupboard. Even still, at that moment, Troy would have taken a fire in his throat for a single ounce of breathable air.

He took a long deep breath and then started to kick and pull, his eyes searching for Mitch.

Mitch was almost surfaced, his upper body out of the water and his lower extremities making progress, when Troy splashed up to meet him.

"Troy!" he yelled, looking back.

"Shit!"

"Kick and pull! Remember, kick and pull!"

Troy watched as Mitch started to pull his core and belly up onto the ice, clawing at it and kicking his legs in unison. Troy turned back to himself and mimicked him. The pressure of the jagged bits of ice cut through his hoodie, and the coldness of the water almost shut him down, but Troy kept kicking.

"There's something down there, Mitch!" Troy yelled through painful attempts at getting air into his lungs.

"What?"

"Something grabbed me. I stabbed it, but it's still down there. We have to get out of here!"

But it was too late. Troy heard the gasp and scream of his friend piercing his ears. He turned in time to see the frightened look of terror on Mitch's face before he was gone, yanked back into the depths of the water.

"Mitch!" Troy screamed! "Mitch! Mitch!"

Troy took a second to gather his thoughts, weighing his options. The words of their fathers came to his mind for just a second; *do not go looking to be a hero,* but the thought only lasted that moment.

Troy took the biggest breath he could and plunged himself back into the ice-cold depths of the lake, his knife still in his hand.

The water burned his eyes even more from the contrast of the night air, and Troy could feel his body beginning to feel the effects of being submerged multiple times. Fighting every urge and instinct that told him otherwise, he opened his eyes wide and began to scan back and forth, searching for Mitch, searching for that Carhartt jacket he had been wearing. But he saw nothing.

He propelled himself downward, making big sweeping strokes with his arms and legs. After three of those strokes, he felt his hands hit the ground, the impact barely registering over the numbness in his limbs and fingers.

The lake was only ten feet deep at its deepest, and that was only in the very center. Mitch's house was where the lake was the shallowest, at six feet or so.

Mitch should be visible, Troy thought. But there was nothing.

Troy spun himself around, taking in everything, searching and searching for any semblance as to Mitch's location. Yet he continued to come up empty handed...and he was running out of time.

That feeling of passing out was coming over him again, the black spots in his vision growing in number, and he felt his chest burn and ache almost as strongly as when he had just fallen in. He figured he had about twenty more seconds at most to get to the surface and try to get oxygen.

Without thinking much of anything but some odd survival instinct in his DNA, he spotted the place where the light was shining through brighter again. It was still just visible through the glossy, dirty water, and he swam to it with everything he had.

In a moment, he was there, and just as his lungs felt like they would give out on him, just as the black spots in his vision closed out entirely, he poked his head up into the night. He took a breath of the oxygen it held.

He sucked it in, coughing from somewhere deep within his chest. He knew he did not have much more time before he would die of hypothermia or shock and that every second he spent in the ice-cold water was another second risking fate. He did what he had been told to do.

There was no way Mitch could have survived being down there that long. There was also the fact that whatever had yanked at him and pulled Mitch down underneath the ice was still out there, lurking. Troy called upon what little energy he had left and brought himself back up to the surface of the frozen lake.

Troy crawled away from the cracks in the ice in fear that he would fall through again, certain he did not have the strength to go through a dive into the water a third time. He rolled over onto his back, allowing himself to breathe and sob.

"Mitch!" he cried, hoping for someone to answer him. Only silence was returned. "Mitch!" he tried again, his words barely making it through. His lungs hurt, and his lips...they were so numb he could hardly speak, let alone cry. He could not feel anything, and he was sure he had frostbite. He figured if he lived through this, they would have to cut off a finger at the very least, if not an arm...if he were not dead. He thought of his hands that would become nothing but a flesh mitt without any metacarpals.

Metacarpals — that was a funny word to Troy. He'd learned it in his high school anatomy elective. It was the scientific word for fingers. *Oh, how it would be funny to see me try to hold a glass of water or carry a lunch tray without any metacarpals! Your anatomy teacher, Mr. Gateman, would he ask you to demonstrate for the class? You and your flesh mitt with no metacarpals? That would be funny, wouldn't it?*

The hypothermia is making you delirious, Troy thought.

He remembered he'd read that somewhere. The cold could get you high with euphoria. That was why those people on Mt. Everest were always found naked. They would feel hot and delirious and would take their clothes off, causing them to die even faster. Troy supposed that was happening to him now.

He thought about how they would find his body in a few days, lying atop the snow. Maybe they would find him lying right above his dead best friend. Maybe he would be naked, like the Everest people. How close he would have been to saving himself and Mitch, but instead, he laid right above him, naked as a jaybird. That thought almost made him give an involuntary and frightened laugh of acceptance.

Troy resigned himself to his fate. He was stuck out here in the cold, which had to be at most in the high twenties, if not a little colder. With the amount of time he had been in the water or felt like he had, he figured he was already on borrowed time. He had no true means of getting out of here. He was sure he had lost his cell phone in the lake.

And besides, Troy thought, *I would not mind death. To die in euphoria like those mountaineers.*

It took what felt like hours laying there on his back sobbing, slowly clenching and unclenching his fingers around the knife he had not let go of. After a while, he tried putting them down his jeans to get some warmth back in them. It wasn't working. It just made his balls freeze.

He was about to close his eyes and give in to the feeling of passing out and dying when he heard it.

His phone. It was ringing. And it was close.

Troy looked over to see that his cell phone was sitting about forty yards away from him, the LED light just shining above where it was sitting in the snow.

It must have fallen out of my pocket when Mitch almost threw me off!

This turn of events gathered whatever spirit was left in Troy. The feeling of hope mustered up every ounce of strength, every piece of his will to live that he had. As he crawled one elbow and knee at a time following the ringing, he said to himself, *Crawl. Crawl, and you may not die here tonight.*

It took him several minutes to get there. He was lucky because the ringing was from an alarm he had set. If it were a call that went to voicemail after the third ring, he would be dead.

No, it was the alarm that saved his life. That meant it was midnight, the time they were supposed to head back to Mitch's. That would never happen again. He would likely never step foot in the Hampway home again. It was too late. Mitch was gone. But this, *this* was his saving grace.

He took a few long exhales on his fingertips, breathing a little function back into them. He swiped until the alarm disappeared. Finding the emergency call icon, Troy tapped at it until it registered his touch.

"911, what is your emergency?"

"My friend and I are out in the woods and fell through the ice. I need help."

"Where are you?"

"The lake. The one by Benson Avenue."

The operator started talking with precise questions, but Troy could not get himself to say anything. He had done all he could, expended every piece of him that was still intact. He felt the feeling of consciousness leaving him, and he could not make out a single word she was saying, let alone answer anything.

He knew he could not hang up. If he stayed on the line, they could track his number, and they would almost certainly fly a helicopter or get a crew out here.

Or, at least that was what he had seen in the movies, which was as good as any scenario he could think of. Maybe they would make it in time, maybe they wouldn't, but Troy had done all he could. He felt himself drift off, and he welcomed it.

CHAPTER 2

Present Day

Troy gripped the steering wheel hard in his hands, concentrating as the rain came down harder and harder. It was making it difficult to see the road, and the pounding of it on his car was drowning out his stereo. It wasn't that he was listening to it anyways, but it was still annoying.

He had only been back in his home state of Michigan for a few hours. Most of that time he'd spent driving on the highway, and a piece of him already regretted this whole trip.

He hated Michigan, and he hated rain.

In fairness, he just hated water in general. It had done too much damage to him in his lifetime already, and he would be damned if he let it get the better of him again. It had already taken his childhood best friend...and his daughter.

Despite the better part of his heart feeling otherwise, Troy drove on, passing turn around after turn around, making his way to good ole Black Lake Township.

He knew this trip would be hard. Everything about it reeked of misery, from the haunting memories of the past to the reason he was going. But that was what you did when your father was dying of cancer. You bit the bullet hard, and you kept on keeping on. Or at least that was what he figured his father would do if the roles were reversed. So that was what he was going to do, or try to, at least.

Louis, Troy's father, had been diagnosed with terminal brain cancer earlier that year. He had been granted a gracious twelve months to live. That had been back in February, which had been around four months ago. Time was ticking, and Troy needed to be there as much as he could, partly for his own sake and partly for his mother's.

Of course, Troy had taken some time off when Louis was diagnosed. He had spent the coin and flown them both out to where he was currently residing in Chicago, Illinois, which, as a teacher, he could barely afford. Although the pay wasn't one of the benefits of being a public school teacher, summers off were, and he intended to spend most of this summer with his father in the *comfort* of his childhood home. Troy figured that was the least he could do for his old man.

Louis had protested, made a bit of a fit in truth, saying it was unnecessary given everything that had happened. He swore up and down that he would not blame Troy if he wanted to fly them out for a few days instead of this elaborate summer trip. Troy almost took him up on that, but when Louis's health had taken an odd and sharp fall (which did eventually come back up some thanks to the advances of modern medicine), Troy had insisted that he stay the summer.

When your father with brain cancer started to lose his mind and see visions, hear voices, and was generally off his rocker, you just got the feeling time was running out.

Although the voices and visions had stopped — that was what his mother had told him a week ago — that clock was ticking like an unregulated metronome playing faster and faster, so you couldn't keep up.

There was another reason Troy wanted to go back home, though he would not admit it to anyone, not even his old man, and in truth, not entirely to himself either. From all Troy was told and admittedly had snooped around for, his ex-wife Becky still lived in the little old house they had bought together. They bought it the summer they had become engaged, which was the summer she had gotten knocked up. That had also been the summer directly after they both graduated from Black Lake High School.

They had not spoken since the divorce, not once.

After the divorce, he had tried a few times. A call on her birthday. Those always went to voicemail by the second ring. A card at Christmas. The occasional email. He had sent her a condolence gift on the first anniversary of Grace's death they had spent apart. That had been the third year after she died. He had given up when it came back unopened, return to sender. He still had that necklace with Grace's birthstone sitting on his dresser. He looked at it every morning.

On the one hand, Troy supposed he did not place the blame entirely on her — in fact, he placed most of it on himself. He was not perfect, and he sure as shit had not handled things like a man, or even well, at all. Not that there was a fucking handbook for losing your seven-year-old daughter to a drowning accident, but he still had not quite forgiven himself for those times. It was like a chipped bone. It hurt like a bitch when it happened, but it was that sharp pain that came from the shrapnel underneath your skin that really made you want to scream.

Troy knew in his heart of hearts that Becky had a right to be angry with him, hate him even, but there was still a part of his mind that wrestled with the idea of them reconciling their differences. He assumed they would never, could never, should never be romantic again, but he still found hope that maybe one day they could tidy up the past. Maybe even have each other as friends. Whatever the hell that even meant.

He still loved her, of course, with every fiber of his being. But Troy knew she could go on, would go, should go on, to marry and mother another child. And as much as it would pain Troy, as much as it would twist the knife that life had placed in his heart, he would be happy for her. The truth was he would even be happy for the son of a bitch that ringed her up because that man would be goddamn lucky to have Becky as a wife and a mother of his child.

Troy sighed and let his grip give a little on the wheel. "Dear God," he said to the empty car. "What are you getting yourself into?"

All this thinking about the past and of Becky had given him a dull headache. He supposed his dad would have advice for a situation like this — that is if Troy gathered the guts to bring this up to him. He wasn't particularly fond of that idea, but hey, his father was the man to go to for life advice.

Louis Kender had always been a hidden gem with consultation and guidance, and the cancer, doom and gloom as it was, had only made the advice far more important to Troy.

So, here he was at the beginning of June, driving to his old hometown in his little car, the only one he could afford, the backseats lined with his three bags. He had two suitcases filled with clothes and one smaller carry-on style bag for his photography equipment. It was the only sort of hobby Troy cared for anymore. He had given it up after everything that had happened, but in the last six months, he had been slowly but surely getting back into the swing of things. Troy supposed it was the whole sentimental thing, with it being the twelve-year anniversary of Mitch's death. After all, it was Mitch who always wanted to see him do it.

"You've gotta take your pictures more seriously," Troy remembered Mitch saying on more than one occasion. "You could really do something with it one day. I mean, really! What if they hung up your photos in one of those five-star restaurant bathrooms? Imagine all the rich, uptight people gawking at your photo of a cow while they take their evening piss!"

Troy would only laugh. "Yeah, maybe one day. But then wouldn't I be one of those pretentious pricks, too?" he challenged.

"Sure. But as long as you take me, I see no real problem with it," Mitch answered. "I could hang around all the rich ladies, find myself a real nice sugar momma!"

Troy laughed out loud, and on the inside, jokes of rich women aside, pondered this and the real life possibility that maybe, just maybe, with enough work, it could be his reality.

But the idea had died when Mitch had.

The rain was pounding even harder now, and Troy flipped his wipers to their max setting, which cleared his vision some, but he still just barely saw the exit sign for Black Lake. He turned off the expressway with a bit of a jerk and onto one of the many backroad streets it would take for him to get to his parents' lake house.

Does everyone here live on a lake? Troy thought.

The question was silly — he'd grown up here, so he knew the answer was yes. Over half the town held some property connected to the town's lake.

That thought annoyed Troy. He *hated* this lake. And he hated damn near everyone that lived on it. Or in the town, for that matter.

Black Lake was a little town. No more than ten thousand people had ever lived there at one time, and that had been when Troy was a kid. Word from his parents was that the place was starting to thin out a good deal, people moving out a little at a time, finding bigger and better places to raise families. Towns with far less catastrophe.

Troy figured those people were the smart ones. Aside from all the misfortune he had experienced in those four square miles himself, along with many others, he had always gotten an eerie sort of feeling about the place. It was like somehow the town itself, or some force within it, had an agenda of its own. And it was a malevolent agenda, to be sure.

Of course, as an adult, Troy knew that kind of thing was bullshit.

A spot in your psyche was rubbed raw and came off the hinges a little when you experienced trauma in your hometown, especially at a young age — or at least that was what he was told after being questioned by the police when Mitch had died.

According to them, he'd had a near death experience which had brought about a hallucination. At first, Troy had not believed it, but eventually, he saw there was no other *reasonable* explanation for what he had seen that night. And considering the alternative option the police had come up with — him actually killing his best friend, even though there was no evidence to show for this — he had accepted the answer.

Ever since that day, they insisted he might have killed his best friend, Troy had hated cops almost as much as he hated that lake.

Either way, he had accepted their hallucinogenic answer. However, that answer had brought about sour feelings that manifested in all kinds of mysterious ways. So, he had always put the thoughts out of his mind. But for some reason, the feeling had come again as he drove through the little back roads. The trees were just a little too cumbersome, the canopy just a little too thick. That was all before mentioning the rain.

Oh God, did it fuckin' rain in Black Lake, Michigan? Troy thought.

Before he knew it, Troy had come to the stoplight and the fork in the road. He remembered this fork all too well. To the left was Mitch's parents' home, where he had spent many days and nights as a kid. He remembered the place fondly, even if he felt a stab of grief hit him, taking the air out of him like a good punch to his mid-section.

After Mitch had died, Troy and Mitch's parents had not spoken much. A call on the occasional holiday was about it, and it had been next to nothing since he had left.

To the right lay the way to his parents, with his dying father. Both choices seemed like the short end of the stick.

Troy sat at the fork. He had not made up his mind if he would make an effort to seek the Hampways out yet. He wanted to; Mitch's parents had been much like his own parents in those teen years. But losing communication had left a bit of a sting on what he had assumed would be both their ends.

Maybe they hate me? Maybe they always did. Troy wasn't sure, but he could not bring himself to find out the answer, so the silence became the more comforting option.

He sat at the light a moment waiting, his left blinker on. He ought to go see them, he knew, but this trip would be hard enough. The Hampway's house was close, though he didn't have to make the trip today necessarily. He could make it another time when he felt a little more prepared.

On the other hand, he weighed that if he didn't do it now, there was a good chance he would go the whole summer without doing it at all.

There was already one place in his parents' house he was going to have to come to terms with—the backyard and the lake where Grace had died—and maybe meeting up with the parents of his deceased friend would be too much?

The light turned green. Troy sat a moment, conflicted, a mix of emotions coming over him. He checked his rearview mirror, behind him being empty, which was no surprise for this time of day in a small town.

His mind weighed the options back and forth. Troy let out a heartfelt and painful sigh.

"Choices, choices," he muttered before he finally flicked the blinker to the right and turned an illegal turn from the left-hand turn lane to his old home. He supposed time would tell what he would do, but today would not be the day he would visit the Hampways.

It was only a few seconds before he saw the flashing circus of blue, red, and white lights behind him.

"Just what I need too, a ticket on my first day back home. Icing on the cake of my negative trip—or, to be even more melodramatic, my negative life," Troy said softly to no one but himself. *Maybe I should stare at these lights until I have an epileptic seizure, just to really drive the point home that I do not want to be here.*

Troy pulled over and put his hazards on. He leaned over, grabbed his license and registration, lowered the window, and turned down his radio. Mitch's father, Dan, had been a cop, and Troy had picked up on how to try and avoid a ticket where he could.

It took a long while for the officer to get out of the car, which Troy found to be mildly annoying. When the man dressed in sheriff's attire approached his window, Troy addressed him kindly. He did know his way around law enforcement by now, after all.

"Afternoon, Officer," he said.

"License and registration. No games," the man replied flatly, barely above the ambient sound of the rainstorm.

"Yeah, right," Troy replied, handing him the paperwork. As he grabbed it, Troy noticed the name on his tag. *Moth. An asshole sheriff with a weird asshole name. Nice.* And then, the officer turned and went back to his car.

He sat in his car awhile, Troy assumed, maybe to avoid the rain that had been coming down. When he finally returned, he handed the stack back to Troy and just looked at him, inspecting him even, before he finally spoke.

"Sir, I need you to step out of the vehicle," the man asked.

"What? Why?" Troy responded.

"Mr. Kender, get out of your vehicle, hands where I can see them," the man said. When Troy took a second to respond, the officer continued, "Now. Are you deaf?"

Troy stepped out of the vehicle.

"Illinois? What brings you out here to a small town like Black Lake?" His voice was low and rather irritable for such a simple question.

"Dad's sick. Visiting for the summer." Troy, having no more patience for playing the ticket game himself, gave back the same tone. "What's the reason you had me get out of my car exactly?" Troy could feel his shirt already soaking and clinging to his skin.

"That's so?" the officer said, avoiding his question. This guy seemed to think he was in an interrogation room rather than a routine traffic violation.

Troy nodded his head. "Uh. Yeah."

"All right. Well, I will get to it then. You know why I pulled you over. You cannot kitty cut lanes like that. If you are in the left lane, you turn left. If you are in the right lane, you turn right, no excuses and no exceptions. You've got a clean record, so I'm letting you off with a warning, but don't let me see it again."

"Won't let it happen again," Troy replied. "Why did you pull me out of the car? I have a right to know."

The officer nodded. "That you do. C'mon this way," he said, walking to the back end of Troy's car. He pulled out his baton with a whack and pointed it at the sticker on his license plate. "Were you aware of these expired tags, Mr. Kender?"

"Oh. No, no, I wasn't. I guess I must have missed it. Haven't been paying much attention to my alerts in the mail," Troy replied, feeling defeated.

The officer lowered his voice to just above a whisper.

"Well, I'll tell you what, Mr. Troy Kender. You best start paying attention in this town. There just might be someone out there looking to find you, and they might get you by surprise if you aren't." Officer Moth clicked his tongue in his mouth before finishing, "Do I make myself clear, boy?"

Troy nodded, now feeling a bit intimidated by the officer, who was standing there with his baton in his hand, gently smacking it into his other open palm.

"Then you best get back in your little shitbox and be on your merry way. And put your goddamn seat belt on. I'm sure you have a daughter or a wife or someone that cares about you other than your dying father, so put it on."

"Right. Yeah," Troy said and got into his car. Mentions of family had lost their initial burn these days. When every student prodded into your life story and if you had kids and a wife, or whatever your story was, you eventually just got used to it. People didn't have boundaries anymore, especially kids. So, Troy swallowed it down as he got into his car. He clicked his seatbelt into its holder in front of the officer for good measure.

"Now, I'm giving you a good warning here. You don't be all out causing trouble during your stay. The locals, they are quiet folk with a lot of…misfortune these last few years since you abandoned this place for some fancy, pretentious windy city in Illinois. Frankly, I think you've got a lot of nerve coming back here after what you did as a kid. A lot of nerve. So, you best be on the lookout and on your best behavior, or I'll have to be around to make sure you never have another chance to come back to this town. You read me?"

Troy was more than a bit thrown back. Abandoned this town? Fancy and pretentious? Didn't the same guy just call his car a shitbox?

Am I pretentious or trash? Was the question that flew through his mind, but he knew better than to say it aloud. He wasn't sure where in Chicago this man had visited, but the neighborhood that held his one bedroom apartment was anything but pretentious.

Troy also wasn't sure any of this was legal, let alone proper protocol. In fact, he was sure it was not, but he exhaled the thought.

"Yeah. No trouble from me. Just read the GPS wrong. Sorry."

"Good day to you, Mr. Kender. Oh, and my condolences for your father. And your daughter," the officer said, then turned and left.

Troy sat in his seat a minute, a little perplexed and frankly frustrated by the odd encounter. It was not like he had the exact protocol for a routine traffic violation, but he was sure something was broken in this experience.

He guessed that was just what happened when you became the sheriff of a small town—your ego went crazy. He wondered if Mitch's father had met this guy yet and if he thought he was as big of an ego man as he seemed to be. Maybe Mitch's Dad, who was a cop last he knew, had run into this guy, and he made a mental note to ask him about it.

And then something hit him—he'd never mentioned Louis was dying. He said he was sick, but he did not say he was dying, did he? And he certainly did not mention Grace, nor had he mentioned anything about his history with Black Lake.

He pushed the thought away as he turned back onto the road. The cop must know Becky, and that was why he accused him of abandoning his hometown and his ex-wife. It was a small town, and there was a good chance they knew each other. Maybe they were even friendly, or more than friendly. And that idea brought up a whole lot of divorced but still territorial paranoia that Troy promptly pushed out of his head.

None of that is your business anymore, Troy, you know that, he said to himself. He wondered if every man in his situation went through this same kind of jealous thing when they went back home. They probably did.

As for his father, no one comes home to visit their parents from halfway across the country for a common head cold or stomach flu.

Of course, the guy assumed his father was dying, and he was, after all. No, what was weirder was why the guy was such a peculiar prick about the whole thing.

Does he know me? Maybe we went to school together. Does he remember what happened with Mitch? Maybe he thinks I did it, Troy's mind whispered.

In a way, you did. You got out, and he didn't. You could have said —

You're doing it again, Troy. Like they tell you in group: you can't keep reliving the memories of the past, waiting for a new outcome. Give it a rest and go see your dad, he thought to himself.

The final road that led to his parents' place was a dirt one, and it blended in splendidly with the thick wood that seemed to be a part of every small town in the Midwest. Troy, having not been back to his folks' home since before his divorce, almost missed it entirely. Or maybe it was that uneasy and nervous feeling he had in his stomach ever since he had turned onto the exit.

He wasn't sure what it was, though he knew he had plenty of reasons as to why he would feel this way. But he couldn't chalk it up to one in particular...well, other than the obvious one of being pulled over and then berated.

His parents' house was an older one, tucked behind the old winding road that was dotted by trees, though not entirely worthy of being called a forest. The nearest neighbor was close enough to hear a yell but far enough that general conversation and play would not be overheard.

It was Troy's childhood home, and the property it sat

on had been the land of make believe for Troy and his friends, especially Mitch, back when they were just kids. They had spent hours and hours running amuck in yards and surrounding woods, which abounded in the small town. Then, during the summers, as older teenagers, they would often have girls come over, Becky being one of them, to take a swim in the lake.

The lake.

Troy had promised himself that he would do all he could to avoid that lake for as long as he could stand. It was too much— too early. The thought of the place sent a sorrowful chill up his spine as he struggled to swallow down the memory.

He was here for his father, and he needed to remember that.

Troy had spent his entire life since he moved to Chicago being single and teaching out in his new school district that had taken a chance on him...which was hard to get when you quit mid-school year with no notice. The principal who had hired him had a son who had died when he was young, nine, Troy remembered, only a few years older than Grace. He had sympathy for Troy. He had said no one ever deserved that kind of pain and gave him the job even with his spotty work record.

He had been given an opportunity, a second chance. He wasn't going to let his stay at his father's house, or his father's approaching death even, sink him back down into the spiral of depression. He would prove to himself this summer that although things had been hard, his heart had been broken, he was starting to pull himself back together. He was almost back to fully functional. He was...moving on, whatever the hell that meant.

When he came to the end of the drive, he threw his car in park and stepped out. He took a moment to take it all in, breathing the cool fresh air of Michigan's beautiful Upper Peninsula. It was much better than the kind of clustered and sharp air that a big city brought you. Out here, he could hear the birds chirp and leaves rustle. He had missed that feeling from a small town, and he hated to admit that he may even have missed the feeling of Black Lake.

Troy walked over to the front door of the home, glad to see it had not changed much at all since he was last here. He had always liked the look of the quaint little place.

He knocked on the door twice and waited, looking down at the concrete porch. He still felt nervous, though he had no idea why.

Probably just being back here, he thought to himself.

In no time at all, the door opened, and he was greeted and embraced by his mother, Tracy Kender. She was a short, slender woman who seemed well aged for her fifty-two years of life.

"Oh, Troy. Thanks for coming," she said as she wrapped her arms around her son's shoulders.

"How is he?" Troy asked in a low voice, returning the embrace.

"He's doing better. He wasn't doing well a few weeks ago, but he seems to have rebounded, by some grace of God."

"That's good, Mom. Really good. Any news on any of the doctors you were trying for?" Troy asked.

Tracy lowered her voice. "Don't mention this to him—Louis will have my head if I tell anyone. But in Marquette, only a few minutes' drive from that apartment we bought when Louis retired, there's a good hospital. You remember Marquette, right?" she asked.

Troy nodded again. Marquette had been a place frequented by his family in his youth. The apartment his mother referred to was one they had bought as a sort of getaway. It made sense given how often they went to the big city when Troy was a teenager (though Troy knew this was all Tracy, and Louis only went to please her. For whatever reason, he loved this old town).

"Well, the Marquette hospital is having clinical trials for your dad's condition. I opted him in. They have to screen and test him down here, then if he passes that, he'll be opted in for this new medication that's supposed to help with his episodes," she continued.

"Well, that would be great. I hope that works out. How does Dad feel about it?" Troy asked.

"Your father is being your father. You know how stubborn he is. He wants nothing to do with it, I can tell, but he's going along with it for me. I think he thinks he won't have a chance in hell being as sick as he is, but I've been praying. Oh, I have been praying every night."

Troy nodded. He was not particularly a fan of this God character that his orthodox religious mother had always gone on about, but he knew better than to speak it in her home and bit his tongue.

Besides, he did hope this clinical trial went through, at least for her sake. He knew the feeling of a guilty conscience and wanted no part of that to be passed on to his mother if she had any regrets when his father died.

So, let her get him into the trials and let her pray if it eases her mind.

"Tracy? Who is it? That Troy?" he heard his father call from somewhere in the house.

"Remember, not a word," she whispered before resuming her normal volume and conversation. "Come in, come in. Your father is just in the kitchen making dinner. I hope breakfast for dinner is still one of your favorites."

Troy laughed a little. It was the Sunday tradition of the family; Sunday was always breakfast for dinner. It had extended all the way to his own family, where at least three Sundays a month, Troy, Becky, and Grace would go over to his parents', and Louis would be slaving away at the stove *and* griddle.

Louis would go so far as breaking a mighty sweat making eggs, pancakes, bacon, hash browns, and the like.

As Troy walked into the kitchen, the first thing that hit him was the familiar smell of food. It was delightful, and he took a moment to take it all in. The smell of his father's cooking brought back a certain nostalgia. Troy clung to it; it was the first decent thing he'd experienced since he had gotten in the car to drive out here. Maybe even before that.

"Troy!" his father called.

Troy looked to his left to see his father setting the kitchen table with three plates and a heaping pile of food on each. His father, who he had not seen since the last visit when he flew them out to Chicago, looked more worn and weathered than he remembered. His once thick head of hair was completely missing, and his skin looked aged and almost had a gray hint to it. He looked every bit the part of a man who was suffering from terminal cancer, but his voice, as Troy would have expected, held no similarity in its tone. It was the same confident one he had always had, which was now in stark contrast to his meager body.

"It's good to see you, Dad," he said as he embraced the old man. It was now that he could feel how much weight his father had lost. By his best guess, it was probably somewhere around another twenty or thirty pounds, which was on top of the previous twenty or so pounds he had lost. Another person would be depreciated completely, but Louis was still hanging in there. His father, who had been an avid fitness junkie, was reaping the rewards of his prior fitness lifestyle.

"Ah. I am glad you could make it, though I will still say you shouldn't have. I could have flown out again, Troy. You did not have to come back here. Back to this town or this house," his father said grimly.

"I'm here for the summer, Dad. And I knew there was no way in hell you'd leave this old town for any more than a week...

and even that would be a struggle," Troy replied.

It was true—this town had a hold over Louis that Troy had not quite been able to put into words. The only way he could really describe it was that feeling he had when he had driven into town. It sank its hooks in you and kept you there for all it was worth.

"You're probably right. At any rate, I am glad you are here, Troy. It means a lot," his father said, still gripping his hand. Troy saw the glimmer of tears develop in the corner of his eye, the first Troy had seen of its kind since Grace had died. His father blinked it away quickly.

"Of course, Dad."

"Well, I suppose that's enough of that. The food is ready," Louis said, and motioned to the table. They all took a seat and ate.

Chapter 3

Dinner had been every bit as good as Troy remembered. He had eaten two servings of everything they had and just barely denied a third when his mother had asked. He only got out of it by promising he would eat it in the morning to not let it go to waste, insisting that he was exhausted from the car ride. He still felt that wave of exhaustion and tension from when he had driven in.

He was staying in the room he had when he was a kid, upstairs and just down the hall from his parents' bedroom. The mattress, along with many of the things in there, was the same, untouched since he had lived in the house.

Troy had spent the better part of an hour tossing and turning in his bed, trying as hard as he could to fall asleep, but with little success. Finally, he gave in and looked at the clock that, at one time, woke him up every morning for school. It read 9:57 P.M. That was not particularly late for Troy. He was used to sleepless nights, so he hopped himself out of bed, careful not to disturb his sleeping parents.

He climbed down the stairs quietly, still remembering which ones creaked when you stepped on them too hard. When he got to the bottom, he slipped his sneakers on and opened the front door.

Troy was surprised to see his father sitting on the top step of the concrete porch, a six-pack of beer sitting to his right. He was puffing on what was likely a very expensive cigar. The deep aroma of the natural tobacco filled Troy's nose. It reminded him of simpler times.

"Didn't know you were still up," Troy admitted.

"Restless night?" Louis answered, turning back to the thin woods in front of him.

"Yeah, something like that. You think you should be smoking that? You got cancer, you know," Troy said, pointing to the stick in his hand.

His father gave a small chuckle. "I sure do. Sounds like a reason to have a few more, doesn't it?"

Louis motioned for him to sit on the concrete step next to him and offered him a few beers. Troy accepted and sat himself down next to his father.

"So, still spending your nights out on the porch?" Troy asked.

"Every one. Though I think now I have some company," Louis replied.

Troy raised his eyebrows, questioning what he meant.

"Coyotes have been coming around these days more and more," Louis said. "Maybe cougars. Soon we will have the wolves and the bears from the next town over."

"You see any?"

"No. I just hear 'em. Sometimes they howl, but mostly I just hear them wandering out there. They are quiet, but if you listen hard enough and long enough, you start to notice it. You start to notice a lot of odd noises. I swear, sometimes I even hear them cackle, like they're laughing. Laughing at me, probably."

Troy gave a puzzled look over at his father again, who had his eyes closed and seemed to be listening intently. Troy did the same, trying to hear what his father was talking about. He opened them empty handed.

"Ah, but what the hell do I know? I am just an old man. I can't hear shit anymore. Half the time, I feel like I am hearing voices that are not even there at all. Probably losing my mind." The pair laughed together at the remark, Troy knowing how true that had become only a few short months ago.

Troy and Louis were sitting on the front porch comfortably, drinking freely from the case of Bud Light that sat between them. It had always been their ritual after the Sunday night dinners, though in the past, it was on the back deck. Troy was not sure if his father had been expecting him and sat out on the front porch as a courtesy or if, after the accident, he had switched his ritual altogether.

Either way, Troy had been grateful when he walked out and saw his father there. It reminded him of a time far away in his teens and early twenties when he still lived in the small town. Some of these times were before Troy had graduated high school, though Troy and his father were sure to keep that under wraps from Tracy. She would've gladly put a ban on alcohol in the house if it wasn't for Louis's standing on traditions.

The pair had been out there for quite a while, Tracy having already gone to bed shortly after Troy had left to try to do the same. The sky was alive and bright with starlight, and the two found themselves enjoying the silent company as much as the conversation.

After a particularly long spell of quiet from both of them, the only noise being the sound of crickets chirping their legs or the occasional coo of a bird, his father spoke what was on his mind.

"They say I've got about eight months left," Louis said. His voice was not broken or filled with self-pity but rather a simple, frank understanding of the future.

"You look damn good for eight months left," Troy replied.

Louis gave a big hearty laugh. "You should tell your mother that! Woman will not let me do a damn thing without being up my nose about it." Louis sighed. "God bless her."

"You think they're right? The doctors, I mean."

"Oh, I have no right to be questioning a medical professional," his father said in a playful sort of voice. "I suppose they might be, but I suppose they could be wrong. I may die in eight months. I may not. It will depend on what the good Lord thinks is right."

Troy nodded. His father had never been a religious enthusiast, but he attended church services with Tracy every Sunday. He had always been insightful and had always believed in a higher power, but many years ago, in another conversation not unlike this one, Troy had asked his Dad if he believed in a man that sat on a throne in the clouds. His father had answered, "I know what I know, and I know what I don't."

But at the same time, clinging to religion was a normal thing to do when people were staring death in the face. Troy figured it wouldn't be too far of a stretch to say his father had done the same in recent times.

"Are you handling it okay?" It was a dumb question, to be sure, but Troy did not know what else there was to really say to a dying man.

"Okay? More than okay, I think. I accept fate for what it is. Life, death, it is all about the cards you play while you are holding the hand. And me, Troy? Well, I have held a full house for a long time now. Sure, we've had some hard times. But in the end, in the same way, I can say it hasn't been easy. I can also say I have been blessed more than I deserve. Don't you think?"

Troy nodded. "I suppose if you look at it in the perfect lighting, it's true."

"Ain't nothing to do with lighting. I've got your mother. I have you. I had a beautiful granddaughter for a short while."

Louis paused. Grace's death was a painful reminder for everyone, his father included. "Son, I'm really happy you made it down here. You know I wouldn't have thought less of you for not wanting to come back home."

"Yeah...well, at some point, I need to accept fate for what it *was*, don't I?"

"I suppose you might be right on that one — *if* it's true, that is," his father replied, and took another sip of his drink. Troy took one from his as well. He was being honest, but keeping things from his father was not something he was ever skilled at, and he sighed quietly.

"I'm worried about Mom, too."

"I suppose you might very well be, and good on you for it, son. But you did not drive all this way to watch a grown woman care for a dying man, did you? At Grace's funeral, she was the only one who could keep it together. My brain is dying, but it has not failed yet. There is another reason you came here. And it does not offend me any, but I am curious as to what it might be that finally got you back down to this place, and more so, why you feel the need to hide from it."

Troy shifted himself uncomfortably on the step of the porch a little. His father could always read him. It made him feel uncomfortable in a way like a vulnerable child getting called out for his secret keeping. Troy supposed he was not going to be keeping it a secret from anyone, including himself, for very long. He had been here for only three or four hours, and his father could see right through him.

"If it doesn't offend *you* that I ask, that is?" Louis said again. It was just like his father to do this too — to kindly, innocently, break into his thoughts.

"I don't know. I guess...." Troy paused to take another sip of his beer. Louis sipped his and took a puff of his cigar. "I guess I was hoping that at some point in the three months I was here, I might run into Becky."

His father nodded in return, only waiting for a continuation like he had known this all along. Which, it was likely, he had. Louis had probably known before Troy even knew himself, or at least that was what Troy presumed.

"It's not like I'm thinking I'll be able to sweep her off her feet, and we'll be able to forget the past and everything that happened. But I just wish we could be…friends? I don't know. We lost a kid together and hating each other, or her hating me, has only added insult to injury."

His father nodded.

"Sounds pathetic, doesn't it?" Troy asked. "Can't let her go. Even after all of it. I probably sound like a horror film stalker."

"I'll tell you what, Troy. I know what I know, and I know what I do not. I don't know nothin' about women—that much has always been clear to me. I lost a granddaughter, but I do not know anything about losing a child or a wife, and I make no try at being a pretender. But I will tell you this—fighting for what you love is never pathetic. If it were, we would not fight for anything. The world may have more peace, but it would be without meaning."

Louis stopped again to take another sip from his can, and upon it being empty, he set it back down, more than a little disappointed.

"I'm not as old as I should be to be this tired. I'm going to have to get going up to bed, but I'll leave you with this: She'll come around, or she won't. It depends on what the good Lord thinks is right. But there's no shame in giving it your best shot, so long as you're watching out for the signs the good Lord is giving you."

"As usual, you're probably right."

"Was that the only thing?"

"I suppose there is something else, though I'm not sure

how I feel about it."

Louis paused, waiting patiently, allowing Troy to dissect his own thoughts.

"Mitch's parents. They, uh…we used to keep in touch a little. Round the holidays and that. His sister, Lucy, too. Last I saw them was at Grace's funeral, but since then, I have not heard a word. Not sure if there was something I should do since I'm here anyways."

This time it was Louis's turn to shift a little uncomfortably in his seat. "I suppose you didn't hear?"

"No. I haven't heard anything."

"I should have assumed as much. We kept it under wraps — the people of Black Lake. The word in town was it was a psychotic break."

"What happened?" Troy asked.

Louis swallowed hard, his Adam's apple bobbing up and down uncomfortably, like a man who tried to swallow back the words that were coming. But the words, they would not go down.

Louis cleared his throat before he began.

"I hate to be the one to break this news to you. Mitch's father, well…." Louis took a moment to word himself carefully. "It seemed like, from everything we heard, Mitch's father went off the rails. Something broke loose, and he…well, he killed them. Both. Lu, that's what Tracy and I called Mitch's sister. She had to have just turned nineteen, maybe. She was going to some university college in Marquette. She was gone most of the time, but she still came home on the weekends, most of them anyway. Working on being a nurse, she was. Lucy, she had a bright future, she did. Dan…Dan shot her first. Then his wife. He shot her too."

There was a silence that was broken only by Troy's hard breath. Troy knew what something like losing your son could do to a person. In his own way, he knew about going off the rails.

"Damn shame, it is. Him and I had become friends. Him

and Lori, they had come over once a month or so. They brought Lucy every so often when she was home. She asked about you a lot. Think she still had one of those little sister crushes on you if I had to guess."

Louis paused again before saying, "After everything with Mitch, he had a real hard time. He attempted suicide. Damn near died, he did. He had been knocking on death's door. He lived, but he was never the same. A few weeks later, he started looking into the other deaths of kids in this area. Adults too, but mostly the kids. You know, there have been a lot of them here. At first, he said it seemed like there had been a mistake in Mitch's death, that there was more to it. We kept that from you. Maybe we shouldn't have, but at the time, we didn't want to drag you through it again. You had just moved, just gotten back on your feet. It just didn't seem right. I don't think it was right to keep it from you now, but then…well, we thought differently."

Louis sighed and drank and then continued. "Was just after you left that he started saying things about how they were all connected—the deaths, I mean. Guess he thought there was a conspiracy or a cover-up. Maybe a serial killer, I dunno. We talked about it a lot. Well, he talked, and I listened. It got worse as time went on, like an obsession he had. At one point, he even tampered with his own evidence. That was when they terminated him. That was when it went from bad to the unthinkable. He started drinking…a lot."

Troy sat his weight back and took another long sip of his drink. It was a moment before he spoke, debating whether he should ask the question. After another sip, he cleared his throat. "Then what happened?"

"He…I guess he took them down to the lake where Mitch had died and shot them with his shotgun. He shot himself right after. They found their bodies lying in the lake face down a few days later when Dan didn't call into work."

"This town has seen some black days," Troy said. "That's awful to hear."

"It was. We should have told you, your mother and I, but for some reason...I guess we just didn't. *Couldn't.*"

"It's all in the past now," Troy replied.

"I suppose it is. I'm sorry no less," Louis said, standing to his feet. He grabbed his empty beer can and turned to leave. Before he stepped back into the house, he clapped Troy's shoulder. "It hasn't been fair for you—life, that is. I am not sure how you do it, not letting those demons in. You're a better man than me, I think."

And with that, Louis turned and left.

Troy sat on the porch with just himself for a while, letting his mind absorb and work through the news he'd just heard. *Went off the rails. Off the rails. He shot them with his shotgun. He shot himself right after.* The phrases kept replaying in his mind over and over again as little pieces of his imagination played the scenario out in his head. When the gun went off, and he saw Lucy lying dead in the water, he halted himself.

Stop. No more.

He closed his eyes again, waiting and listening for the howl or whatever his father had tried to describe, anything to take his mind off the morbid movie in his head, but all that returned seemed normal, at least to Troy. The crickets chirped as they always had, and nothing seemed out of place. There was only the occasional snap of a branch, and he had an odd sensation come over him. Like there was something there that he couldn't see, but it could see him. Like a pair of eyes watching him, analyzing him in the dark.

He brushed it off as the consequence of working through the news he had just heard and set his can on the porch next to him.

After some time, Troy felt the exhaustion of the night's

story, and his trip begin to wane on him, leaving the eerie feeling behind. He shook himself, ridding his brain of the last bits of the fragmented imaginary film of Dan Hampway killing his family, before grabbing what was left of his trash and turning to go inside. Just before he did so, he turned one last time to get a glimpse of the tree line, the feeling of being watched almost gone, but not entirely.

From the corner of his eye, he saw the rustled movement of something leaving the trees for the shelter of the thicker woods, the small fleeing noises causing him to startle just a little. When he turned his full attention to where it had come from, though, all trace of it was gone.

"Coyotes," Troy whispered as he walked inside.

CHAPTER 4

A summer week went by with no incident. Troy had spent much of his time idling in and out of the house, making his way to the little downtown sector of the town. It was a good spot for taking pictures he figured he could sell to some side project, or whatever else, for a few hundred bucks. It wasn't much, but it housed a lot of joyful memories from his early days, and he enjoyed reliving them. The pictures came out good enough for their intended purpose.

He had met up with a handful of friends on separate occasions to chat and catch up at the local restaurant or small-town bar and grilles. It wasn't anything special, but it filled the later hours when his parents were out about their own business. In the week Troy had been at his old home, his father already had a doctor's visit, which bore similarly non-conclusive news. It was spreading. It was slow, but the disease was still moving its merry way along, and any day now, Louis would start to see the effects of it rising again. Memory loss, mood swings, odd sensations, dizziness, a loss of equilibrium, even loss of eyesight, and the potential for the return of small hallucinations had all been mentioned, though none of these were a guarantee.

The silver lining for these appointments was that he was

still currently eligible for clinical trials in Marquette. There were a few more tests that needed to be done and a few more meetings, but Tracy was glad they were getting closer. Louis was not so pleased with the news and left for the garage.

Louis wasn't working, at least not in an employed sense, due to his condition, but he was often out in the garage working on various projects — namely his truck. It was his stress reliever. He had driven it to its breaking point, fixed it, and repeated that cycle for damn near twenty years. Troy spent much of his time out there with his father, who seemed to enjoy the company.

Tracy worked her normal shifts at the local knitting store. It was a small place, maybe eight hundred square feet, and the kind of business that only survived in a small town like Black Lake, where the older women population had idle time and craved companionship. It seemed to suit her, and it kept her busy enough. Louis later told Troy that she had picked up extra hours when he had to stop working...and that he had been stashing away cash, along with his life insurance policy, so she would be taken care of when he finally kicked the bucket. Troy only nodded in return, not having grown accustomed to the idea of his father's inevitable passing or his rather laissez-faire attitude that was coming along with it.

The next Sunday came and went much like the first, though he had woken up late in the house alone, only greeted by a note on the dining room table.

> *Took Dad to another appointment in Marquette. Might be a while. Call you when we are on our way home. Pray for the best!*
> *Love, Mom*

Troy nodded to himself. This was good news. A third appointment meant he had passed stage one of screening — or at least that was what his mother told him last time they had spoken about it. This was not often, considering they always had to do it outside of Louis's earshot.

Troy, for the first time since he was a kid, said a silent prayer for his father that he would make the qualifications for these clinical trials.

Troy walked around the house aimlessly for a while, being careful to avoid the back half of the house, which he had been successful at doing since his arrival. He had an unspoken agreement with his folks. He didn't want to see the place Grace had died, not yet anyways, and they had been kind enough to accommodate that so far, or at least Troy thought so, figuring it wasn't by chance that he hadn't had to go into the kitchen for the entire week.

He went back to his room and figured he would try and wait it out. Waiting around aimlessly to hear his father's news was driving him mad, however, and soon enough, he found himself digging through his old things.

Finding his old boxes in the closet, ones he had left at his parents' place after the divorce, seemed like a good enough task. Between these boxes and whatever Becky had sitting in her attic — or more likely had thrown away — he had seven years of his life that he hadn't seen in two, sitting in cardboard around the town.

Troy opened them up, looking through them to kill time, starting with the biggest first. The first and second boxes were filled with old books and DVDs, a few items of clothing, and a handful of wrestling medals he had won.

That reminded him of his father. Louis had wrestled, too. At one point in time, where that rusty old truck sat, they'd had a small set of wrestling mats. Louis and Troy would spend many hours drilling moves. It was no wonder Troy had been only a few matches short of being a great. He still remembered how Louis had been to every match — every single one, even those out of state tourneys in Ohio and Illinois. He would always be there, sitting as close as he could, screaming his head off. Those times out there in the garage and those long Saturdays with just his team and his dad were some of Troy's favorites.

Troy sighed. He wondered if, in his father's current state, he could yell like that if his life depended on it. He was so frail now. Far from the man that had come to every match and far from the man that had been able to toss him around the garage.

The third box was smaller and lighter, not much bigger than a shoebox. Troy ripped the tape free, lifted the top, and removed the packing paper to find something that made his heart leap but also sink at the same time.

There were notes and another even smaller box inside. Troy remembered them well. He opened the little box to find the watch Becky had gotten him for their one-year dating anniversary still sitting in its case, untouched from the last time he had worn it.

It was a rather expensive little thing for a teenager to give their high school boyfriend. It was simple but well made. Nothing flashy, but high quality. Troy loved that watch. So much so that he'd had to leave it behind because, to him, it represented those better times too well.

That year Troy had gotten Becky a necklace. He remembered going into the Black Lake jewelry store with her just to look. He remembered seeing her face when she saw the little sapphire pendant. Troy also remembered her face when she saw the almost six-hundred-dollar price tag. So, much like she had, he started saving pieces of his check. A week before their one year, he had just enough money, went to the store, and bought the necklace. Becky had cried a little when she opened the box. Just like Troy was starting to develop a tear now as he stared at the watch. Troy wondered if she still had the necklace. He thought probably not.

Troy placed the watch back in the box and turned his

attention to the notes.

The notes were from the same anniversary as the watch. Becky, always the extravagant gift giver, had written a total of three hundred and sixty-five love notes that she had packed into a jar — one for every day of the next year.

The tears were starting to come now. Troy closed the boxes and put them back in the closet. He didn't feel like digging up old memories anymore.

He turned to his bed and grabbed a pair of headphones from his bag, and put on his favorite record. It was one that had nothing to do with love, or family, or his other broken things.

In a short while, Troy had dozed off again, claimed by a terrible, unshakable exhaustion that going through old memories always caused. He was always dancing on that tight rope of living in the past, feeling he had things to work through but wanting to move on and put it behind him. The tightrope of guilt from the past and hope for the future. That one was a bitch.

When he awoke, the sound of his playlist just a hair too loud in his ears, he let the thoughts of Becky and his childhood dating leave his mind. There were more pressing things, like how his stomach was growling. He could feel it bubbling around, desperate for some food. Troy sighed. He had been avoiding the kitchen well to this point. However, he could argue that he had not been avoiding painful memories.

What is the point? You are going to have to come to terms with it sooner or later. And you are going to have to come to terms with Mitch, and with Becky, too, he thought. *It's not like the past gives a shit how delicate you are.*

Troy mulled the idea over in his head. Maybe he would go into the kitchen but avoid the windows.

Would it be easier one small step at a time? Or should I rip the Band-Aid off and walk right out the sliding glass door and see where Grace died for the first time since the accident?

He could see the place vividly in his mind now, filled with its perfectly sitting lily pads and beautiful beach sand. The perfect sight to remind someone of how painful death is when it occurs at a place so perfect.

The rumbling in his stomach, this time growing even painful, decided it for him. He would let fate decide what he would do with the glass door, but he was starving, so with that, he sat up and walked himself into the kitchen.

At first, he made himself walk in slowly, cautiously, stopping at the entrance to shuffle through the cabinets, looking for something to eat. His stomach was aching as he looked through each one, coming up empty-handed except for two pieces of bread. He looked through the fridge, and his eyes lit up at the carton of eggs. He pulled them out, as well as the skillet, and turned the stove on.

Using the stove was safe. It didn't face the window. Troy let himself relax a little. He cracked a few eggs and threw them in the skillet, then turned back to the cabinets, being careful to keep his eyes away from the window, retrieving the toaster. He slid the slices of bread in, spun himself, and turned the coffee pot on just like he used to so many years ago.

Becky had said he was always a dork for watching those cooking shows, but she did say it came in handy for a nice weekend morning. She said he had taken after his father, which she liked, and so did he.

Becky and his parents had been close. They all got along very well and genuinely enjoyed spending time with one another. But it was Becky and Louis who had grown a special kind of bond. During those early dating years, when Becky would come over, she would often beat Troy to his home from his shift at work. His mom and dad would always be around, giving Becky company. She was part of the family well before they were married.

Sometimes Troy wondered if Louis was ever upset with

him for spoiling the life they had all shared. He knew this was ridiculous, but his mind still teased. He knew his father missed Becky. They all did.

Troy could remember vividly waking the girls up to breakfast in bed, all made with toast, eggs over easy, maybe a pancake or two, and for Becky, a nice, sweetened cup of joe. Then that same Sunday night, Louis would cook breakfast for everyone, and they would compare the two like a real cooking show.

It felt like it was yesterday, but it felt like yesterday was a lifetime ago. A wave of sadness had cropped over him.

Becky. It had been years since he talked to her. Years. He had not made any effort to contact her since he arrived in town. He was still wondering if he should scratch the whole thing, just try to move on and forget it. But his father's words rang through in his head. *But, I will tell you this, fighting for what you love is never pathetic, son. If it were, we would not fight for anything. The world may have more peace, but it would be without meaning.*

Without meaning. That was one way to accurately describe how he had been feeling these days.

But still, he wasn't sure why he was even thinking about her or tormenting himself by going through old boxes of their things. She had made it clear she had no interest in ever seeing him again—that much he remembered. But a small piece of him thought that maybe, just maybe, if he saw her, he could fix... something.

Sure, they may never be together again, but they did not need the hate. The animosity.

Troy felt himself grab his phone without really thinking about it and thumb through for her number. Becky Gordon. Her maiden name.

He almost clicked it, the skin of his thumb hanging only millimeters above the screen. He could call her, he supposed.

There would not be much harm in attempting a single phone call, would there?

He pushed the thought from his mind and closed out the call function. Maybe in due time. Maybe.

Troy shook his head. If only he could see her, talk to her now as a grown man.

This is the kind of conversation that should be in person, he thought. *Even if she hates me, she will put it aside for one cup of coffee, right? I mean, shit, we were kids when our lives came crashing down. Just two twenty-five-year-olds who'd just lost their baby. What marriage could survive that? It's a wonder we even made it those sixth months after Grace's passing.*

Well, "made it" is a bit of a stretch, isn't it? his mind teased. Those six months, Troy had emotionally abandoned her, and he knew it. Not only did he know it, but he hated himself for it. Troy had always heard that the loss of a child can bring parents together or drive them worlds apart. For Troy and Becky, the wedge could not have been thicker.

The smell of charring turned his attention from his thoughts and to the eggs.

"Ah!" he said and quickly moved over to his now burnt eggs and threw them on his plate. He walked over to the counter and threw his toast on it as well. Both were more than a bit overdone.

Troy sighed again. He had been so sure of this trip, so sure he was ready for it, that it would be good for him. But now, just being here in this house, everything seemed to be going...not the way he had intended, to say the least. Like this burnt meal was a metaphor for the bigger picture.

He took a few absent bites of his egg-soaked toast as he peered out the kitchen window to the dock, out to the lake. He had been avoiding this for the better part of a week now. He figured soon enough he would have to face it, and now seemed as good a time as any.

Besides, if it were not so horribly sentimental and memorial, he would have taken a picture of it. He assumed he could freelance the view, sell it for a few hundred bucks or something, but he knew he would not. Places with these kinds of memories were not meant to be stored on a picture. They haunted you in your dreams, returning to torment you while you slept each night.

The memory came flooding back at just the sight of the place.

He could see it so vividly, so...lifelike. It was far crisper than any photograph he had ever taken. He was sitting on the edge of the beach, just sitting there watching Grace fish off the dock with her little kid fishing pole. They had picked it out together a week before when *she* had finally decided that *she* was, in fact, old enough to go fishing with her daddy. It was something she had accompanied him on but never actually done herself.

"Dad, I am seven years old now. I am old enough to have a fishing pole and catch the fishes!" she had said.

"Can't argue with your logic, Gray. I am going fishing at Grandma and Grandpa's. Guess we will have to get you your own before we go," he'd replied, and then they were off to get her one.

After they bought the little fishing pole, she spent hours on the beach trying to catch something. She spent that whole week out there but had turned up empty handed every time. Grace had begged her mom to let her go on the dock but had been shot down immediately. It was Troy who made the compromise.

Grace could go out on the dock, but she wasn't allowed to go past halfway and had to fish off the side when she was on it by herself. There always needed to be an adult watching, no exceptions. Grace was grateful and promised to listen well, and listen well was what she did. She was exactly where he had shown her to be. The water would barely be up to her chest at that height, so even if she did fall off the dock, which was unlikely anyway, it was hardly something she could drown in.

Grace also didn't put up any fight when the occasion came that Troy had to go grab something or take a call. She would wait patiently on the beach until he got back, just as she was told. She had not caught anything yet, but she seemed happy enough with the compromise for the first while.

After about an hour, the story had changed.

Grace was starting to grow a little frustrated that she still hadn't caught anything and wanted to try and get the bigger fish that were, in her mind, just out of her reach.

"The fish!" she said, "The fish are just at the edge of the dock, Dad. I can see them from here. They are hyyyouuugge!"

He had to admit that his kid was cute and quite the lawyer, but Troy had shot that down and calmly explained to her the reasoning and reminded her of the deal they had made.

And he made a promise. Daddy would go fishing with her out on the little paddle boat later, and they would go for the biggest ones out at the deeper end, but only if she promised to listen. So, she sat right where he showed her while he worked on his computer editing pictures he had taken earlier that summer.

He had been freelanced to work on making pictures for Black Lake's website. It was a new thing the little town was exploring, and they had asked him to take them. This was a big opportunity for Troy and something he really wanted on his resume, so he had been spending much of the last few weeks getting the perfect shots. Then he'd spent much of the last few days editing them until they were as close to perfect as he could get.

This could be the springboard! Troy had remembered telling Becky. *This could really be something that gets me out there, you know. Really gets Kender Photos moving!*

Becky didn't necessarily disagree with Troy, he remembered.

"You are good, after all," she had said. "I just think you're doing this little too pro-bono. The pay is not great, and it is taking up much of your summer off. And to be frank, I think this project is a bit more of a stress to you than it is worth."

But Troy had stuck with his guns, and she had supported it after stating her piece. That was how Becky Kender did things. And that day, while Troy was working on the set of photos, she had placed her hand on his shoulder, kissed him on the cheek, and told him they were turning out better than she had even expected. Since compliments were not given lightly by Becky Kender, that meant she thought they were damn good. And they were.

That day was still crystal clear in Troy's mind as he stared out the window.

Troy even remembered smiling. That was the cutest seven-year-old girl you ever did see. And he was damned proud of that. And damned proud of Becky. She was the epitome of motherhood, and she was the biggest part of why Grace was such a good kid. Troy was a good father, but Becky truly was the glue that held their little family together, and he never forgot that, nor did he let her forget it.

Troy remembered the summers filled with happy laughter out on that beach, even now as he looked out the window two years later.

But Troy remembered the fall even better. He remembered the yell of his mother, screaming his name and something about Louis being hurt. He had looked over to see his father had fallen on the ground, clutching his head in his hands, his mother coddling over him, panicking.

"Dad? What happened?" Troy cried as he ran over to the group of three, Becky and his mother, who were helping his father to his feet.

"I dunno. I just.... I guess I must have tripped. My head felt like I got hit with some kind of migraine. I lost my balance, and then my foot caught on something. Goddamned deck needs some work done to it. Knew I should've done it months ago," he said as he pulled himself up. "Man, that really did a number on my knee. This goddamn deck is all warped and...."

Troy remembered he had stopped listening at that point. He remembered his name being called. And he remembered the voice of Becky, the way it cracked when she said her daughter's name.

"Troy?" he heard. "Where's Grace?"

"She's just fishing on the shallow part of the dock," he replied.

"I don't see her," Becky said, her voice picking up.

"Honey, she's right—" Troy looked out and pointed to... nothing. Grace was missing from the dock, her fishing pole sitting on it right where she was supposed to be.

"Oh, God. Troy, you left her by herself on the dock. Oh God, oh God, oh God!" Becky said, her voice nearing panic instantly.

She was clutching her pale white face, the blood drained from it entirely. Her breathing was growing rapid, and in seconds she was hyperventilating. Troy remembered each breath as he began to fuel panic of his own.

"No, no. No, I'll go find her," he said. "Grace!" he yelled. There was no reply. "GRACE!" he screamed again as he was running to the beach as fast as his legs would carry him. He leapt over the knee-high brick separation of grass to sand on the beach and screamed once more, this time his voice cutting into his lungs. "GRACE! Baby! Where are you?" he cried.

He was twenty yards away now, half down the beach and to the dock. The fishing pole was clearer in view, and so was her little toy tackle box. The string on the pole had been broken.

"Gray?" he cried.

His mind teased him as he screamed again.

Where is she? She is going to pop out at any moment, like a sick joke. She will be in trouble for that. You do not scare your dad like that, sweetheart, he would say.

He would ground her from the dock for a few hours. It would be funny later in life when they told her first boyfriend. Something they would all laugh over at her embarrassment, but she would deserve it.

You do not scare your dad like that, sweetheart. You almost gave your mom a heart attack!

That was when he saw it. The little seven-year-old body was face down in the water, barely afloat on its surface, still partially submerged.

Troy remembered running harder. He remembered diving off the dock. He remembered reaching her body.

He took her in his arms and swam back to the dock as quick as he could. It felt like minutes before he reached the dock, but he knew it could not have been more than a handful of seconds.

Troy vaguely remembered not knowing how she had gotten so far out there. She had to have been more than forty yards past the dock, but it all vanished in a flash. He remembered reaching the edge of the wood, throwing her limp body out of the water and onto it. He climbed himself up with her and began performing CPR, trying to remember everything from those classes he had barely paid attention to.

She was not waking up.

Ten compressions and then a breath—or was it two? Or was it thirty breaths and a compression? In the end, he couldn't recall what he had done. Under that kind of pressure, he was told, almost no one could be expected to.

Those words didn't matter, not to any parent in his

situation.

Still, for two years, he'd asked himself, would things have been different if he had just remembered how many fucking compressions it was? Would his whole life be different if he had just paid attention in those stupid fucking classes the schools make you take?

Troy remembered brushing her hair away from sticking to her forehead and blowing air into her lungs with no result. Back and forth, he went from mouth to CPR, back and forth, back and forth, with nothing but her limp, blue body.

He remembered her ribs breaking under the pressure, the noise and the feeling. The cracking of her bones had radiated through his own arms.

Troy had screamed then.

He was crying, sobbing, screaming. He kept pressing down repeatedly until someone pulled him off her. It had been an EMT. Troy had not noticed that almost nine minutes had passed since he had gotten out of the water.

Troy remembered the look on the man's face after he checked for a pulse. That concluding, clinical shake of his head to signal that she was dead. That *his* baby was dead. That *Grace* was dead.

Troy remembered yelling "No!" as he pushed the EMT away and started compressions again. Everything after that was a blur.

His recollective vision was cut off as he bent down and grabbed another bite of his breakfast. He played around with it on his fork before finally putting the bit of it in his mouth and turning his attention back to the window.

He never asked who had called 911. He assumed it was his mother, probably, since Becky had been hysterical...which was to be expected. He certainly was by the time it was all over. But in the end, Troy had guessed it hadn't really mattered who called.

Still, it was those questions that kept you up at night, waking you up at three in the morning when the nightmare of that day came crawling into your bed with you.

Those memories haunted him every waking moment and then again in his dreams. Every day for the first year, those thoughts replayed for him every second of every agonizing day.

He had attempted suicide that year—he had failed. The district he was working for had to put him on leave, and he continued to spiral downward. He was unable to leave the bed. The thought of attempting to take his own life again, this time with no mistakes in the process, even seemed to require a mental energy he couldn't muster.

Eventually, the school said they needed him to return, that the bereavement period was over. He told his principal to go fuck himself. That was what got him fired.

He was put on medication, and that helped. He bounced back a bit. He started to implement some amount of coping, started going to group therapy sessions...it seemed like things were picking up a little.

That was only for Troy, though. It was shortly thereafter Becky had asked, as gently as she probably could, for the divorce.

In a simple year, his life had crumbled.

Troy assumed she had wanted one for a while.

At least she had the courtesy to wait until I was...stable. Whatever the hell that means.

Troy felt the formation of a single tear in his left eye. He blinked it away and turned back to his food, and looked out the window as he ate.

Aside from the terrible memories of this beach, he would admit there was quite a view from this window. An outstanding view, in truth. Clear water, as clear as he had ever seen. A very white beach. It was a beautiful spot right in the backyard of his parents' property. It had a special kind of allure, as did many places in the town of Black Lake, Michigan. That was surprising considering that this was Upper Michigan, where spots just like this one were a dime a dozen.

But still, there was a special allure to this one. To this town, even. He guessed that's why so few people left, even with all the terrible things that happened there year after year.

The lily pads floated in the water so neatly, and the unoccupied brush that laid out on the other side of the lake was unkempt and wild, beautiful in all its glory. Troy hated it, but he could not help but notice how at peace the lake was, resting quietly out there as if that summer had never affected it.

The sudden ringtone of his phone on the counter made him jump back and caused his plate to go crashing to the floor, shattering to pieces. It was his mother calling, a call he should have expected, but it had startled him, nonetheless.

"Hey. Yeah?" Troy answered, holding the phone to his ear with his shoulder while he grabbed the broom and swept up his mess.

Louis and Tracy were finishing up and were going to be leaving in a few minutes. They would probably be home in about an hour and a half, given it was Sunday and there wouldn't be much traffic on the road.

No, they did not have any news to report or really anything noteworthy at all. Things with Louis were the same as they had been at the last check-in and treatment. The doctors had run the same tests they always did, and those would be back in a few days, so it was just another waiting game to see what lay underneath the surface of Louis's illness.

Before Tracy ended the phone call, she asked if Troy could run to the store to grab a few things for dinner that night. Troy obliged, jotted the short list down, clicked the phone call to a close, and swept up his mess. The flashback was still running through his mind with vivid detail, even as he left for the store.

CHAPTER 5

When Troy's parents returned, he opted to skip out on the family dinner. He was tired *again,* and he had had a long day... and though he might not admit it, looking out to the dock had brought back a flash of emotion that left him feeling drained.

He laid in his bed that night tossing and turning, only falling into the shallowest of sleeps, before waking himself up again with another flash of memory or thought. In the hour or more since Troy laid down, he had not slept a wink.

Frustrated and irritable, he sat up, rubbed his face quietly, walked down the hallway, and stepped out to the front porch. When he opened the door, he saw his father sitting down by himself, looking out into the woods that encompassed their home.

"Didn't think you'd still be up," Troy said. "Do you still come out here *every* night?"

"I don't sleep much anymore. Besides, your mother would throw a fit if I smoked this in the house," he said, puffing from another cigar. "You?"

"Yeah, it seems insomnia might be running in the family." Troy took a step out onto the porch. "Care if I join you?"

Louis moved himself and the few cans of beer over to make room for Troy, who promptly sat down next to him.

"You know, Dad, alcohol kills, too," Troy said, in a way that one says the truth to someone they knew it would make no difference to.

"That's what they say, isn't it?" Louis answered.

They looked out into the woods together for a minute. The sounds of an owl hooting and the chirping of insects surrounded them. Troy gave an audible sigh.

"Got something on your mind?" Louis asked.

"Not sure. But I know you'll get something out of me."

Louis laughed at this. "I may be dying, but I'm still your dad, Troy. Go on, tell me."

Troy paused. "Do you have any regrets?"

"Well, of course — we all got some. Big and small. I suppose if I thought long and hard, I could fill a room up with a list," Louis said. "You have one weighing on you?"

"It just seems so...trivial, I guess," Troy replied, almost second guessing bringing it up.

"I'm not so sure it would be, given the right perspective," Louis replied.

"It's...I finally.... I looked out to the dock for the first time today," Troy said, his words tripping over themselves.

Louis nodded. "I try not to do it too often if I can help it."

"It was just so vivid. Like it was yesterday. So...real."

"You are handling it okay?"

"Well enough, I guess," Troy said, though he wasn't entirely sure he was being honest. "Say, do you remember her elephant? The stuffed one I got her right before she was born?"

"How could I forget? She carried that thing with her everywhere. She would have glued it to her hip if you had let her. What about it?"

"I don't know. It probably sounds stupid, but.... Sometimes I wish we had not buried it with her. Sometimes I wish I still had it, you know?"

"At the time, you thought it was what you should do. That is not trivial at all. But sometimes, we must learn to live with those choices, even if we think we might have been wrong in hindsight. Change what you can change, and learn to live with what you can't, as they say."

"Yeah, I suppose you're right."

There was a time before either of the two spoke again. They sat there on the porch looking out past the yard, seemingly looking at something but also at nothing at all. After a while, Troy heard a tree branch snap from somewhere out there.

"Thought I might've heard something in the woods the other day," Troy said. "What do you think?"

"I think I've been hearing them when I'm out here late at night. Have you *seen* anything?"

"Not too much. Just something brushing up. Whatever it was, it seemed like it was checking me out."

"Sly little things they are. *Something's* been getting closer and closer."They sat there quietly awhile before his father spoke again. "Have you called Becky yet?"

Troy fumbled around with his thoughts a little while. He had been meaning to, that was half the point of this trip, but something was holding him back. Fear maybe? Nervousness? He was not sure.

"Not yet." Troy took a can from the six-pack and cracked it open, downing a third of it in one big gulp.

"Well, do it when you're ready, but remember that Father Time does not answer to any of our plans."

"I was hoping I might run into her, you know, face to face. Thought that might make it easier...or at least —"

"You think it will be easier if you trap her?" Louis interrupted.

That was not exactly the phrase Troy wanted to use, but admittedly it did seem fitting enough. Troy sighed and took another drink; Louis did the same.

Louis paused a moment, thinking deeply before he spoke again. "If she's anything like I remember, trapping her would not be a wise move on your part, son."

"I wish you weren't, but you're probably right."

"That was a fiery one, that girl. If it were me, I would not want to sneak up on her. Could backfire on you. If it were me, I would give her a warning. Let her know you are around town and plan to be here awhile. Do you remember what I said last night?" Louis asked.

"Yeah, yeah, I do. Something about giving it your best shot and watching out for the good Lord."

"I'm not saying I'm right—"

"But you probably are, as much as I wish you weren't. What time is it?"

Louis checked his watch, which he still wore on his right wrist. It was actually a watch that Becky had gifted him for his birthday a few years ago, Troy remembered. One to match what she had gotten Troy.

"Half past eleven. It is a little late, but I would guess she is still up. From what I remember you telling me, she was always a bit of a night owl."

"I guess I'll go call her now and see if she picks up before I start having second thoughts," Troy said. "Hey Dad, one last question."

Louis nodded.

"You can be honest. Do you blame me for what happened between Becky and I? I know how much you loved her."

Louis shook his head. "No, Troy. I don't blame anyone. You're right. I loved her like my own daughter and still do. But, no, Troy. I do not blame you for the things that happened. If it had happened to me and your mother, I'm not sure we could have handled it any better. Now, I think it's about time you tried to make that call, if you're going to."

"Thanks, Dad. I might try her tomorrow. It's been a long day down memory lane already," Troy said.

"Do it when you're ready, but don't wait forever, is my advice," Louis said. "Goodnight, Troy. See you in the morning."

"Night, Dad," Troy replied as he walked into the house.

***

Louis took another sip of his beer and gazed out into the forest that lay just beyond his property. He had a strange feeling he had not had in a while...not since Dan Hampway had murdered his family. He pushed the thought from his mind. That was ghost talk. That was nonsense.

Louis stood up and took one last look out into the woods that surrounded his home. It surrounded them, the house and the Kender family, from front to back. Without the mailbox and the little road that led to their home, you probably would not even be able to see the place from the main street. At the time he and Tracy had first bought the place, Louis remembered, it had been a huge selling point. To be a bit more isolated and off the beaten path, just a hair away from the neighbors and what little business there was in Black Lake.

But now, for whatever reason, it had been growing on him more and more on how trapped he felt. Trapped in his home and trapped in his illness. But he would never leave, even if the walls caved in. Louis Kender wouldn't leave this place except in a pine box.

Louis took the last big swig of his beer, put out his cigar with the rest, and tossed them both in their respective trash. He grabbed the remaining half of his six-pack to head into his house. As he grabbed the door handle and gave it the small turn to open, he heard something behind him, from out in that tree line.

It was a cackle — animal like, but almost... too close even... to resembling a human laugh. A laugh that reminded him of Dan

Hampway when he had gone insane and killed his family.

Why that came to mind, he had no idea.

You're almost mine, a voice seemed to whisper in his mind. It sent a chill up Louis's spine.

In the instant it was there, it was gone again. Louis turned and surveyed the woods that lay in front of him, with nothing but trees and leaves to return his stare.

Louis rubbed his eyes with his free hand, trying to clear some of the exhaustion from his mind. It could not have been a laugh. It was the cackle of a coyote getting just a little close and a little too excited, and his dying brain had morphed the soundwaves just a little.

They said that was a side effect, didn't they? he asked himself. *Yeah, yeah, they had mentioned something about hearing...and even hearing* things. *And besides, a coyote howling was not too far off anyways. They were just getting a little too comfortable.* He would call the city about that tomorrow morning after he had some sleep. With some rest, he would feel a little more ahold of himself.

This was residual guilt for hiding the Hampways from Troy. Funny, he'd brought up regret since that's what Louis was feeling now.

But still...that sure as hell sounded like a....

He pushed the thought from his mind one final time.

"Damned dogs," he said as he turned and headed inside.

CHAPTER 6

Troy had woken up himself, something he often loved about the summer months. No alarm, no commitments. That was one benefit of being a schoolteacher, that was for sure. And when he had gone out into the living room, he was not surprised to find the rest of the house empty.

Louis had made the point clear that he was to continue the rest of his time allotted to him by living as close to the life he had as possible. He was not able to work much anymore, but that didn't mean he wasn't going to do the things he enjoyed, which was generally working on some kind of project around the house or in the garage.

That seemed fair enough to Troy—even his mother knew better than to throw a fit about it. Troy imagined she was probably off somewhere with her girlfriends, having lunch or running errands, though he was not entirely sure.

She had mentioned how Louis had begged and pleaded with her to keep up her normal routine when he had initially gotten sick. Reluctantly she had done so. Troy thought this was probably a good thing for her. She still needed a life after his father died eventually.... He brushed the end of the thought away.

Troy slipped his shoes on and headed outside and into

the stand-alone garage that sat only a few dozen yards from the house. He could hear the radio playing before his father was in sight, and when he stepped inside, Louis was slaving away on his old pickup truck. It was a rusted old thing, and Troy did not get why his father did not just buy a new one. But his father was weird that way.

Louis had always held onto things and places, even if it was time for a change, because of the familiarity. He figured that was why Louis would not move even after what had happened at his home — even when the very sight of his own backyard was upsetting to him. Troy also assumed that was why the garage was a cluttered mess.

"Some things just hold on to you," he remembered his father saying when he was just a kid. At that time, Troy did not understand just how true those words could be. As an older man, he had learned not to question his father as often. The chances were high that Troy would see it for himself to be true in a few years' time.

"Hey," Troy said.

"Oh, hey there, son. Didn't know you were up yet."

"Just woke up. Where's Mom?"

"Beats me. Oh, she's out and about doing whatever it is that she does on the weekday mornings. Remember, I said I didn't understand women and their girlfriend days," his father replied. "I'm glad she takes them, though. Took a lot for her to finally let go and keep enjoying herself. Enough of that, though. How'd you sleep?"

"Well enough. Still working on this old thing?"

"Yep. Replacing the alternator. Went out on me last week. Damned thing. Suppose I should buy a new one someday, but I was thinking, what would be the point? Besides, sometimes some—"

"Some things just get a hold of you?" Troy finished.

"That's right," his father said, and winked.

"Speaking of which, have you ever thought about cleaning this place out? I can help if you want," Troy said. He glanced around again. Outside of a small workbench and the space around his old pick up, the garage was littered with old stuff, some of it being Troy's. He saw everything from his first bike to the set of weights he'd used when he was a teenager with Mitch.

"Oh, Troy. I should, for your mother's sake, when I'm gone. But as long as I'm still here, you know I will never do it. Keeps the memories alive, you know. I appreciate the offer, though, but the day is freely yours."

"If you're sure. But I'm here to help. Besides, some of this stuff is so old. I mean, not like you're going to be using these," Troy said, picking up the weights. They were surprisingly heavy. Well, not that surprising considering the last time he used them, he had lived in this house.

"I remember you used those every day when you were in high school, so here they will live! Maybe if you and Becky reconnect, you'll want to use them again," Louis said with a chuckle. Troy laughed a little too. "You got any plans for the day?"

"If you say so. Here if you change your mind. Nothing really set in stone, no. Figured I would go out and about at some point. See if there aren't some shots I can get for my next project."

"Say, how has that been going? I've been meaning to ask, but it seemed to have slipped my mind."

Louis had always been supportive of Troy's pastime, so long as Troy pursued a stable career or schooling. In fact, it was Louis who had bought Troy his first real quality camera for Christmas the year he had gotten serious and even paid the money for his first photography class.

Troy had spent the first year taking pictures of everything he could but found that his true passion was in scenic shots, and

Black Lake, along with its surrounding areas, was a hell of a place to take them.

Even after Grace's death and his subsequent move, Troy had found himself still thinking of Black Lake and its potential shots when he was lacking inspiration. Of course, his mind would then drift back to all the misery he'd had in that town, and he wouldn't pick his camera up for the next month, sometimes more.

I guess even now, I get what he means. Some things just get a hold of you.

It had taken three years for Troy to make any traction doing anything with his collection of photographs. Once it had taken off, it really got moving, though. By the time he was twenty, it had become a real source of secondary income. Nothing major, even at its peak, but he had made a few thousand dollars a year off his little side hobby...and his father had respect for that. And Becky had respect for the cash that had paid for those earlier diapers and doctors' visits. Troy remembered selling his first photo to some advertisement place for seventy dollars. He had hoped for more but remembered the wise words his father had always given him.

"Remember...people have all kinds of pastimes, and they can cost a pretty penny. Hardly anyone makes a dime back from it. Take the money and be damned proud of what you did."

Troy brought himself back to his conversation. "Not so hot. Kind of just getting back into it, but I am starting to make a little ground again. Who knows, though? The market in Chicago is a lot bigger than here. I might get lucky."

"Luck won't have much to do with it. You are good, Troy. Always have been. Glad to see you picking it back up."

"Thanks, Dad." The comment had left Troy with a smile.

After Grace died, he had hung it up for quite a while, and it was not until he picked his camera up again that he realized how much he had really missed it.

There was something about the seclusion, about the patience of it all. Walking around in nature for hours, finding the right lighting, the right scenery, the perfect shot. There wasn't much to do back in the city of Chicago—the bustling city was the stark opposite of Black Lake. Troy had found himself having to drive over an hour to find any kind of something that reminded him of what it was like when he was a teenager. But now he was back in Black Lake, and he figured he ought to have at least a few dozen good pieces before he left. If they sold…well, he might just start making a name for himself in Illinois.

"Well, I won't keep you then," his father said.

"You sure?"

"Troy, you're going to be here the whole summer. You cannot spend every waking minute of it by my side waiting to see if I keel over. I've had this same conversation with your mom at least fifty times. It makes me feel old and broken and sad. Besides, don't you have someone else here you ought to put a little focus on?"

Troy blushed. "Fair enough."

"Do me a favor, though. Why don't you take my ole revolver, just in case you run into some coyotes?" his father said, unclipping his holster and handing it over. "They seem to be getting closer and closer. Think one of 'em was just up against the tree line last night when you went upstairs. Either that or a damn cougar. Cats are almost as bad as the dogs this year."

Troy thought of his sick father out on the porch alone at night with a predatory animal a mere thirty yards from him and what would happen if a man in his condition faced that.

He was pulled from his demented daydream when his father cleared his throat. "You remember how to shoot it, right?"

Troy nodded. Even as kids, they had always been warned about coyotes. Troy had always assumed it was a bit over the top, given he had never seen any. That was until the neighbor's dog had been torn to pieces.

Tracy wasn't keen on her teenage son shooting guns in the woods, but Louis still insisted that he take him out shooting, saying, "He needs to learn sometime. Why not now? What if our son is the next dog?"

It was a bit morbid, but hey, it got Tracy to ease up on her protesting.

Troy was excited, though the first shot of the .357 damn near took his arm off. Still, it remained a fond memory, even if it was a distant one.

Looking back, Troy figured it may have been more of an excuse for Louis to shoot his gun than an actual protective course of action. But hey, it was a fond memory of shooting his revolver either way. He figured it was probably the same now, but still, he supposed it would not hurt any. He took the loaded, but sheathed, gun and adjusted it to his belt.

"I'll see you in a few hours."

"See you."

Troy turned and headed to grab his things, his father's revolver by his side.

At first, Troy was not sure where he was heading, but he found himself trotting down a familiar way that he had gone so many times before. The woods were home to a lot of memories, good and bad. He was not sure why he was going, or even if it was a good idea, but he let himself be carried there anyway. He found his feet carrying themselves there for a reason he could not explain.

He had spent many summer and winter nights sitting out on the edge, or sometimes in the depths, of that wood by himself. He would be out there for an hour, sometimes more. Often by the end, he would find himself crying over the events that had plagued him in this town.

After Grace had died, however, Troy had not visited the place where his friend Mitch had drowned. It was too much.

Although it had been years since Troy had been in these woods, he still remembered them well. He trudged through them, steering clear of the way that led to that wretched lake. He did not know exactly why he was here, to begin with, but that place was not somewhere he was ready to go...not yet anyway.

It was not too long before Troy found himself where he knew his heart was taking him — the hill. The small hill that resided in the wood had served as a place for many fond memories he had once had, both with Grace and Becky, as well as Mitch.

It wasn't a particularly large hill, but in the winter months, it served as a good enough spot for himself and Mitch to build forts and go sledding as kids. Then as teenagers to get away from it all and snowboard a little. In the summer months, they shot BB guns at pop cans and occasionally even his father's revolver, which he was never formally allowed to do alone.

As he had gotten older and met Becky, he had taken her there. He had even had some romantic moments there that he did not truly care to bring up with himself.

As a parent, he had taken Grace and Becky there again, not wanting it to be left to rot with his friend's death. He wanted to share it with them, like sharing a little piece of the friend he had lost.

Becky had thought it was a bad idea at first, but she came around quickly. They weren't serious, but they had been dating when he died, and she'd watched over the years as it ate at him. Although unorthodox and sometimes even unhealthy, she let him cope in the ways he felt helped.

He took them sledding in winter, and they played in the stream at the base of the hill that eventually led to the large wretched lake. They were fond memories, and there were many of them, but they brought a feeling of sadness with them as Troy scouted the place out, looking for potential pictures...mostly for his own keeping.

He knew he could never sell a picture from here. He wouldn't, or couldn't, even put them in his portfolio. This place just held too much of him.

When he looked around, he saw the shots, but he saw the memories too. He smiled at a few and sighed at others. He wanted to leave, and he wanted to stay, but he reminded himself why he had come here. He needed to put the past behind him sooner or later, and it was better to do it on his own terms.

Behind the lens of the camera, he would be safe from the life that had haunted him here.

Troy lifted his camera and placed his eye to the viewfinder, bringing the scenery into his vision. It was as good as he had hoped. He clicked the shutter button, causing a quick and distinct click, a flash, and then the picture was taken. He took a few steps to his left and took another. A few steps forward for a third, and so on until he had at least two dozen pictures of the stream from various angles and viewpoints.

He spent a few minutes going over his pictures, finding that they were, as he expected, mediocre. He went through the lot of them, assessing what needed to be done for the next round when he noticed the lack of any real noise.

The woods were quiet, deadly quiet. He could not hear a single bird chirp or the rustle of anything on the ground. It was an odd feeling, one that anybody who spent as much time out in nature as Troy would know was not...normal.

Louis had mentioned coyotes, cougars, wolves, and even bears. Admittedly, the bears and wolves were less common, still having not made their way into their town on the regular. But those animals, despite cute teddy bears and cartoons, were a real danger.

The spook of it was how the noises of prey animals

stopped when the predators were around. That was a scary close comparison to what he was feeling now. Not to mention, no matter how much Troy tried to get the idea out of his head, whatever had grabbed him in the lake, whatever had grabbed Mitch, was likely still here too. It would be preying on whoever was unlucky or dumb enough to be out by Blake Lake alone. Someone just like him.

"Don't start down that rabbit hole," he said to himself, shoving the thought from his mind. "You know that kind of thing is bullshit."

As if in some weird answer, a universal attempt to prove him wrong maybe, Troy was startled and nearly jumped from a sharp noise that came from behind him. The cracking of a branch that could not have been more than forty feet away. It was sharp and loud and hung in the air like a gunshot from his father's revolver.

He turned around as quickly as he could, his free hand already running to the revolver on his hip, ready to blast any predator species...or any ghost spirit that was waiting to make a jump on him. Troy imagined that skeleton hand thing grabbing his ankle and his lungs begging for air as he was yanked deeper underwater. If that thing was back to finish its work, Troy would blast that fucker in two.

But what is a bullet going to do to a ghost? Troy thought. *Nothing is what a bullet would do to a ghost, but more importantly, why are you entertaining this idea?* His inner dialogue played like the voices of a mad man and the voice of a rational, reasonable man of science dancing together in thought.

When he turned and regained himself a little, he wasn't surprised to see there wasn't anything there. No ghost waiting to finish the work he had started on his soul, and there was no coyote or cougar or bear waiting to wallow him in its grasp, either.

There was only, as Troy should have known, the ordinary sight of trees.

He looked around left to right, trying to find the source of the noise, but when he found nothing, he gave a sigh of relief.

He was in the woods, after all, and sometimes noises just happened. There was always a culprit, even if you didn't see it. The squirrel running through looking for food, or a bird that landed on a branch unfit for its weight.

He clicked the latch back over the holster and steadied his breathing, letting his hands stop their shaking.

Letting the past get to you, huh? he thought. *Remember, you came out here to prove to yourself and everyone else that you were ready to start life again. The window got to you. That was a step backward. Now it is time to start taking steps forward. Ghosts aren't real. Not if you don't let them be in your head.*

Once he had gotten back to his normal heart rhythm, he looked for a place to sit.

With some care, Troy lazily walked over to a small tree that had fallen over some time ago. He imagined it had been there a while since he vaguely remembered it and took a seat. He rubbed his eyes and then brought the camera up, looking at its screen, flicking through picture after picture.

They were not bad — nothing great, though.

Troy sighed. He could probably use a break. Despite what the average person thought, taking professional pictures was not some easy job that required no thought. It was a tiring job, if not physically, at least mentally, and Troy felt that feeling of burnout revisit him.

He figured he owed it to himself to at least give himself till noon when the lighting might be better before he headed back home. Besides, as of now, it was not like he had anything to do.

He supposed he could call Becky like he said he would. But if he had any hope of her picking up or even answering a text, he would probably need to wait until she was off work. Which he assumed would be around five, though he realized he had no idea what she had been up to the last two years, and for all he knew, she was jobless and homeless. He made a mental note to ask his parents when he had arrived home.

Troy looked around. By his best guess, it was probably close to noon, and the Michigan sky was hazy and dim through a cloudy mid-morning. This was the kind of weather he hated. It reminded him of that day.

That dreadful day his daughter had drowned.

A cloudy day, even in the summer, was not much of a day for fishing or to play in the lake, or the dock, or really in general. It was a day to stay indoors, or at the very least relax in a hammock or out on the deck. It was not a day when a little girl was supposed to drown.

But she had, oh she had. And the weather, the woods, and this town reminded Troy just a little too firmly of how it had happened. And how it had happened not so long ago. The thoughts and memories attempted to flood in at that moment, but Troy forcefully pushed them away.

Pushing the thoughts from his mind left an empty space that was almost immediately replaced by a sense of vulnerability. Of helplessness. Hopelessness. And in some way, like he was being...watched.

Troy looked around his surroundings. He did not see anyone or anything. In fact, he seemed to be as he should have expected, completely alone out in these thin woods. Troy remembered that the nearest house was close to an hour's walk away, maybe more. But still, the feeling crept over him slowly and surely, and Troy felt an uneasiness take over his chest, his heart beating just a beat too quick.

He checked again, mostly to try and ease himself. Just as he predicted, he was alone. The thought of that seemed to only make the feeling grow worse.

Alone. He had been alone for two years. He hated that feeling.

He brought his eye up to his viewfinder and brought the stream back into view — he was here to take some damn pictures, after all. Or at least that was what he muttered to himself, his heart still racing just a little too fast for a summer stroll.

Troy clicked the camera, bringing the picture into a frame. He shifted the point of view and took another, and then a third.

He looked down at his work. The first two were not his best, but they were better than the last, and he supposed that was a good thing. There was something about the third picture he had taken, though. Something he could not quite explain. It was like, in the very place he had taken this picture, where the frame landed on the hill, something had happened there.

It took him a minute of staring before he realized what it was. Troy remembered when he and Mitch had come out here a year before he died, at this very spot at the base of the hill, to snowboard. It was early January, and the two had walked the fifteen-minute stretch out from where Troy was now to where they entered the part of the woods that held the stream and the hill, though you couldn't see it until you were up close.

There had been footprints — footprints on a brand-new fresh coat of snow. It had only stopped snowing a few hours before, and it had accumulated several inches. That meant whoever had made those tracks had been there right before they were.

At first, it did not seem like much to either of them. This wasn't exactly privately owned land, after all. They reminded themselves that even though the weather was harsh, it wasn't like it stopped Mitch or Troy from going out there.

But as time went on that day, Troy thought more and more about it and wondered who the hell would be out in this part of the woods an hour after a snowstorm. Sure, Mitch and himself had come out here in the cold, just after snow, but during? It was not like it wasn't possible. It just seemed...weird.

That day probably wouldn't have held any special significance at all, and Troy probably would have just forgotten about it all together had it not been for the disappearance of Deja Johnson, a seven-year-old who walked home from school almost every day with a group of neighborhood kids. Word was she did not walk home with them that day.

The kids at school had told reporters she had been acting weird for a few days, that someone had been calling her name, telling her to come and play — to follow the voice to all kinds of different places on the outskirts of town — but none of the other kids heard it. They just heard Deja say she had been hearing it, and everyone knew Deja liked to tell her stories. That day, the day Troy and Mitch had found the footprints, she had walked off into the woods in a trance-like state and had never returned home from school.

There was never an official reason.

Of course, there was major consideration to abduction, especially seeing that they never initially found a body. But Deja had been acting weird for a while before then. Some assumed she had run away from home, others thought she had something awful happen to her, and she just...lost it. Nobody in town knew for sure.

What they did know was that her body had turned up in the woods at the base of the lake on the other side of where Troy and Mitch lived several weeks later. The body had been found sitting upright, legs and feet crossed, at the base of the lake, so close that if it had not been winter, the tips of her toes would have sat in the water.

The word was the body was found entirely intact. There was not a trace of damage — except for her eyes. They were missing and had never been recovered.

Or at least, that's what the new town legend said.

Troy and Mitch never went to the police after finding those footprints.

"We can't. We really shouldn't have been out here. And who knows if they were hers or...anyone else's, anyway?" they had said. "It's a coincidence. It has to be. She walked off into the woods by herself, got lost, and died. That's it." That's what the pair of boys had told themselves.

They never said a word. Troy was pretty sure Mitch had forgotten anyhow and never knew how to bring it back up. That was one more thing on the list Troy had hated himself for. For as many people who vanished or died in Black Lake, Michigan, he would have thought he would have said something. But a fifteen, almost sixteen-year-old Troy had convinced himself that a seven-year-old girl went crazy and walked off into the woods somewhere and died from the elements.

Troy shuddered when he thought of what might have happened to her. Abducted and never seen again until she was found dead in the woods with no eyes. He shuddered again, now knowing how close he could have come to that same abductor, the footprints from only minutes before he made his own. Still, the pair had never said anything.

Days become weeks, weeks become months, and months become years, and eventually, the memory of finding those footprints had thinned from his mind — until now.

Troy took a deep breath and deleted the picture. He turned around and away from where he had taken his shot, where he had seen those footprints that might have been from the person who took Deja. Or maybe it was just another person using the woods as an escape or a shortcut to somewhere in town. Either way, the thought chilled him as he turned away from where those footprints once left their mark.

He brought the camera up again, figuring he would probably call it quits after this final wave of pictures. He was growing tired and impatient, and that feeling of unease had still not left him.

When he investigated the camera, he took a quick look at the stream. Troy felt himself almost involuntarily bring his gaze up toward the top of the hill at the start of where the stream began its flow.

There was not much of a shot there—there was not anything remarkable about the hill. In fact, it seemed perfectly normal, except for what he thought he saw atop it. He squinted, trying to get a better look, and eventually turned to zoom in with his camera.

It took one click at a time, the magnification growing greater and greater. With each careful click, the picture came clearer and clearer into view. At first, he did not believe it, but when he was finally zoomed in as far as the camera would go, the thing on top of the hill had materialized.

There was an outline of something up there. Something almost like a person, but dismembered—like whatever or whoever it was had been in a terrible accident. It was a good distance away and hard to see clearly, but as Troy squinted, he swore he could see the face of the thing.

It appeared burned or scarred in some way, with eyes that appeared to be nothing more than holes. And it was staring back at him with those dark empty sockets. Troy could not quite make it out from here, but he felt its eyes fixated on him, burning a hole through him from the camera lens.

The figure was so still, Troy had almost decided it wasn't a person at all but rather a tree or shadow that looked like a figure. But just as Troy was going to make his mind up on that, he saw the arm come from its side and...wave.

Troy felt an icy chill run through his body. He drew his

face from the camera and blinked, the feeling coming over him even more strongly, the sounds of the woods and stream behind him drowned out by the thumping of his own heartbeat.

He put his eye back to the viewfinder and brought it to the spot he had been looking at, but the figure was gone. There was nothing, not a single trace of the presumed man that had been standing there.

Perplexed and confused by his contradictory visions, Troy found himself moving toward the place where the shadowy figure had stood. His heart was racing, and in the back of his mind, he considered how this might not be the best idea.

A stranger in the woods, one who was watching him, or whatever else this odd person might be doing, could and probably should be considered dangerous, especially in a town like Black Lake. Especially after the memories he had just recalled. But for some reason, Troy could not explain, he felt himself push those thoughts away and carefully place one foot in front of the other in the direction of the hill.

After climbing the mound to the spot Troy was sure he had been looking at only moments ago, he was not met with anything out of the ordinary. Troy looked around for a minute, finding the exact spot he had been looking at, looking for the person that had shown up in his viewfinder. There was no human life on the hill at all or any semblance that there had been one in quite a while.

What was in front of him, however, was a small tree — more of a sapling, really. It was about his height and already had quite a few different branches pointing out in all directions, the thickest of which stuck out at Troy's shoulder level and blew in the wind.

The odd thing wasn't the tree. The odd thing was the clothing hanging from its branches. There was a winter hat on top. The ends of the sap's branches had gloves on them. The bottom even had a pair of shoes. A pair of elementary school girl jeans had somehow been shifted along the branches and placed on the tree. What covered its middle was a thick Carhartt jacket, its branches sticking out of the sleeves like arms.

Troy looked at it suspiciously. That explained why he thought it was a person. It sure as hell did look like someone — or at least it would from a distance. That was easy enough to explain. What wasn't so easy to understand was why anyone would do such a thing out here in the woods.

The even more peculiar part was the how. How could someone get all these mismatched clothes? They were from different ages and different genders. There had to be eight articles of clothing spanning different ages, from a young elementary aged girl to an early high school boy.

And how did they get them all to fit on this sapling? It looked almost as if they had always been on the tree because you could not fit a pair of elementary girl jeans around the branches the way they had been fixed. Could you?

Maybe you could if you spent a great deal of time with it. Troy himself didn't see how, but then again, it wasn't like he was out here looking to put pants on trees. He assumed then that it was possible. But again, why?

He turned to where he had come from and climbed down the hill again, staring up at the thing. Troy laughed to himself. The answer was obvious enough when he thought it over, wasn't it? He decided yes, yes it was.

Of course. You're a schoolteacher. You know the answer. Kids do weird shit. And they do weird shit to mess with guys like you, out in the woods by yourself. This was probably some high schooler's idea of a funny prank joke. It might have even been from last Halloween, for all you know!

Troy mulled that thought over. It seemed plausible enough. A group of kids came out here and figured, what the hell? We'll throw a prank on some pair of kids out here after dark trying to get lucky with a blow job. That would be rich to those kids, rich even for Troy. He could picture it now, a pair of teens doing what they shouldn't, then shitting their pants thinking someone was watching, only to find out it was a tree with a fucking coat on it. He could imagine the looks on their faces.

Troy laughed at himself again. "Yeah, that explains it. Little paranoid being back home, aren't we? Freaked yourself out from morbid stories of the past?" he asked himself.

Still, in the back of his mind, another thought lingered.

What if the same thing that took Grace all those years ago put these clothes on the tree? What if these were the clothes of his victims? And then he caught himself. *Thing? Victim? Really, Troy? You are not even going to think it's a human being? You are going to jump straight to a* thing? *You paranoid bastard!*

He looked down at his camera and checked for his last picture, just as a last resort. In the clearness of the photo, it was simply a tree — a tree with clothes on it.

Troy sighed, a bit with relief and a bit with exhaustion.

Is this what Dad felt like? Seeing things? Hearing things? Troy remembered when he first dealt with Mitch's death, and then Grace's, how the doctors had told him he was hearing and seeing things that weren't real. That's what they had told him. They weren't real. But these things sure felt real while they were happening.

He set his stuff on the ground and bent down to lean against the tree. He pulled out a bottle of water from his bag and took a couple of thirsty sips from it. Troy closed his eyes for just a minute, still continuing to get a hold of his nervous breath.

In and hold, one, two, three, and out. That was something he'd learned in therapy right before the divorce. When you felt like you were about to have an episode, breathe in, hold, hold, hold, and breath it out.

Bring yourself back to center, they had called it. He did

this twice before he heard it.

"Daddy?"

He thought he heard the whisper. It was so small, though. It could have been anything. He could have just imagined it, or that's what he told himself.

"Daddy, over here."

It registered in his mind, alarm setting in since the last time he had heard that voice had been just over two years ago.

But it couldn't be! That was Grace's soft voice he had heard!

"Help me, Daddy," he heard again.

This time he was sure of it. That was his daughter's voice, right behind him. He spun to meet it, half expecting to see her standing there.

But how? She is dead, he said to himself. *I buried her!*

Troy unclipped the button of the holster, pulling out the revolver. He could feel the cold steel in his hand, his finger just inside the frame of the trigger. Whatever the hell was going on, that was not, could not, be his daughter.

"Who's there!" he screamed, panting, pointing the gun in all directions. "Show yourself!" He was spinning himself around, trying to find where the voice was coming from.

There was nothing there. The wind was blowing hard, and the leaves were picking up in the air around him. He heard the whistling of them blowing around the trees.

That must've been it. These woods are freaking you out, Troy. You need to get a hold of yourself. There was a tree that some kids had messed with. That's all. There was no voice of a young girl, no voice of your daughter. That was the whistle of the wind. Don't let yourself hear what isn't there.

Then there was that cackling sound, the awful cackling sound from the other night out with Louis. It sounded so much like a laugh. The one the coyotes sometimes make, his father had said. There was no ghost, but he remembered where he was. This wasn't the city of Chicago. This was the wilderness in the upper half of Michigan. There were coyotes, bobcats, cougars, and even occasionally bears.

Fear struck him again, but in a different way, as he remembered how a bear had killed someone in a neighboring town before they put it down back when he was a kid.

There are animals, but there are no such things as ghosts, he told himself.

"See? Don't get yourself so riled up," he said aloud, and turned. "You can shoot a wolf or coyote."

But with that, he picked up his pace as he grabbed his things and headed back the way he had come. Troy kept the gun unholstered, just on the off chance he was being stalked — though he reminded himself to put it back in his holster, maybe even leave it in the car when he rolled home. Louis was always on the defense about his past episodes, but Troy didn't need his mother, or anyone else in town, thinking he was off his rocker and walking around with a six-inch revolver. Especially not now with how on edge he was.

It took a bit for his heart rate to settle back down, though it did by the time he had gotten back to the little stream, but by then, he had walked over half a mile with innocence.

He sighed and marched his way back to his house, forcing himself not to look at where he had found those footprints so many years ago. In fact, Troy had rushed out of the woodland so fast and had been so paranoid that it didn't even register the kind of coat that was on the tree.

It had been a Carhartt jacket. The same kind and color that Mitch had been wearing twelve years ago. Troy had been so caught up in his own worry and thought he never noticed the name that had been on the inside collar of the coat.

The name read Mitch Hampway.

CHAPTER 7

Troy closed the door to his car and started the ignition. A few minutes after he had gotten home from his photography session, his mother had said she needed to run to the local department store to grab last minute things for the rest of the week. Since he was on edge from being in the house and the events in the woods, Troy had said he would be more than happy to go. Tracy, who seemed to be stretched a bit thin that day, had been very grateful. She went so far as handing him a full list and her card, but Troy had declined, saying he had no issue paying for his keep.

The department store was on the far side of town, the side of town where Deja Johnson had lived, down by the highway he had taken to get to his folks' place. It was not too far off, but the township speed limits the whole way made it feel like it might have been on the other edge of the world. A nice and easy twenty-five miles an hour with littered stop signs. But it was the kind of drive Troy could use after the day's events.

He clicked the car stereo system onto some radio station playing a country tune. Troy was never a huge fan of country, but he would always take it over the silence of a lone car ride. He hated that more than any kind of music—that silence. That reminder he was usually all by himself.

After a handful of songs from shuffled stations, Troy arrived and pulled into the parking lot, and entered the big box store, list in hand. He took his time, plugging in his headphones and not in a hurry to find a cart or go shopping, really. He had been in the house quite a bit, his normal summer routines of photos, exercise via long bike rides, and running errands being thrown off living back with his parents.

He had spent quite a lot of time with his father, but he had spent almost the same amount of time just lounging around. This made him feel a bit guilty and a bit antsy to get out and about again. Not to mention he felt a little unproductive, given he had not even tried to get a hold of Becky yet.

His father's words rung in his ear. "Trap her?" He supposed he was not exactly trying to avoid her, but he had not really gone out to the store with the hope of running into her... or had he? He wasn't entirely sure, and he was not sure he really cared to know, so he pushed the thought from his mind.

The first half dozen items on the list were simple groceries and easy enough to find. Bananas, bread, Tracy's favorite ice cream, and a two-liter bottle of soda. There were a couple of household items that took a second to find, but he managed and threw them in the cart as well. On his way out, he grabbed a few cases of beer, some deodorant for himself, and a pack of razors. He lazily threw them in his cart and proceeded to check out.

On his way home, before he even left the parking lot of the store, it began to rain heavily, the droplets of water crashing loudly against his windshield. He turned his wipers on full blast and turned the radio back on.

Rain always gave him an odd feeling, made him more emotional and trapped in his own thoughts. And at Black Lake, it rained a lot, even for a city in Michigan. That had been part of the reason he had moved out of state, not just a few towns over. It was depressing and often reminded him of what the past had haunted him with for whatever reason.

That thundering sound of hard raindrops on the roof of his car almost drowned the sound of the knocking on his window — almost, but it didn't.

Troy turned to see who it was, and to his surprise, it was none other than his favorite enforcer of the peace, Officer Moth.

He rolled down his window.

"Don't worry, Officer, I got that light fixed a few days ago," Troy said, trying as he might to conceal the irritation in his voice.

"Great. I didn't come by for that, though," he replied loudly, his voice just over the sound of the rain hitting the ground. Droplets of it gathered around the brim of his hat and were even dripping into Troy's open window, though Officer Moth made no acknowledgement of soaking his interior.

"What can I do for you then?" Troy asked.

"A little birdie told me about your trip into the woods earlier. I just wanted to let you know the area is now under private investigation, and we have a strict no trespassing policy."

"Investigation?" Troy asked, wondering how a "little birdie," who Troy had not seen at all in the woods, could have gotten the word to the officer in such a short period of time.

"It has been linked to a prior murder case. The murder of a young girl named Deja, along with others. It's an old case, but we happened to have found some evidence that may link to her death. You wouldn't happen to know anything about that or the clothes we found on a tree, would you?"

It was a pointed question like Officer Moth already knew the answer but was baiting him.

Instinctively, though, Troy had no idea why, he replied, "No."

"That so?" Moth asked.

"Afraid it is," Troy replied. "Though I was out there today

and saw that tree. Just thought it was a bunch of kids with their pranks. As a teacher, I see that kind of thing often."

Officer Moth eyed him suspiciously.

"Sorry I couldn't have been of more help, but if there's anything I can do, please don't hesitate to ask," Troy concluded.

"I'm sure we will be in touch, Mr. Kender. I told you this once already, but I will say it again; I'd be careful where you're going from now on. You might find yourself in trouble if you keep poking around."

Troy nodded silently.

This guy is off his rocker, he thought. *I haven't poked around anywhere...but now I want to.*

"You have a good day now, Troy. And stay out of trouble. And out of the rain. I know how much you hate it," Moth ended, tapping his window.

Troy rolled it up and waited for the man to get into his police cruiser and drive off before he left.

He sighed. This guy really had it out for him. As much as his false accusation only made Troy want to snoop around and find exactly what was going on and why he had felt so harshly towards him since their first encounter, Troy knew it was better left alone.

Moth was the cop, after all, and cops with a complex in a small town had a handy way of making your life hell if you did not appease them.

No, this would be far better handled by calling the sheriff, or even the county, at the end of his stay, right before he left, and let them know what a real piece of art they had for a town cop in Black Lake. That idea made Troy calm down a great deal. *Diplomatic but effective,* he thought as he pulled out of the parking lot.

As he drove, Troy lost himself in reminiscence. Mitch's house was a left hand turn away, not too far down the road. He had not thought much of the news of his friend's father, Dan Hampway, mostly on purpose. When Louis had given him that news, it had given him a chill he had been avoiding since.

Troy remembered as kids, he and Mitch would be out and about, causing havoc around the small town of Black Lake. One time Troy remembered well happened right before Mitch had passed. The two boys were walking along the sidewalk in the emptied town square. It had been late at night, and the two had the next day off from school. The snow had started falling at three in the afternoon, and now in the evening, it was still falling hard and fast.

The pair of boys had been wearing their varsity jackets, which they had both gotten that year for football and wrestling. Both being fairly standout players had meant making varsity in their second year a breeze. School pride was an understatement in Black Lake and the surrounding small towns, Troy remembered.

Looking back at it, as silly as he thought it was for someone who hated his hometown, football was king, and in winter, so was wrestling.

Neighboring schools always battled it out for district and state championships. The entire county seemed to flood these games and matches. The bleachers were always packed shoulder to shoulder. Parents would scream and yell at one another, often cursing, sometimes getting thrown out for swearing at the ref. Occasionally a parent would even attempt to get physical with another kid's father, and there would be an arrest. This didn't happen often, but it was not unheard of in Black Lake. It was all a bit overdone for Troy's taste, who much preferred to play his sports without all the theatrics. He figured that was why it all happened that night so many years ago. People treated small town sports like religion, and eventually, people were bound to get hurt.

When they were about halfway back to Mitch's place,

which was on the outskirts of the inner town area, they started hearing shouting coming from in front of them on the opposite side of the road. It was a group of kids, maybe three of them, about their age, wearing Riverland Highschool jackets — the rival school and the team they had beaten by one match in the district championships, a match they weren't supposed to win.

Ben Mavis, captain of Riverland and the undefeated 145 pounder, had been known as a tough wrestler...and a dirty player. He had gone on to win states three years in a row and was looking at college scholarships from all over in his senior year. He had also been talking shit everywhere he could about how he was going to put down the Black Lake team, and everyone assumed it was a done deal.

That was until Troy had cut down to Ben's weight class and talked trash of his own.

When the two squared off, Troy remembered Ben squeezing his hand hard, digging his nails into his wrist. They were long, longer than legal length, and he had somehow gotten away with it at the check in. Troy only laughed.

The match was short and quick. Troy had gotten two points ahead by the end of the first round, landing moves he barely remembered, as if it were somehow destiny for him to win the match.

The second round, he wasn't as lucky, Ben having scored once more than Troy, leading to a tied match going into the final round.

Troy went out confident but also levelheaded. Ben had gone in for a takedown, antsy and impatient, leading Troy to score on a reversal. Troy was going to be able to pin him and pin him fast. In response, Ben had flipped over and swatted at Troy, landing his finger — and fingernails — in Troy's eye.

The match was paused while the doctors were brought in. Troy was fine. He had said as much, but there was a nice fingernail cut along his eye, and he struggled to keep it open even after the medical clock time was completely drained.

Ben was disqualified. And due to this match and mistake, Riverland had lost as a team as well, losing their seat at the championships.

Troy was not sure now, in the falling snow of a weeknight, what the hell Ben Mavis was doing out here in Black Lake. There was not too much to do aside from the little shops, which were almost all closed, but he supposed it didn't matter.

He was not sure if Ben recognized him or if it was just the jacket, but either way, he supposed that didn't matter either.

In an instant, the group of four were within feet of Mitch and Troy.

"Say, Troy, why don't we have a little rematch of districts?" Ben yelled.

Troy rolled his eyes. "Lay off, man. It's just a sport."

"Just a sport? I lost my scholarship on that match, you little shit."

"Maybe next time, don't be a cheating pussy, eh?" Troy heard Mitch say back. There was a moment of silence between the boys. Mitch was always one to escalate things.

"What did you just call me?" Ben replied.

"I said…." Mitch cleared his throat dramatically, "You are a cheating pussy. Was that clear enough for you?"

Troy only heard the yell and cry of Ben as he lunged forward, swinging his fists at Troy. The other boys split up and went after Mitch, who had been a bit bigger.

Troy had seen it coming just in time to avoid most of it, but the cheap shot still landed on the back of his head behind the ear. He felt his balance and equilibrium thrown off and took a few wobbly steps backward to regain himself.

It did not take long, and Troy had gotten himself up and squared off. Ben had taken another shot, which Troy blocked and countered with his own. It landed on Ben's cheek, but it did not seem to cause much damage.

Ben threw another and another. Troy had stepped back twice and then threw a punch of his own and grabbed ahold of Ben. Holding on tightly, he used the slipperiness of the snow-covered sidewalk to his advantage and tripped him, causing them both to fall to the ground.

They wrestled around on the ground for a minute, both trying to get themselves the upper hand, neither really doing much of anything. Troy looked over at Mitch, who seemed to have caused one of the boys to quit, and the other seemed to be losing.

Ben used this time to get the upper hand and rolled over, pinning Troy to the ground. He rained down hit after hit, Troy just barely able to cover up his face. He was able to block most of them, but the blows that did get through were hard and painful in the cold air.

It was Mitch who came to his aid and rescue. He had apparently gotten the upper hand in his own scuffle and was now ready to be of help against Ben.

Ben was so entranced in raining down shots that he had totally forgotten about Mitch, giving him the opportunity to crack him hard against the temple with his knee. Ben's body weight shifted from the blow, and Troy rolled with it, now gaining the upper hand.

Troy landed a few punches of his own before he saw the car lights. They were flashing their brights and getting closer.

"Troy, let's get the hell out of here!" Mitch said, helping him to his feet. And like that, they were off. They sprinted as fast as they could, leaving anything they had bought from the store behind them in the snow.

The woman had gotten out of her car and was screaming something about calling the police, but the pair of boys paid her no mind as they ran away.

In ten minutes, they were back at Mitch's house, standing in the front doorway panting and gasping for air. They were still covered in snow and, due to the urgency, had not been quiet about going inside.

They heard the footsteps of Dan Hampway coming.

"What's this all about?" he called. When he entered the room, he spoke again. "Jesus, what happened to you guys?"

"Ben. Mavis. Attacked us. The car saw us. We ran," Mitch said in blurted fragments.

"Whoa, whoa. Slow down. What happened?" his father asked.

When Mitch regained his breath, he recounted the story with every detail. His father only sat there listening and nodding until the end. Being that Mitch's dad was a respected officer of Black Lake, the pair feared they were about to be heavily disciplined...and were shocked when Dan Hampway broke out into a chuckle of laughter.

"Well, did you guys win? You look pretty banged up." Dan had always hated that town, and he especially hated that stuck-up prick from Riverland and his douchebag father even more. Dan had him thrown from games and matches on more than one occasion and was familiar with the family dynamic.

"Oh yeah, we won," Mitch said again.

"All right. Well, I don't normally condone fighting, you guys, but in this case—" Dan was interrupted by the knock at the front door. "Shit. Go somewhere. Downstairs!" he whispered.

The two quickly shifted around and did as they were told, hanging on the top steps out of sight.

"Hey there, Officer LaQuesta. How are we doing tonight?" Dan said.

Looked like the bystanders had called the cops, and Ben had given their names. Typical. Especially in a small town where almost everyone knew each other.

"Hey, Dan. You see Mitch or Troy around? Heard there may have been a scuffle."

"Can't say I have, Officer."

"You sure? And stop with that officer talk. You only call me that at the station, you know that.."

"Sorry, Brandon, just habit. I am sure. They went out early in the day, and I have not seen them since. Probably over at some girl's house. I can try and call 'em if you like?"

"You're positive they aren't here, Dan?" the officer asked.

"Haven't seen them. Why, what happened?"

"Well, you know Cassandra from the library?" There was a pause where they assumed Dan had nodded. "Well, it seems she thought she saw them getting into a scuffle with some kids from Riverland."

"Oh, man. No, can't say I know anything about that, other than I know that Ben Mavis kid has had it out for the boys for a long time now. Troy especially. I told them, I said, 'No fighting! Not under any circumstances. If they hit you, just take it and turn the other cheek like you're Jesus H. Christ resurrected, and head yourself home afterward.' I said, Don't want no troublemaking from our family, or Troy's."

The officer sighed. "I always had a bad feeling about those kids over at Riverland. Especially after that match. I was there, you know, where that kid threw a temper tantrum after losing to Troy. Me and Louis had quite the laugh about it."

"Well, technically, he was disqualified for cheating. Would be weird for that Ben Mavis kid to come out here with the snow and all, wouldn't you say? Wonder what that boy would try if they were all out alone together...?" his father said, the enunciation almost causing the young boys, who were only around the corner, to bust out laughing.

"I guess you could say it is a little odd. So, you haven't

seen them?"

"Nope. Can't say I have. But I'll call Mitch and be sure he wasn't doing anything he shouldn't," Dan replied, dropping the voice acting.

"Let me know if anything comes up?" the officer asked.

"Will do, Brandon. Anything else?"

"Like Jesus H. Christ," he muttered, laughing to himself. "That was good, Dan. That was good. No, if you haven't seen them, then I suppose not. I will keep looking to see who it might have been then."

There was silence for a second, then, in a hushed voice, the on-duty officer said, "Say, you hear anything more about that Deja girl?"

"Nothing new, no. But I got to tell you, B, just between us...."

Dan's voice dropped so low the boys couldn't hear him. He undoubtedly knew they were there, standing on the steps. His voice trailed off. Try as he might, Troy could not make a single word out.

"No shit," LaQuesta said. "You'll keep me updated on anything else you hear? You know I'm the new guy, so I'm not in your girls' club yet." Both men laughed at that.

"You will be in time. Black Lake has some weird traditions about it, like keeping secrets about these types of things. I'll keep you updated. Take care, Brandon. Drive safely."

There was a pause and then the sound of the door closing. Mitch's Dad came around the corner.

"All right, you two, best stay out of trouble for a while. And Troy, get some ice on that bruise. That is not going to look good. I doubt Officer LaQuesta will give you any trouble, but some of those new officers down at the station do not know me as well. So lay a little low, would you?" Dan said, and left.

The memories came back so vividly to Troy.

Dan Hampway had been a well-respected officer in their little community. He had probably been on the fast track to being the sheriff at some point. He was calm, cool, and level-headed from all that Troy had remembered.

Even at Mitch's funeral, he was devastated, as any parent would be, but not in a way that signified he would become... unhinged. And even after, Troy remembered he never seemed to have any ill will or anger. Just questions without answers. Troy wondered to himself what could possibly make a family man, a respected police officer who had seen plenty in the small town of Black Lake, kill his own wife, his daughter, and himself. Troy felt a weird pit in his stomach. Something about the whole thing did not sit right with him. In that memory, Troy thought it seemed like Dan had known that, too.

Troy was brought back to the present day as he neared the intersection that led to his parents' on the right and the Hampway's old house on the left. Troy drifted over to the right-hand turn lane.

He supposed if Dan had really lost his mind in some weird post-traumatic situation, then he didn't need to go see the place. But still, he wasn't sure if it was some kind of sentimental bargain from the memory he had just relived, but he wanted to see the place at least once before he left. Maybe he could make a connection. Or maybe he just needed to satisfy some weird notion in his own mind.

Troy was not sure which it was, but either way, before he made it to the end of the intersection, he found himself with his left turn signal on, headed for his second childhood home.

CHAPTER 8

Troy was not sure exactly what it was that made him pull up to the old house, but there he was, sitting idly in front of Mitch's childhood home. There was a foreclosure sign out front only a few feet from where Troy was parked. It had been for sale for two years, he had heard, and the price had kept dropping lower and lower.

Even as the price fell season after season, no one had bought it. Everyone in town seemed to know about its history... and it was not that long ago that a cold-blooded double homicide/suicide by a man who had a psychotic break had occurred.

The place looked run down on the outside. Troy looked at the broken window that stood on the second story of the home, where Mitch's room used to be. It had not been fixed, and it looked like old damage. The paint around the sill was peeling, and the siding looked like it was falling off.

It seemed no one cared anymore. He remembered Louis telling him the city, the realtors, or everyone in town had more or less given up on trying to sell or rent it, and it had become a bit of a local hangout for kids or drug users. In the short time since Troy had moved away, it had gone from a nice enough house of a well-liked officer of the law to a rundown joint that seemed like it hadn't had any love in five years or more.

That was funny in some way to Troy, the way delicate things seemed to take so long to build and were so fast to fall apart. Much like his marriage. Much like his psyche. Much like his life, he guessed. It had not taken long after Grace died for all of those things to fall apart as well.

He could have seen himself in Dan's shoes, at least to a certain degree. He had attempted suicide after Grace died, and he watched his marriage crumble. He had failed, he had gotten better, but he still had the memories and damage to prove it — the scar was still there on his brain. He still couldn't take over the counter medication without bringing on memories of that night so strong he grew nauseated and damn near foamed at the back of his mouth.

As Troy looked at the window, his mind trailed off. He was not sure how it had all spiraled out of control so quickly for him. One day he was levelheaded and handling himself well enough, at least considering the circumstances. Then the next, he had cracked like an egg.

He had odd hallucinations, first audibly and then visually... much like the thing he had seen ten years ago with Mitch, and far too close for comfort to what had happened earlier in the woods. The thought of falling off that mental cliff again made Troy shudder.

Professionals claimed all of it had been induced by trauma, and he suffered from a fragile psyche from a near death experience and trauma in his youth — that he was basically an egg predisposed to crack at any given minute.

Funny how they say that like it's not your fault like that's supposed to make you feel better, Troy thought. *Like being a fragile egg is something to be proud of.*

In time, after he had gotten professional help and after Becky had left anyway (the damage being done, the redemption being too little too late), he had come to accept this diagnosis. Post-traumatic stress had brought about a trigger for his otherwise likely avoidable schizophrenia. At least, that was what the doctors had said.

He took the medications, and he went to sessions, therapy, grieving groups, all of it. He got better — at least he could function in society well enough. He was a well-liked teacher and neighbor — in more ways than one, he had moved on from his past. But something had still never sat right, no matter how many times he was told that extreme cases of life and death — such as a near death experience that claimed the life of your best friend or the guilt brought on by the drowning of your daughter — would bring on things that specialists in the field were just now beginning to understand. He never fully bought it.

Had Dan gone through all that? Taking the same steps for his own family? Was it just not enough for him, too? he asked himself. *Or was what he went through just too much?* Much like it had been too much for himself. No matter how many grief sessions he attended, no matter how many therapists he saw, no matter how many prescriptions he tried, it didn't matter in the end. Even as his life slowly started to come back together, it could never undo what Troy had seen. *Was it that way for Mr. Hampway?*

He had seen something that day. He had felt it, this presence in the lake. It had come after him. It hunted him, found him, and took him under the water. He had escaped, fought his way out, and it had claimed his friend. He had felt it. That feeling there was something there, something wrong. Something evil. And the day Grace died, he had felt it too. It was only in hindsight that he knew it, but he had felt it. He was sure of it.

There were other times too.

He had that feeling on and off his whole life that he had lived in Black Lake. It was like a warning call. He would get that feeling that something bad, something terrible, was lingering in the air around him. Then something would happen. Something tragic. An accident down the road claiming the lives of a trucker and a family-filled minivan. Someone's child was murdered. Some teenager committed suicide. A girl walked into the woods to never return, her eyes missing from their sockets. Or your best friend fell through the ice, never to be seen alive again. And they all happened in or around Black Lake, Michigan. He had almost forgotten what it had *felt* like until he had driven back into his hometown.

Troy quit bringing it up with the people around him, namely his parents and his wife. They started talking about paranoia and his medication. He kept it to himself and started flushing the pills down the toilet. When Becky caught him in the act for the third time, she had enough, and shortly thereafter, she had left.

Had Mr. Hampway done something similar? his mind flashed. Troy found it odd, constantly comparing his story to his friend's father, but it naturally seemed to fit in. This both comforted him, feeling like someone would understand, and scared him, given how Dan Hampway's story ended

Troy could not blame Becky — she did not understand, and she was worried. She was grieving the loss of her daughter and felt she could not be responsible for Troy's life and her own. So, he gave her the house and moved away. She told him she did not hate him. She felt sorry for him mostly, but once it was finalized, they had not spoken a word, and that felt a lot like hate.

Troy wondered if Dan had gone through something like that in his own marriage. If his wife and Lucy hated him. That thought made Troy sad. He knew, at least in a way, what Dan had gone through, and he wasn't sure he deserved that kind of resentment from his own family. He didn't blame them, though, just like he didn't blame Becky.

The whole thing was fucked.

Looking up to the house, the flood of memories seemed to only grow stronger. How many hours had Troy spent in that little house, looking at Mitch's family as an extension of his own? Surely it was close to the number of hours Mitch had done the same with his family.

The sight of the house in all its broken glory almost left a tear on his cheek. His eyes fluttered around the place, taking it all in, when his eyes landed on that far left upstairs window, the one where Mitch's room used to be.

Troy was not sure what made him park the car and open the door. He was even less sure what made him exit his vehicle. Even less sure was the reason why he had walked up to the failing home. He just knew he did.

"I shouldn't be here," he said aloud, "But I have to be."

A few mindless steps led him to the front porch, standing in front of the front door. Standing there, he could even remember the smell of Mitch's mother cooking that same stir fry she had always made. He caught the imaginary smell of the cookies she would bake. She had always baked cookies. Usually, she made a few sugar cookies, even if there was not any real occasion for them because she knew those were Troy's favorite.

He sighed.

It stung, knowing what had happened to his friend's family. This town had an awful way of making its residents the victims of its cruelty.

The Hampways had that happen twice — once when Mitch died and once when Dan lost his mind and killed the rest of his family. It really had done the same to the Kender family. First Troy damn near met death, then the accident and Grace was gone. And now Louis was dying, too.

It was kind of funny to Troy — not in the ha-ha way, but in the sad kind of way that makes you breathe out a laugh right before you start to cry. Crying felt a lot like what he wanted to do now.

But Troy let himself remember, before the night on the snowmobile, when this house had brought with it most of the good memories of his younger years. God, he had spent so much time here in this very house he was standing at.

Video games, playing guitar — poorly — or doing silly workouts in Mitch's room because they had watched too many '80s macho-man movies. Troy laughed at these memories, not from sadness but genuine happiness. They had been so young and innocent back then.

It was in this house they had sat around and talked, too, about the future and where they wanted to go. Mitch had thought about enlisting in the army. Troy did too, then he met Becky and had forgotten the idea. He never wanted it as much as Mitch did, anyways. Come to think of it, he really was only going to follow Mitch.

God, how he missed him. Twelve years had not been nearly long enough to unpack the damage the night had caused. And that, he supposed, was why he opened the door.

Surprisingly to Troy, it was unlocked. The door creaked on its hinges as Troy gave it a gentle push. The interior of the house seemed, from what Troy could see in the doorway at least, to be in the same repair as the outside. Troy took a step inside.

The home carried a smell with it, like rotting wood and animal shit. There was another smell, too, a wretched strong one that Troy could not place no matter how hard he tried.

Natural gas, maybe? No, no, that's not it, and thank God for that. A natural gas leak in a house in this amount of disarray — well, there was no telling how long before he got ill. Or blown sky fucking high with the roof and the walls. It would rain down blood like he imagined in that one heavy metal song he listened to on the drive into town.

It's not natural gas. It's not the wood that has its own distinct rotting smell…. Then it clicked as the word "rot" ran off his tongue. The smell was of something dead.

It made Troy's nostrils flare, and he thought about turning around and leaving, but he did not. There was something else that was weird and holding his attention. The inside of the house seemed like it had not been cleaned out since...what happened.

Oddly, most of the Hampway's old furnishings were still in their remembered places. The couch was still in the living room but with a big tear on it. The bookshelf was still at the foot of the stairs, stripped bare though and crooked now. This did not seem like a place that had ever been listed for sale, even though he knew it had been.

Troy brushed the thought from his mind. Maybe his father was wrong, and it never was listed, to begin with. Just not worth it on anybody's end.

So here it is, my best friend's childhood home, left to rot, loot, and squat in, he thought, bitter and resentful.

He kept moving through the home and up the stairs to the bedrooms.

Inspecting the rooms upstairs, Troy noticed as he made his way to Lucy's room that every door was cracked open. He resolved to shut them as he walked into Lucy's room.

He had only been in here a couple of times in his youth, but he remembered it. It still had the pictures on the walls. A couple of aged photographs of her and her friends on the first day and last day of high school. There was a college textbook sitting on a desk, unopened.

"Human Anatomy: Volume 12." That brought back what his father had said. She was going to school to be a nurse out in Marquette. That pained Troy a little. She could have had a good life, even after everything that happened with Mitch.

Did Dan wait for her to come home from school, or was it just happenstance? Troy shoved that thought from his mind. The thought of Dan waiting to do his deed when his daughter was home from college was too dark. Too far into Dan's mental break. He did not want to go there.

It was weird seeing her room so mature. The last time he had been in here over twelve years ago, he remembered posters of boy bands and teen girl drama shows that would no doubt be outdated by today's pop culture.

Troy remembered how Lucy was always kind to him and even remembered when Mitch had told him that Lucy had one of those older-brother's-friends crushes on him like Louis had said. He thought it was funny then. He had never found her to be more than his friend's sister but knowing she had still checked in on him with his parents pained him a little. The last time they spoke was at the funeral. They did not talk again after he skipped town. Now, he just felt sad.

I should have checked in on her, too. Seen how she was doing. How everyone was doing. The guilt was hitting him like a clean shot to the liver, threatening to buckle him over.

Troy left the room before the tears could start.

It was in the hallway walking to Mitch's room that Troy started to get the start of that feeling he had gotten in the woods like something was there with him. He attempted to let the feeling pass as he went into Mitch's bedroom. It didn't.

Mitch's room was exactly how Troy remembered it. Nothing looked like it had been moved after he died, though it was uncharacteristically clean of Mitch. That was depressing in its own unique way.

Troy walked over to the nightstand table and chuckled. This was always where Mitch had put his nefarious smokables. Troy had always thought this was about as ridiculous as anything, but Mitch had said, "Hiding in plain sight is the way around my folks. They would never guess it's here."

Troy laughed. He never was caught, so he supposed in

some way Mitch was right about the nightstand. He put his hand on the handle and pulled it open. What he saw was not anything of nefarious inhalation but something that surprised him.

Sitting in the nightstand was an item he had not seen in over twelve years. An item that held a mixture of emotion and a haunting recollection of why he was standing in this empty house. Troy reached down and wrapped his fingers around the hunting knife he had used the night he had almost drowned. This was the knife that, in some way or another, had saved his life.

Troy unsheathed it and looked at the blade. It looked the same as it had before everything happened. Like the events that had forever changed his life had no effect on this untethered metal.

He rubbed his thumb across it in the way you do when you are testing a knife's sharpness. It was as sharp as it had been twelve years ago.

Clutching the knife in his hand, he felt the flashback of the phantom feeling on his leg from when whatever it had been grabbed him in the water. He remembered stabbing and flailing with the knife, trying to get free.

That sick feeling he had gotten in the woods, the one that had been growing in him since he had entered the old Hampway residence, even the town of Black Lake as a whole, had spiked. The hair on the back of his neck was standing, and that feeling that someone was watching him had peaked.

Troy dropped the knife when he heard the bang. He rushed out of Mitch's room to where he had heard it, which was down the hall in Mitch's parents' room. The door was closed shut.

Fear engulfed him.

He stood in the hallway, his heart beating hard and loud in his ears, but not so loud that he could not hear what was coming from the other side of the door.

The laughing.

He could hear laughter and thumping coming from inside Mitch's parents' room. It continued as he was in the hallway with his heart thumping hard and trembling beginning in his hands. It sounded like something or someone was just on the other side of the door with a faint, menacing cackle. Troy closed his eyes for just a moment as he swallowed hard, trying to make the fear go with it.

It stayed with him, glued in the pit of his stomach.

Standing there, he weighed his options. He could leave now and forget this happened. Forget he ever even came to this house and be on his way. Or, he could face what was in that room, face what had been his worst fear for twelve years. Or to see nothing and confirm that he was rolling down the hill of psychological collapse.

But Troy knew he would never forget if he left now. He would wonder every day, every miserable day, if he was going crazy. And when would it end? Troy knew when. When he put a barrel in his mouth and pulled the trigger because eventually, this would come to a head. And the head it would come to would be the back of his. Sprayed against the wall would be a mixture of his blood and brains as he asked his dear god, the one he never believed in, to make it stop. Please, make these delusions stop!

He took a step forward, and another, and another until he was standing at the closed door. The noise had stopped by now. It was dead silent, deafening in its eerie stillness.

He wrapped his hand around the doorknob and twisted it open.

His eyes dotted left to right as he searched for what had been making the noise a few moments earlier, and that was when he saw it.

Huddled in the corner with its head in the small trash can was a small animal, with its grey and black spotted fur matted down by mud and dirt. It was throwing things out of its way, digging deeper into the can. As it found what it was looking for, it pulled away, and Troy saw that it was a raccoon.

CHAPTER 9

Instinctively he flailed his arms and yelled, "Get! Get!"

The raccoon hissed and groaned, making a sound that was all too familiar. It was almost, but not quite, the laughing noise.

In a rush, Troy felt a small wave of relief but was still on edge. Raccoons could have rabies, after all.

Bending down, Troy grabbed the first thing he could get his hands on to throw at the animal, a broken picture frame that was sitting on the dresser against the wall. It crashed against the floor, sending pieces of it flying at the animal, scattering every which way and effectively scaring it off. It ran. Troy sighed.

A raccoon. Better than a delusion, I suppose, he said to himself as he let the final waves of relief rest on him, his heart settling back to normal.

Still, Troy felt himself wanting to leave after the odd encounter. Though the groan of the raccoon was close enough for Troy to count it, it wasn't the exact same laughing noise he had heard in the woods. That kept the back of his mind wandering a little too much for his liking.

Heading out the door and down the hallway, tracing his footsteps back through the home, he was almost out the front door when he stopped just in front of the entrance to the basement.

It was the one place he had not been in yet. He had so many memories of it as a kid, playing video games or those scrappy wrestling matches that gave you rug burns for weeks. The doorway held him there, inviting him with so many pieces of his past that he could not resist the urge to see it.

His thoughts went back to the time Dan had gotten them out of trouble with those neighborhood kids and how they were sitting on the basement stairs just listening. He found himself walking down those same stairs now.

What he saw when he made his way to the bottom of them was surprising. His chest skipped an even larger beat than the potential rabid raccoon had caused.

There were papers strung up all along the room.

Photographs, news clipping, a map with markings on it — all thumbtacked into the drywall. Troy took a step forward to examine them.

In the first photograph, he recognized the face of the four-year-old boy who had drowned in a kiddie pool.

He was a neighborhood kid, Troy remembered. *Jayce was his name, I think. His family lived up on the hill just by the lake. Well, his mom did. Word was she was running from her abusive husband.*

This was the photo taken at the scene, his face puffy and blue and bloated. It reminded him of his daughter's face. He turned away from the picture.

Almost a dozen of these horrific pictures were hung. A newspaper clipping was posted next to each photo, color-coordinated with a dot on the map of his hometown. The titles of the articles read things like, "Missing Girl Found Dead in Black Lake River! Probable Kayaking Accident." Or "Missing Teen Turns Up After Storm: Probable Suicide in Black Lake."

One stood out that said, "Another Teen Goes Missing in Black Lake." He glossed over the stories, and his eyes found his. "Snowmobiling Accident Leaves One Teen Dead, One Alive in

Critical Condition."

Troy flicked his eyes away from it. He had not seen this article in over a decade. Reading it a hundred times as a teenager had been enough.

Having no desire to relive his personal nightmare, Troy looked away, stepping back and seeing the wall as a whole.

Seeing these pictures all strung up like a display of the worst events in Black Lake's history not only frightened some instinct in Troy but also made his stomach drop at the sight of them, threatening to empty its contents.

The words of his father rang in his head as he thought of Dan gathering these pictures and taking them to his basement wall. "He went off the rails."

In echo of this, there was writing everywhere, scribbles of chicken scratch with different theories.

SUICIDE EPIDEMIC
SERIAL KILLER
CHILD MURDERER
WHAT HAPPENS IN BLACK LAKE?

Then it was blank for a few inches before another, more furiously written question made Troy feel the tension of that night twelve years ago.

WHAT LIVES IN THE LAKE?

But the last one made Troy feel sick to his stomach.

It was in smaller writing, all lower case, a staunch contrast to the rest. It was like this word was the last and final result. The end conclusion of all his research.

Seeing it in writing, its five letters was what made it real. It was circled furiously like Dan had traced a circle every time he found a new reason to believe this was the real reason Black Lake had a black cloud over it. By Troy's best guess, it had to have had forty circles around it.

It read one simple word.

devil

Underneath were three more notes tacked to the wall and one picture with a question above it. It said:

Where is it?
What does it want? *Who* does it want?
How do we kill it?

The photo beneath that question was what made Troy look away. Now regretting coming here at all, he reserved not to return as he walked up the basement steps, out the front door, and into his car. Trying to forget the picture of the knife he had used to cut away bushes that tangled his feet in the lake so many years ago.

***

Troy took a big sigh. Given what Louis had told him, he scolded himself for not staying away from the old Hampway house. As Troy got into his car, he silently reprimanded himself for reopening old wounds.

"That house is as broken as I am," he said to himself, putting his car in drive.

He looked up to the old house for what he suspected would be the final time, and something caught his eye.

It was as if he could see the dark shadow and silhouette of someone standing at the window of Mitch's room. The shape of the dark lines was so accurately close to what he had seen in the woods before he found it to be only a tree.

But that's impossible! I was just in the house. In that room!

But still, whether it was the light, the reflection, or the

way the blinds stood, Troy was sure he had seen someone up there. Someone was up there with a pair of black and terrible, expressionless eyes staring down at him.

Troy blinked.

The familiar wave of eerie cold was passing over him, and he dropped his gaze from the window. In that moment, his body felt as cold as the ice he had fallen through twelve years ago.

It passed, and he brought his eyes back up to the spot where he thought he had seen the small outline of the shadow... but there was nothing there. Nothing but the white, dirt covered blinds that had to be over a decade old.

Troy shook his head, a feeling of silliness coming over him. That was three times now since he had been home, four times if you counted the time on the porch and twice today, that he had felt unsettled by a presence that had turned out to be nothing. That familiar feeling coming and going and the fright he had felt, partly because he thought it was real and partly because he thought his mind was imagining the whole thing. He didn't know which he would prefer at this point.

He put his foot on the brake and threw the car in drive.

Slowly he inched forward up the pavement, keeping his eyes half on the road in front of him and half on that empty window in his rearview mirror, still unsure of himself. He headed back onto the road in the direction of his parents' home, only letting his eyes drop from the window as he drove away, the feeling of being watched having not quite left him.

He felt the unseen pair of eyes from that window, the ones he had imagined, beaming a hole in the back of his head the entire way home.

CHAPTER 10

By the time he got home and pulled into his parents' driveway, he had convinced himself it had been all in his mind. Another hallucination brought on by seeing that house...that house in all its broken glory, and the memories and grief of not only losing his friend but the family, too.

These little glimpses had happened to him, even after he moved away...but only every so often, and they were never that extreme. But seeing that house alone had been a bad idea, given how he had left town in a mental state barely above functioning. He did not speak a word of it, even when his mother asked for the reason why he was so pale.

"I haven't eaten much of anything today," was what he told her when she asked. It wasn't exactly a lie—he hadn't eaten much of anything, but he left out the reasons why.

The figure in the window. Dan had "Gone off the rails." *Big time. Is that happening to me?*

"Well, dinner's almost ready," she said, assuring him that would fix the problem. He headed to the kitchen and sat with his family, the terrible feeling of being watched from that window almost gone—almost, but not entirely.

No, Troy still felt as if something were watching him now.

But he didn't dare speak a word of it.

When dinner was over, Troy found himself out on the porch with his father yet again. This was their new normal: performing their old and now renewed nightly ritual of a cold beer on the porch steps, looking out into the edge of their property.

"Any words with Becky?" Louis asked, raising his eyebrows.

"Not really," Troy said. "Haven't made much of an attempt, if I'm honest."

Louis nodded in return. They sat there a while, quiet, listening to the birds chirp, an occasional owl hoot, and the rustling of life just outside the line of their home. It felt like forever before Troy finally cleared his throat to break the empty space between them.

"I went to Mitch's old house today." His words were careful, though he wasn't sure why he was admitting this at all. Not only would that have been illegal, but it was also a bit insane.

Louis nodded again, as if this was not surprising but an expected statement.

"Felt surreal. Can't believe it's been twelve years, you know?" Troy said, and took a swig of his drink. "Sometimes it feels like it still only just happened. Like I was right there on the lake with him. I've wondered if his parents blamed me for it, but I guess now I'll never have the chance to ask."

"You know, we talked a lot after everything, Dan and me. I don't think his parents held any contempt for you, Troy. I don't think anyone blamed either one of you for being kids. You were sixteen. You guys were a little careless, sometimes even a little stupid. But it was both of you, and you were both just that — kids."

"I know. It's just—" Troy stopped, seemingly unable to find the words.

"Guilt's a funny thing, you know. It comes in weird ways.

Worry. Anger. Panic. Sadness. Sometimes to escape it, we might even project our own feelings onto other people. But remember, it was Dan that had told you two, just as I had, to be sure one of you got home alive. He told me that one day, he said he was glad one of you did, even if it wasn't his own son. 'Better one than none,' he said. 'Troy was like a second son to me, Louis. Always had been. Always will be.' That was one of our last talks on this very porch when he said that to me." Louis's voice was true and sincere, and Troy knew he was telling the truth. His father had not ever been much of a liar — he was an honest man who even hated holding secrets. That was probably where he had gotten it from.

Troy sighed. "Do you think it was fate? Do you think he was doomed to it? To fall apart, that is? Or do you think maybe there was something else?"

"You know, Troy, I have wondered about that a lot in this very spot."

Louis paused for a long second as if contemplating each word. He took a careful, contemplative hit of his cigar. When he spoke, he was as careful with his words as one might handle a sharply pointed knife.

"I think this town, Black Lake, can get ahold of people. I am not sure how or by what means — maybe it is just the side effects of living in a small place, I do not know. But I feel it every day. I know others feel it, too. I venture to say you have felt it at times, even. Us old-timers, we feel it stronger, I think. We have lived here longer, and it seems this town just gets ahold of you and does not let go.

"It can drive you mad, a little town with so much misfortune. A place like this could make anyone do a number do crazy things. Or set events in motion. Or, whatever you'd like to believe." Louis finished, took a sip of his beer, and then put it back down. "Eh, what the hell do I know? Just the ramblings of a dying old man. But I am feeling a bit tired, and my head hurts, so I think it's about time I head to bed." With that, Louis up and left.

Troy quickly finished his drink and threw it in the trash before he headed inside himself, his eyes scanning the area around him before he went upstairs to shower. As he did so, rubbing himself clean and drying himself off, his mind kept teasing at Louis's remarks.

It was a weird place, this town. The woods seemed to have some odd sense about them — the town square even felt a little on edge most of the time. The only word Troy could really think of was that, at times, it felt like there was something paranormal here…and it was malevolent.

Louis's words rang through his head. *We have lived here longer, and it seems that this town just gets ahold of you and does not let go.* He figured that was part of the reason Louis had never left and part of the reason Troy had come back even though he did not need to. Once Black Lake got its hooks in you, it seemed like they were forever dug in.

Troy was almost dry and had taken a moment to look at himself in the mirror as he ran the towel through his hair. The reflection of himself showed that he looked tired and worn down, but it still only looked half as bad as he felt. His time back in Black Lake was draining him, that he was certain of.

Lost in a daydream, somewhere off in distant memories, he was rattled back to life by the screaming sound of Tracy calling for him.

"Troy!" he heard his mother cry from somewhere else in the house. "Troy!"

"What?" he called back, throwing his old clothes back on.

"It's Louis!" she cried, her voice loud and concerned but calm and rational, too. Troy launched himself out of the bathroom and into the hallway before hopping down the steps two at a time.

"Dad?" he yelled. "What is it? What is it?" He sprinted through the house to where his mother's voice had come from, dodging the walls and furniture in his way.

When he finally arrived at the entrance of the kitchen, he felt water brush his feet, and then he saw what the problem was.

The first thing that registered in his brain was the sink. It was overflowing with water, spilling out of its mouth from the faucet onto the floor in a big sloppy puddle.

His father was laying on the floor, still conscious but slumped over, while Tracy was trying to get him to his feet. It appeared by the cut on his head that he had smacked it on the kitchen counter when he fell. A thin line of blood was forming from it and landing in the puddle in diluted red.

"What happened?" Troy yelled, rushing over to his father and helping his mother usher him onto his feet and into a chair.

"I'm all right. I just...slipped," his father said with slurred speech.

"He...he was just helping me clean up here. I went to put the dish rags in the washer, and then I stopped to fill the cat's food bowl. I couldn't have been gone more than five minutes, and then when I came back in here, he got all delirious. It was like he didn't know what was happening, and then he lost control of his legs and fell. And he cut his head on the counter on the way down," Tracy said, her voice only a little calmer than it was a moment ago.

Louis was gingerly rubbing his right temple, right along the cut that had not yet stopped bleeding. He was pale as if all the blood had been drained from his face from that little cut, but as the moments passed, the color seemed to return, albeit slowly. After more time passed, he seemed to grow a little more coherent.

"I'm all right, I'm all right. I just stumbled."

"Louis, you were mumbling to yourself, and then you just fell over limp!"

"Have you called an ambulance?" Troy asked. Tracy shook her head.

"I am not getting in one of those things. I am *all right*. I have an appointment next week and can tell the doctor then," Louis protested. "You're already dragging me around this goddamn state every other week."

"Dad, listen — you fell and hit your head pretty hard. You have a nice gash on the side of your face. Not to mention you are as pale as snow. I am calling an ambulance. You need to get checked out. You could have a concussion or internal bleeding."

"Goddammit, I said I was all right. I slipped and fell. There was water on the ground, and I slipped, and I *fell*." Louis's voice, although not exactly aggressive, was rising in frustration.

"Dad, there was water on the floor because you left the sink on to overflow while you were having an episode," Troy replied.

"I told you, I am fine. It's over now. I am fine, and I am not getting in no goddamn ambulance," Louis said.

"Your stubborn old ass!" Tracy said, slapping him against the shoulder, hard. "If you do not go, so help me, God, Louis Kender, I will end your life myself. Troy *is* calling the ambulance, and you *are* getting in it!" She was damn near shouting now, and she was crying.

The look of fear and despair on her face was long and drawn out, the look of cool, calm, and collected having completely left her. Tears that had been welling in her eyes spilled over in mass as rows of them filed down her cheeks in swift and precise lines.

After a moment, Louis sighed, giving in. "Fine. Call the ambulance. But I am not staying overnight in a hospital. I'm not dying in one of those crowded rooms, you two hear me?"

"No one said anything about dying. Just checking up," Troy said, the number already dialed and ringing.

Tracy, wiping her tears, muttered something to herself

before walking out of the room, apparently frustrated, and grabbing things they may need in case they were to stay overnight. She was careful to stay out of the eyesight of Louis as she collected an assortment of clothes and toiletries for a three-night stay.

Troy sat in the room after the phone call, the ambulance on the way. He and his father were the only two in the room, Troy sitting across from his father, who was sitting hunched over in a chair, his hands laying on the dining table and staring down at it.

"How're you feeling?" Troy asked. Louis did not answer. "Dad?" he said again, and made a small tap against his forearm.

At the touch, Louis perked up strong and fast and grabbed Troy by the wrist hard and strong, to the point of hurting where his fingers dug into Troy's skin. Louis's eyes met Troy's, and in a low, raspy voice, he whispered, "It isn't over. He is coming. To finish what he started."

Troy's eyes widened, and he pulled his hand away. "What? Who? Dad?" he said in stammered breaths, but Louis had released his hand almost immediately. He seemed to shake something off and come back to normal like he was coming out of a trance.

"I'm sorry," he said, releasing Troy's arm. "I'm not sure why I did that."

"It's all right, Dad. You are sick. The doctors are going to check you out, and we'll get this figured out, okay?" Troy said.

Louis nodded in a way that showed he understood and understood that he did not have much choice in the matter, either. He rolled over and vomited twice.

The ambulance arrived in what felt like no time at all. After the medics did their onsite routine, they put Louis on the stretcher and wheeled him into the back of the ambulance, much to Louis's protests.

"I can walk!" Louis shouted. "At least let me walk to the

ambulance, dammit."

"Mr. Kender, we aren't going to let you walk. You had a head injury and then vomited. You will absolutely be doing no walking. Please lay down while we get you in the ambulance... on three...1...2...3...."

Troy heard his father complaining yet again. "Don't know why I couldn't just walk—would've been much easier for everyone."

Then the response from the EMTs. "Mr. Kender, it would be easiest if you cooperated, sir." The sound of his mother apologizing followed. From what Troy heard, the ambulance personnel told her it was no problem. They saw this with men his age a lot.

Troy laughed a little. His father was something else.

But what had happened earlier? He guessed he would have to figure out later, as his mother was now approaching him.

"Okay," she said. "Okay. It's okay. He'll be okay. For now."

Tracy had regained herself quickly and was now calm but rigid throughout the entire ordeal. She handled herself like a woman who was coming to terms with whatever she had to do. Someone who had done this before and was tired of crying. She still needed to occasionally, of course, but only in short, controlled bursts. Her burst was over, and she was back to clinical. His father was right—she had been the only one at Grace's funeral who had held any semblance of sanity together.

"I'll follow behind you," Troy said to his mother, who had already gotten in her car.

"You sure?" she asked. "You don't have to come, Troy."

"Of course, I'm coming," Troy replied. "I'll meet you there." And he turned and got into his own vehicle.

Louis's words rang in his head, bouncing back and forth like a pinball game the entire drive. *It isn't over. He is coming. To finish what he started.*

CHAPTER 11

The distance between the Kender household and the nearest local hospital was normally a twenty-minute drive. Given they were following an ambulance, it was shorter than that, but the time felt like it was going by slower, each second passing in Troy's ears with his heartbeat dragging along as slowly as it could.

His mind was filled with what had happened when his mother had stepped out of the room. His father had grabbed his hand, hard, and had mumbled something. Something about it not being over and someone coming back...to finish what they had started. For a split second, Troy's mind wandered and froze in one small flash of thought that landed on himself and Mitch at the lake twelve years ago.

He brushed the thought away quickly.

Paranoia on my end and a man suffering from a brain tumor that is quickly spreading and getting worse. That is all that was.

Troy chanted that mental thought to himself all the way to the hospital.

When they arrived, Louis was taken somewhere in the back of the hospital, where they were to do initial testing for signs of a stroke or some other explanation for his sudden episode. This had happened a few times before, Tracy explained, but each had come back with no cause other than as a symptom of an illness he was already fighting and losing to. That was the sad-funny thing about this kind of disease—everything was so hard to explain, she had told him.

After a few long minutes of the two sitting side by side, hardly another word spoken between them, Troy finally broke, cleared his throat, and asked what had been on his mind.

"You said he was muttering something to himself, right?" Troy asked.

"Yeah, right before he fell. He started mumbling all kinds of weird things. I hope he's okay. God, I hope that this doesn't disqualify him from the trials," Tracy replied.

"Did you catch what he was saying?"

"Oh, not a lot, really. It didn't make much sense to me. Something about how it is not done yet. It is not over. Then he mentioned something. It sounded kind of like a name. I think it was—no, that couldn't be right," she replied, brushing her own thoughts aside.

"No, what was it?" Troy said.

"It kind of sounded like the start of him saying Dan's name, but that doesn't make any sense. Why would he say Dan Hampway's name? I probably just misheard him. Must've been something else."

Troy raised his eyebrows but kept his voice cool and collected. "Does he normally do that during these episodes?" His own mind was spinning with why Louis would mention Dan Hampway. The pictures on the walls, the knife, the...the breakdown he had. He kept this from his mother as he waited for her to respond.

"Sometimes yes, but normally it's something I can't understand," Tracy said, "Why?"

"Did you hear anything else?" Troy asked, waving her question away.

"No...I mean, yes, he did say one other odd thing. Something about how 'it is back, he is back.' Something like that. Why, Troy?" Tracy asked, this time more firmly.

"I don't know. Just seems odd to me," Troy replied, standing up and rubbing his face and then promptly sitting back down. "Seems like some pretty weird stuff to just start calling out, don't you think?"

"Not really, no. The doctors said it is a side effect they have seen before. I guess I have not really thought much of it other than that. Now that I've come to think of it, Dan might have been what he said. Your father and Dan had become good friends, and when he died...it took its toll on your father. And Louis did mention you two were talking about Dan out on the porch, so it probably wasn't far from his mind."

There was a long awkward pause. His mother was right, but she didn't know that Troy had just been at the Hampway home. She had not seen what he had seen.

Was it a coincidence, his father having an episode and calling for Dan the same day Troy visited? Maybe. But maybe there was something more.

Tracy just stared at Troy, a little puzzled by his questions. Troy's mind was spinning. The words from earlier that night still rang through his head as if they were just spoken, that figure in the window coming back to his vision. He shook them away.

"Yeah. Side effect. You're probably right," Troy said, not wanting to share with his mother that he had been to the house, knowing she would sincerely disapprove. "I'm going to go grab some water from the vending machine. Want anything?"

"No, that's all right. I'm hoping they transfer your dad to a room soon," she said, still giving him that look of bewilderment.

Troy nodded. "Dad's going to love to hear that. Good thing I'll be getting water when you let him know."

He headed off down the hallway in search of the vending

machine. When he found one, the hospital being a maze of poorly coded signs pointing every which way, he put his card in and grabbed himself two water bottles.

"Three bucks? For water? Christ, the medical services never fail to nickel and dime you," he muttered to himself and drank the entire first bottle in big, heaping gulps, trying to clear his head.

Coincidence. It was a coincidence. But he wasn't so sure. He was starting not to believe coincidences existed as one stacked after another. *There's something else going on. I know it. I'm not sure what, exactly, but there's more to this. It's time I quit telling myself differently.*

Then, despite his groaning of prices and his mother's decline, he bought her a soda anyway, and his father one too.

When he arrived back, he found the row of chairs he and Tracy had been occupying empty. He waited around for a second, and just as he was about to leave, his mother popped out from down the other hall.

"Troy, they got your dad a room now. It's just down here," Tracy said, beckoning for him to follow.

Troy went with her, handing the drinks over. She took them and smiled. They entered his father's hospital room together, and Tracy set Louis's soda down on the table.

It was a small room, one for non-emergencies, but with his own room, Troy figured Louis would probably be spending the night there. He sighed at the fight he saw coming when his father finally put two and two together.

The three of them sat in the room together. Tracy and Troy were sitting on the uncomfortable chairs so typical of a hospital room while Louis cursed and complained about how he was all right and they were only going to find what they always found with him, which was, as he accurately said, nothing. He began to complain about how he wanted to go home, to sleep in his own bed, and how he hated everything there was about hospitals. Troy didn't disagree...hospitals were the only thing that could get his normally cool-headed father into such a whirlwind.

After a while of it, Tracy threw her hands in the air. "I've had enough of this. The doctors are doing what they can, Louis. I will go see when you can go home, but I am warning you, Lou! If your attitude is not changed by the time I get back, so help me, God!" She stormed out of the room.

"What's her problem?" Louis said quietly when she was out of earshot.

"I think it's you, Dad," Troy whispered back with a sly smile.

"What did I do? I hate hospitals. She knows that!" he said, and then busted into a round of laughter that Troy reciprocated.

When the laughter died down and a few silent minutes had gone by, Troy tapped at his father's hand to regain his attention.

"Hey. So, Mom said you were muttering something to yourself. Something about *it* being back?"

Louis looked up contemplatively, then he sighed. "I can't remember. Hardly ever can. Seems like my memories are starting to go quick these days. Sometimes I do remember one thing, though." Louis paused and cleared his throat. When Louis spoke again, his voice was low and trembling. "Sometimes, when this kind of thing happens, I go...somewhere else. Like I am not here. And I see this man. Well, more like this thing. It's kind of like a man, but it doesn't have eyes. It has eyes, I mean, but they're just dark holes that are empty and black. It just stares at me from a distance. It just sits and stares with those eyes—those horrible, horrible eyes."

Louis was out of breath from just telling the story, the fear exhausting him.

"It stays far away from me, usually, but lately...." Louis' voice dropped even lower. "It's been closer. Stalking me. It feels like—like it's one of those damn coyotes or wolves or something, just waiting for me to slip up so it can make its move. It feels like...." Louis swallowed. "It sounds ridiculous, but it feels like I'm being hunted." Louis ended in a shudder that shook his hospital bed.

Troy shot up. "This man...this thing...can you remember anything else?"

Louis blinked a handful of times before answering. "I can't remember. I can't remember. I can't remember." His voice was rising, growing impatient. "I can't remember."

Troy looked at his father, afraid that he might set off an alarm or something. "Dad, it's okay. It is okay. Let's just stop talking about it."

At the sound of Troy's voice, Louis seemed to regain himself, like he had been in one of those trances again. Nodding, he turned his attention to the window across from him and sat there, the thoughts still seemingly plucking away. It took the reappearance of his mother in the doorway to shake Louis from it.

Troy sat in his chair with his chest pounding through his shirt. This was starting to add up to more and more. His father seeing the same thing he had seen in the woods, maybe even what he had seen with Mitch—this could be no coincidence. It was all connected.

No, no, that is just too much. Too crazy. There may be something nefarious afoot, but that is just too much.

He was shaken from his own thoughts as Tracy cleared her throat and spoke.

"Louis, they are keeping you overnight. Possibly longer if you don't get ahold of yourself and let them take the tests," Tracy says.

Louis started a round of grumbling and groaning about how much he hated it already and how awful a night at the hospital would be, even occasionally throwing a few obscene words in no one's direction. This made Tracy respond with a stern look, and Louis finally stopped.

"All right. Well, Troy, why don't you go on home? There's nothing left to do but wait for the tests anyways," his mother softly said, doing her best to ignore the commotion from Louis.

"What about you?" Troy replied.

"I've been here before. I am sure it will not be the last time, either. You're the one on vacation, so why don't you go on home, and I'll give you a call if anything changes?" Tracy replied.

Troy fumbled around with the idea in his head. He hated hospitals almost as much as his father did, but he did not totally feel right about leaving either. On the other hand, he was sure his mother was doing this with some purpose. Probably a mixture of dealing with Louis, his own hatred of hospitals, and herself feeling too exhausted to have any more company in the situation.

Finally, after taking a long, careful moment to decide, his mother spoke up again. "Besides, someone's got to watch the cat for me."

Troy had only seen the cat a handful of times, maybe three, since he had gotten into town, and although he didn't want to leave his mother and father alone in the hospital, he was still grateful for the excuse. He hated it here, with its long hallways filled with sick people, its empty chairs that were entirely too uncomfortable. Not to mention the three-dollar water. He hated that about as much as anything else. The entitled attitude of making your stay with your sick family all about making a profit.

"You sure?" Troy asked, first looking at Tracy and then at Louis.

Louis shrugged in return. "Just because your mom is forcing me to be here doesn't mean we both have to be miserable. Go on home and feed the cat, son. I'll be out tomorrow morning."

Tracy rolled her eyes in reply. "You'll be home when they

release you," she said to Louis. "All right, Troy, I'll just use the restroom, and then I'll walk with you to your car." Tracy left the room for the little restroom right down the hall.

"You sure you're going to be all right?" Troy asked, his question pointed toward Louis. But Louis was not looking at Troy—he was looking at the same odd spot out the window of the hospital. "Dad?" he said again, and touched Louis's arm.

Louis seemed to bolt back to life. This was becoming too creepily common for Troy.

"Yeah, yeah. I'm going to be all right. You go on ahead and get out of here. I think it is about time you made that phone call to Becky anyways. It's long overdue by now, I think." Louis waved him off just as Tracy was coming back into the hallway, announcing she was ready to leave.

Troy hopped in his car, asking again if Tracy was sure they would not mind that he was leaving. Reassuring him, she closed the door, and Troy closed the window and drove back to his parents' house, confused, scared, and depleted.

CHAPTER 12

Troy woke up that morning to the empty house. It felt quiet and a lot bigger than it was without anyone else inhabiting its space. He thought of how his parents might have felt waking up here every morning, just the two of them, while his father was dying. A pang of guilt passed through a knot in his stomach.

I should've been here more. I should have stayed at the hospital. I should be with him now while he has some time left.

But his mother had been right, as she almost always was when it came to Louis. It had pained him for Troy to see him like that in the kitchen and in the hospital. There was no doubt he felt more than embarrassment at the ordeal and was probably giving the nurses hell as part of the consequence. Louis was a thinker, a blue-collar intellectual, but in his own funny way, he was more than a bit odd and tended to get hung up on things from time to time. This was another trait that Troy had inherited directly.

The rumblings of an empty stomach were what brought Troy out and to the kitchen. He had not eaten anything at the hospital, nor had he eaten when he came home; instead, choosing to crawl right into bed. He was paying for that this morning with big sweeping stabs of a stomach that was completely empty.

The chairs and mats of the kitchen were still a bit off

from the events of the night before, and Troy took a second to rearrange them back in place before heading over to the counter and scrounging around for something to eat.

He sat there awhile with one of those cheap cereal bars, taking small absent bites out of it, looking out that same window he had before. That window that held the frame of the scene that had changed and ruined his life.

Troy wasn't sure if this was exactly the healthiest thing for him to be doing emotionally. He had gone out of his way to see this place once, and he had. Did he really need to see it again? Relive all of this again? He was not sure, but he did not feel that same pang of shock, guilt, and frustration he had felt the first time. He felt it. It was still crawling in, but it was less, and Troy figured that ought to be a good sign, at least for the moment.

It was early, no way past ten, but the sun still bore down on the sand, the grass, and the water that seemed to shimmer in its reflection from the lake. The shrubs and untamedness on the other side of the place seemed to be alive with morning life, and Troy realized the window was open as he heard birds chirping.

How he remembered summer mornings and nights with Becky and with Gracie, his sweet, sweet Gracie, out on the beach. It was part of the reason they had come to his parents' house so often when everything seemed so less traumatic in their lives.

Without really thinking about it, Troy moved over to the glass panel doorway and looked out to the yard with a better view.

In sacrifice, he could not hear the chirping of the birds anymore or the rustle of the trees with every gust of wind. He looked around to make sure his mother's cat, the one he could not ever remember the name of, was not lurking around to make a break. When he concluded that she wasn't, he cracked the door open.

The morning air felt light, and for the first time since he

had been home, he felt good, even pleasant, with the sun against his skin. Still barefoot and in sweats from the morning, he stepped out onto the wooden deck absently.

This was the spot where they'd had all their cookouts and family get togethers.

Graduation parties, birthday parties, college grad parties, finally nailing the teaching job parties...Becky getting a promotion party. The house of Louis and Tracy Kender was not an enormous one, but it had been the life of his childhood memories, many of which he had been reliving since he got home.

Before Troy knew it, he was walking around reliving it. He remembered the wrestling matches with Mitch out on the grass or in the sand in the summer or running across the same beach trying to get in shape for the upcoming season. It had been Mitch's idea, of course, but Troy had followed without hesitation.

Oh, how silly they must have looked back then! Kids being kids, boys being boys. He imagined the summer nights the pair had spent here, just as many, maybe more, that he had spent over at the Hampway residence. The residence that had fallen to shambles since Dan had lost his mind and...and....

Troy stopped the thoughts. These were not the things he wanted to remember during this trip down memory lane. He resettled himself, shaking away the feelings of pain and guilt from his body.

This house was also one of the reasons Becky had always loved coming over as a teenager and was where many of those young love memories were made. They would sit on the little wooden swing set off to the side, just by the beach, and watch the life and water for an hour, sometimes more, her head on his shoulder or his lap. He almost laughed to himself as he sat down on it, remembering that this may have very well been the spot he had fallen in love with her. No, he was sure of it. He fell in love with her right here on this very worn-down rickety swing.

There are so many memories at this place. He could hardly count them all, and with each passing second, another would come, and then another, like a collage of pictures he had taken and permanently etched into his memory.

Troy found himself walking without really meaning to, only noticing when his feet hit the cold sand underneath them. He was standing on the beach, a mere thirty-five feet from the dock where his daughter had lost her life.

He felt himself go cold, a chill feeling running through him as he looked out into the place. He had not been that close to it since she died, and he had not really meant to come this far. Looking out into the lake, he could see that it was as calm as he had thought back in the house, and that gave him a resentful feeling.

Don't you know what had happened here? he asked the world.

The trees, the birds, the lily pads...didn't they know? That his daughter was taken from them here in this very spot? He gave a stiff laugh to mask his grief. No. No, they didn't know. And even if they did, why would they care? Of course, there would not be anything different on the surface — why would there be?

Troy was about to give the place one last glance before he left and made his way back inside, the sight of it beginning to really create an uncomfortable feeling in his chest and eyes. They were starting to grow heavy with tears he did not want to shed, not today. As he turned to go, his eyes just scanning the last of the beach as he pivoted on his back foot, he saw it.

There was something there. Something floating in the middle of the lake. At first, he could not see it, could not quite make out what it was. Troy squinted and let his vision come into focus. It was neon yellow and floating in the water, unlovingly.

Troy's eyes widened, and he felt his feet move on their own accord, propelling him toward the lake as words began to form in his mouth.

"Oh my god," he whispered at the realization that there was a little person, a child, floating in the lake. He was readying himself, taking another two steps closer, then picking up pace as he neared the dock, breaking into a full sprint through the sand, almost tripping over himself as he did so. He was met with a hard landing as his first foot hit the wood of the dock, the force coming up through his knee, but he didn't mind that now. He picked up his pace, ready to dive in, again.

But when he reached the end of the wood, prepared to jump ten feet forward, he braced himself for an abrupt halt, almost falling in. He peered out to the edge, looking down.

There was nothing there. He looked left, and he looked right, scanning the lake back and forth, up and down. There was nothing there or anywhere. There was no body to be found out on the lake anywhere.

He slapped himself on the face. "Christ, Troy. Get it together. You're going crazy," he said to himself. He turned and marched himself miserably off the dock and back onto the sand.

Troy turned and gave a final look, just to be sure he had not missed anything.

He had not. The lake was still entirely devoid of people or bodies. He turned back again and started heading for his parents' house.

He stopped halfway when he heard the giggle. He turned back to the lake in disbelief. He could not believe what he had just heard, but that giggle was unmistakable. It was the giggle of his seven-year-old girl. It was Grace.

But when he turned around, again, there was nothing to greet him. Everything seemed ordinary as it always did—the house, the beach, the lake. Nothing out of the ordinary at all. But Troy could not shake the feeling of unease from his vision or the sound he had just heard. He rubbed his eyes and massaged his temples.

"What is happening to me?" he said to himself, dismayed and scared, as he marched away, the sound still ringing in his ears.

CHAPTER 13

Troy hopped in his car. The grocery store was not far, and even though he had already gone for Tracy, he figured he needed to get out of the house before he went thoroughly insane. He was expecting his father to be home soon. Based on what his mom had told him they should be leaving after a few more quick things with the specialists, but until then, he wanted to burn as much of his time away from that lake and dock as humanly possible.

He pulled up into the lot of the grocery store, parked, and walked in. He was not sure what he was here for anymore. He figured it was probably to get out of the house more than anything, so he walked in, not really knowing where to start.

Troy grabbed a cart and started walking down aisles aimlessly. The place had changed a little, of course—it had been two years—but for the most part, it was basically the same. He even thought he recognized a few fellow patrons from his younger years of living here, but they did not seem to recognize him, so he didn't say anything.

It was a familiar place, the local shopping plaza and the family owned stores. Really, the whole town felt that way, but he felt like he did not quite belong here anymore. That he was not a part of this community like he once had been. And he supposed it was probably true. He had moved on, moved to another town, another state. When he and Beck had gotten a divorce, he ran away.

But for whatever odd reason, it also felt like Black Lake had called him back. Like this town had weird unfinished business with him. When he first arrived and had these feelings, he shook them off as ridiculous. But now...now he had the feeling, maybe even the awareness, that it was true.

He also felt like a quitter. Maybe that's why Becky would not answer his calls in those early months. Maybe she hated him for that. Maybe she wasn't wrong.

But it wasn't totally my fault, right? Our baby had died.

Their sweet, sweet seven-year-old had drowned to death in a freak accident. And he stood by Becky. He stood by, and he took the blame. He had tried to make it work—oh god, how he had tried—but it was never enough.

It was not enough. He had fallen into that dark spell, that dark place, and it wasn't like he was really in any position to deal with that. And who could blame him? No, he had lost a daughter, then he had lost himself, and finally, he had lost his wife ...and the blame was easy to place. The more he had thought about it and the longer he had to reflect on it, he had put all the blame on one person. That blame, that hurt, he placed it squarely on his own shoulders.

Troy was abruptly thrown from his daydream by the crashing of his shopping cart, the clanging of metal on metal pulling him back into reality.

"Oops. I am so sorry about that. I wasn't paying any at—" He stopped in surprise.

"Troy?" the voice called to him. For a long moment, he didn't believe it. Not until he heard her voice again. "Oh, Jesus Christ," the voice of the formerly known Becky Kender muttered.

"Beck?" Troy managed to get out in a flustered grasp for

words as he stood with his mouth slightly open from surprise.

He supposed it should not have been that weird—it was the main grocery store in town. And wasn't this what he had been planning in the back of his mind all along? Against his father's advice, hadn't he been avoiding the call he knew he should make? He had excuses—his dad being in the hospital, that was exhausting. But still, had he not brushed the thought away last night and even today?

Yes, yes, he had. In some weird way, he had been hoping to organically bump into her. And now he had.

But now, being faced head to head with meeting Becky, he felt his heart skip a beat.

"What are you doing here?" she asked. Her voice was not warm or inviting. It was hostile.

Troy swallowed hard. "I'm here for my dad. He's sick. Had some time off work, figured maybe it would be good for me to come back and try and, you know...." Troy wasn't sure what to say. *Watch him die? Be there for him? Heal from this old town before my old man kicks the bucket?*

Despite the joke, that was certainly part of it. But what was the other part? To find Becky and profess his undying and unadulterated love and the misery the last two years had given him? Probably as much the second as the first, but he also knew the aisle of the local market was probably not the best place for it, so he changed the subject.

"You look great, Becky." And it was true. The events two years ago had aged her some, sure. It had aged him too, so it was no surprise. But underneath it, he could still see the gorgeous woman he had married. She even wore her hair the way he had liked, even after all this time, even though she hated doing it that way.

Was that on purpose? he asked himself. *Or does the new guy she is with now like it that way, too?* Troy stopped himself. *You don't know if that is even true about her being with some other guy, Troy. And even if she is, that's not your...his what? His problem? His concern?*

No, it isn't your business.

"Thanks," she said, and started pushing her cart down the rest of the aisle.

"I tried to call before I even came out here, though I'm sure you know that," he said. "I was hoping maybe we could meet up for coffee or something while I was in town."

"Troy, don't," Becky said flatly, pushing her cart past him.

"Beck...c'mon. Talk to me," he pleaded. He was sure this would be his only chance. He could not let her go without putting up at least some kind of a fight.

"No, Troy. Just stop," she replied again.

Troy could not help himself. He reached for her and gently touched her forearm. She pulled away and pushed her cart further, now almost entirely past him.

"Becky, please," he called again, tearing up just a little. He swallowed hard, forcing the emotion down so he could give himself to a rational conversation with his ex-wife.

"Don't touch me. Do not look for me. Do not follow me. Just leave me alone," she replied.

"Beck, I only wanted to talk. Just one day. For thirty minutes, that is all I want. I just wanted to see how you were doing, and to—" he started, but he couldn't finish. He could feel his voice cracking now. He had not prepared himself for this. And between it and the hallucinations he was having this morning and the day before, he figured he was going to break at any second.

Fearing that he might, making a fool of himself to his ex-wife in the supermarket aisle, he closed his eyes and took a breath. He listened.

"No, Troy. I said no. You may be visiting your parents, but that does not mean I want you to track me down and find me at the fucking grocery store. If this was your grand plan, to come back home and sweep me off my feet, consider your mission failed. I have moved on, Troy. There isn't any room for you anymore."

The words hurt. They cut at him a little deeper than he would have cared to admit. He wasn't sure he had come out here to sweep Becky off her feet the way she put it, but now that it was out there in the open, he wasn't so sure that was *not* what he was trying to do either. "Becky, please. Give me half an hour. Just over at Bruegger's. I will buy you your favorite cup of coffee. It's still that triple Venti half sweet, non-fat, caramel Macchiato? Probably two shakes of that chocolate stuff and three shakes of the sugar. Maybe two. It just depends on if it's sunny or not. You always said you liked the extra sugar, but only when it's cloudy." Troy paused. Becky didn't reply. "That is the one, though. I'm sure it is. It ate up all my checks from my first job. I know you remember that." Troy paused.

He could tell Becky was a little taken aback, maybe even a little impressed by his memory. Troy knew he would never forget. That had been their first date and almost every Sunday morning thereafter for years. It had only stopped when Grace had— He pushed the thought out of his mind and continued talking before Becky could object.

"And if you never want to see me again, I get it. I will throw away your number and leave you alone. Just please, consider giving me *twenty* minutes even, Beck. It's been so long." His voice was shaking and barely above a choked whisper. Troy figured he probably sounded rather pathetic right now, but he did not really care. This was likely the only chance he was going to have, and he would be damned if he did not swing for the fences with everything his heart had left.

Becky seemed to mull the idea over in her head for a minute. He was sure she was thinking about how much she didn't want to go, but the very fact she was contemplating this and not bolting out of the store gave Troy a sense of hope on the edge of the cliff. His heart was pounding hard, his breath a burdened chore as he waited.

A minute or twenty passed, Troy wasn't entirely sure which, before she finally broke the silence.

"Fine," she said. "Fine. Twenty minutes at Bruegger's tomorrow at five. You buy. Nothing more."

"Thank you," Troy replied, regaining some color in his face.

"Don't be late. The clock starts at five whether you're there or not," Becky said in return.

"I'm always early, you know that," Troy said.

She nodded and then turned away, pushing her cart down the rest of the aisle and eventually out of sight.

CHAPTER 14

The summer night air was wet and warm, but Troy still felt the chill of Black Lake come over him as he loaded his groceries into the back of his car. He did not know how he had done it, gotten that date with Becky, but he had. That was what warmed him in that cool breeze.

Somehow, he had gotten it. It seemed his father had been right after all. There was still a shot in the dark. They needed a face to face, something organic and unplanned, and somehow, he had not gone and screwed the whole thing up.

His parents were on their way home now — they had called just as Troy was paying the lady at the register. Even with self-checkout being available, Troy had a weird thing with wanting to use a traditional register if it was available. Louis had told him once that someone was making a living at that register, and those self-scans were taking over people's jobs. Troy had not used one since. It also gave him a minute to stand idly and think about what news his parents had delivered to him.

The news was not good, but he supposed it wasn't bad either. There was no real answer other than a side effect of whatever was going on in the inner workings of Louis's brain from the disease. They supposed it was something that would happen with more frequency as the cancer began to run its course, but nothing seemed to be alarming the doctors any more than before. As for now, he was still up for consideration for the clinical trials, though Troy worried at this rate that his father would be dead before they even started.

When Troy arrived back at his parents' house, it was still empty, however. He suspected they would be home soon and hurried to put all the store-bought items in their places. The dizziness from the night's event with Becky replayed through his mind as he sat himself down on the living room couch, waiting for the arrival of his parents.

After what felt like twenty minutes or so, he used his phone to check what time it was, only to find it was dead. He sighed and stood up. Troy walked into his bedroom to plug it in, only stopping to go to the bathroom on his way.

He stepped into the room, taken aback by the cold air that touched his skin, sending a shudder through him. He'd had the chills since his encounter with Beck, but this was significantly colder, even to the point of unreasonable discomfort for a summer evening. It had to be at least twenty degrees colder in here than in the living room he had come from. He rubbed his upper arms where the goosebumps had already formed.

Troy let his eyes dart around the place and eventually settle on the window, where he saw the blinds swaying from the warm summer night breeze. He didn't remember leaving them open, but it seemed logical enough. Still, the air in the room was far colder than it had been when he was last outside, which was less than half an hour ago.

Quickly he walked over to the window and closed it, but only after taking a second to poke his head out of it. The air outside was the same temperature it had been, if only slightly cooler, nowhere near the coldness of the room the rest of his body was standing in.

He removed himself from the window, a bit perplexed, and closed it with one forceful push before remembering why he had come here in the first place. The sound of the front door swinging open released him from his trance.

"Troy?" Tracy called. "We're home."

Shocked and startled, he recovered himself and called back. "Be right there."

"How was everything?" he asked once he had made his way down into the living room where his mom and dad were. His mother compulsively rearranged the cushions, and his father placed his summer hat on top of the coat rack.

Louis wiped a bead of sweat from his brow, reminding Troy of the contrast in temperatures he had just discovered. His mind teased him again of his past with this town. When his mother spoke, the thoughts left.

"Went okay. Nothing really to do, and nothing really to report," Tracy said.

"Like I told you would happen. Was a waste of time," Louis said. Tracy shot him a disapproving look, to which he defended, "What? It was," with a shrug of his shoulders.

"Anyways…," Tracy said irritably, "the clinical trials are still on. At least for now. We should hear back soon. At least that's what they said when I called them on the way home. Hopefully, they'll call in the next few days. They start soon," Tracy finished, her voice growing anxious.

"Good Lord willing, I'll just keel over here," Louis mumbled.

Tracy shot Louis the worst look Troy had ever seen on his mother's face. Louis must have caught it because he changed the subject as quickly and innocently as possible.

"So, what's the good word with Becky?" His words pointed to Troy.

"About that…I actually ran into Becky at the store," Troy

replied.

"And...?" Louis asked, waiting for the rest.

"We're going to meet up for some coffee," Troy replied. "Tomorrow at five."

"Great news, son. Now, don't screw it up," Louis said with a wink.

CHAPTER 15

Troy was tapping his finger along the edge of the farthest back table of Bruegger's Coffee and Cafe. He was early, as he'd said he would be, and he was nervous, which he'd told himself he would not be. Yet here he was twitching his finger on the edge of the table. Aside from yesterday, he had not so much as said a single word to his ex-wife, and somehow, he had roped her into coffee.

He had no idea how he had done it, but he had, and now he needed to not screw it up.

Bruegger's had not changed much. In fact, it really had not changed at all, from what Troy remembered. The two currently working employees, a young man and woman that were both his age, were Deion Brown and Adriana Perez. He remembered them both from school. The three of them were never more than friendly acquaintances back then, but as they were making the small amount of orders, he could tell there was some chemistry between them now.

The quiet lulls in between customers, which were frequent and long at this time of day, gave Troy the idea that they were probably romantically involved now. Troy supposed that was a bit of an assumption—he didn't know if they were—but it was interesting to Troy every time he heard of a new couple that had gone to school together without dating even once, but through fate ended up together in the end. Even if he'd had the opposite happen to him.

They were both nice enough when he ordered, nodding, asking how he had been. They kept it short. They didn't mention Grace, though he could see through those smiles into that pity most of the town's residents so often gave him. He hated it but expected it and didn't take meaningful offense.

Troy did wonder, though. *What do people think? Becky and I lost a child, divorced. And I split town. What kinds of things do these people say when I am brought up?* Troy knew he wasn't the centerpiece of conversation — he wasn't that egotistical — but Becky still lived in town, and so did his parents. He was sure at some point he was brought up, even if it was just old friends of his reuniting and shooting the shit.

Was he looked at as a stain on this town? A cursed roach? A witch? After the amount of bad luck he had in Black Lake, he wouldn't be surprised if people truly believed him to be a bad omen, carrying with him disaster everywhere he went.

He pushed the thoughts from his mind. Did he really want to know? He thought he did, at first. With further examination, he wasn't so sure.

On that note, Troy ended his people watching and turned his attention to the coffee on his table. It was still steaming from the top of his cup. Troy reached over to the packets of sugar to his left and poured three of them. That was how she liked it...or used to, anyway.

He stirred it around and gazed out the window of the little small-town coffee house, a wave of memories flooding back to him.

This had been their first date.

God, that felt so long ago, but he could relive it like it was yesterday. He had been so nervous, even more than he was now, as he waited for Beck to show up.

He remembered how she was ten minutes late, and at first, Troy had figured he had been set up. He was so disappointed he damn near slid out of his chair and sulkily walked his teen self-back home. Then he heard the little dinger ring as someone entered the store. Lucky for Troy, he had not left yet, because when he looked up, there she was.

She was beautiful. Not in the same way she was as the full-grown woman he had come to know and love over the years they were together. But it was then, as a junior in high school, that the seed of his love had been planted. And even after all this time, all this...unfortunate chaos his life had brought him, he still was. He figured he always would be.

The ring of the door, the same ringer he had heard so many years ago, took his attention away from the daydream. Becky had just walked in, but there was not much of a smile on her face, not like his vivid memory had. No, she looked impatient, maybe even a little irritated. He waved her over.

"Hi," she said as she sat down across from him.

"Hi," Troy replied, his voice sheepish and timid. "I got your coffee for you."

"I see that," she said. "Thanks."

There was a brief pause before either one of them spoke again. It was long, drawn out, and awkward. Troy wasn't exactly sure what he had imagined, but this was not what he was exactly hoping for the first time since the divorce, and likely the last time he would have to talk to Becky.

"Listen, Troy. I am not totally sure why I agreed to this. I'm not. We decided to end things for a reason. I am sorry your dad's sick, I am. And I hope your mom's well. But after everything, I just— Look, I know we were basically kidding ourselves, but I just don't know —"

"Beck, I'm sorry."

Troy did not interrupt her to be rude. He just needed to get out his piece before she took up and left, which looked like it was coming his way quickly. He figured the time he was promised was ticking away, and it certainly was not going to be twenty minutes, more like twenty seconds. The words spewed from his mouth as if he could not get them out fast enough.

"I'm sorry. I shouldn't have shut you out. I was a kid, and I was stupid. I was so...lost in my own grief that I did not see yours. I'm sorry, Becky, I really am," Troy said. He could feel his face was hot and tingly. He didn't want to cry again, not like he had in the supermarket, not here. He breathed in, resolving that if she left, he would wait to break down until he was in his car. There, he could at least do it without prying eyes.

"I know you are, Troy. And I am sorry, too, but my point still stands," Becky replied. Her voice was not cold—no, it was more...sad.

"And that's okay. But you did promise me twenty minutes, and it has only been three if you do not count the ten minutes when you were late. I am just asking for twenty minutes. Nothing more. Promise. After this, you can take off, and we can go our separate ways. I just...I feel horrible being on these terms, Beck. I really do. I cannot sleep when I think about it. Twenty minutes, that's all I ask...and you did say yes, you know," Troy said with just the smallest hint of a pleading smirk at the end.

***

Even through his emotion, he gave her that same smirk he had always had when they were kids. And for a moment, just a blip of a second even, she felt something for Troy she had not felt in years. Longing. A dull ache that was familiar from the first few months after they had divorced.

Becky closed her eyes, exhaled, and opened them just to close them again.

"Twenty minutes. Please," Troy said, hanging up his last-ditch effort.

Becky looked up to him before she spoke. His eyes were big swirls of red-rimmed color. It was obvious to her he had been crying often since he had been home. Or maybe it was for two years now. Maybe even longer. As bad as things had been at their worst, how much of it was really his fault? It's not like he wanted his best friend to die and him to survive. It's not like he did anything, not really, to let Grace die. Now, his father was dying. She felt the slightest piece of guilt for the harsh judgements she had made.

All that, and he's still here to see me, too, she thought. *Like I'm still the priority in his mind. Like when we were kids.* The guilt wasn't what made her reply, though. That made her want to leave and never see his face again. It was that achy longing feeling that took her by surprise again. It was stronger than that gross guilt feeling. It was the feeling that kept her glued to her seat.

"I suppose I did say I would give you twenty, didn't I? Twenty minutes. But no more surprise visits after this, Troy. I mean it," Becky replied, and took a sip of her coffee.

Troy nodded slightly, sighed a big huff of relief, and sat silently for a minute before he began.

"How's the triple Venti half sweet, non-fat, caramel Macchiato with—"

"Three sugar?" Becky finished. "You remembered after all this time?"

"Yeah. Think I have grown a bit fond of it myself, though my coffee house is nowhere near this place. It's a big name, sure, but it isn't holding a candle to ole Bruegger's Coffee and Cafe."

That was one of the few things he had missed about this little town. There were not many things he did miss, five maybe, and he guessed four of them could be Beck, but one of those things was Bruegger's.

"You know, when I was sitting here waiting for you, I got

to thinking about the first time we went here. Do you remember?" Troy asked.

"Of course, I do. Our first date, how could I forget? You got a plain black coffee. You said you liked it, but it didn't seem like you did to me." She gave half a laugh at the recollection, which she stifled quickly.

"Funny story about that. I remember you saying you wanted to go here, and I asked if I could take you. You said yes. My heart skipped a beat then. But then I got to thinking...oh no! I do not have a job or *any* money. How was I going to pay for it? This place is great, but it isn't cheap, that's for sure."

Becky nodded in agreement. This place was great, but it was certainly *not* cheap.

"Anyway, so on my way home from school, I stopped here and looked at the menu and saw that it was expensive, even for the *cheap* stuff. The counter people were looking at me all funny, so I left before I saw the whole menu," Troy said, laughing."So, I go home, and I'm looking all around my room for spare cash, and I can't find any! I checked the washing machine for dollars, quarters, anything! But all that looking only resulted in fifty cents. So, I did what any rational sixteen-year-old would do—I walked into my dad's room and found his little stash. It was a jackpot for me. He had a couple of hundred bucks, maybe. I took a five and three ones because that's what I *thought* he wouldn't notice."

Becky lifted her eyebrows at his annunciation.

"Yeah. I'll get to that in a minute," Troy said, addressing it. "So, I take the eight dollars and fifty cents. I was an hour early. That is how nervous I was. Oh, God. An hour! I sat at this very table and twiddled my thumbs for an hour! God, I was weird."

Becky laughed at this, throwing her head back and covering her mouth. "You say it like it's changed or something. You are cute in that quirky way, I do admit."

"All right, all right, I am a bit odd. Anyway, so you were

late, and I damn near left! I was two seconds away from leaving out the back door of this place, tail between my legs when you walked in and... you took my breath away from that second. Think I fell in love on the spot, if I'm honest. It was either here or my parents' porch swing that summer. One of the two."

Becky was blushing just a little. She remembered this vividly herself. Troy was selling himself a bit short, as he always did.

He was a handsome kid and a nice guy. She had been equally nervous, but her best friend, Sophia, had made her wait... and wait...and wait. It was only at four, their designated meeting time, that Sophia gave her the keys to the car and let her leave.

"So, I sat back down and waited for you. You sat down, and we started talking, and then we realized it was kind of weird we were in a coffee house empty-handed, so I asked what you wanted. You said a 'triple Venti half sweet, non-fat, caramel Macchiato.' Still, I don't really know what is in that, but I went up there, repeating it to myself to make sure I did not screw the whole thing up, by the way!"

Becky laughed because she had heard him whisper it, too. "I am not so sure about the whisper part. I heard you all the way up to the counter!"

"When I got to the register — be ready for this, Beck — I saw it was basically all I had. So, I ordered it and got the cash back and then ordered mine with what was left. I had three dollars. All I could get was a plain coffee. And I hated it," Troy finished. Now he was really starting to laugh, and Becky had joined in. It felt so nice...so natural.

"And all these years, you never said anything!" she accused him. "I ordered you a black coffee every time we came here, and you drank it."

"Well, yeah! What else was I going to do?" he asked.

"You could have said something, at some point, at least.

You didn't have to keep it up! Or steal your dad's money!" she said. "I could have paid for myself had you said something!"

The whole story was funny. It was cute. It was their story. But it did not feel awkward or weird to talk about. In fact, it was kind of nice. It felt like they were reliving memories of other people. Becky liked that—they reminded her of easier times. Times before the accident.

"What was I going to do, Becky? I was a kid! Probably more important was that—I was in love! So, I sipped that horrible plain coffee, and when you left, I went home and rinsed my mouth out with as much water as I could. But here is the best part. I got home, and my dad.... Well, he was waiting for me when I walked into the kitchen, his stash laid out on the counter."

"Oh, no!" Becky said, her laughter taking off yet again. Louis had always been an intimidating guy. He was not angry or rude or anything. He was just that kind of guy that intimidated you, especially young kids, and especially the sixteen-year-old Becky Gordon.

"He was so mad, Beck. I thought he was going to put a hammer to my head or something! Then he asked why, and I said was taking you out on a date. He asked to see a picture of you, so I pulled one up on my phone and showed him. Can you guess what he said?"

Beck shook her head. She had no idea.

He cleared his throat and postured up a little, giving the best impression of his father he could manage.

"'That is a beautiful young lady, son. And she graced you with a date. Now, you go along, and you make sure you do everything right, or she'll ruin you, boy. She'll ruin you and leave you wishing you had. Oh, you owe me a weekend of yard work for that eight-fifty.'"

"Anyways, he always loved you. Like a daughter of his own. Pretty sure that is the only reason he bought that overpriced security system from you in the first place. He still has it, by the way."

"Really? And c'mon, it's a good company!" Becky said back. "They make good equipment. And believe it or not, they finally actually gave me that promotion they always talked about!"

"Maybe it is, but it's still way overpriced. That is good to hear about the promotion, though. I am happy for you. I know how much you wanted it," Troy replied with a smile.

"How is he? I used to run into him and your mom in town. Not a lot, but every so often. I heard he's pretty sick," Beck asked.

"He's been better. Only has a few months left...which is why I am here, you know. But he is...." Troy searched for the right word, "He's managing."

"I'm sorry to hear that, Troy. Give him my regards?"

"Of course. I think I let him down hard when we...you know. But, he will be happy to hear from you. He hasn't stopped talking about you since the first night I got into town," he said. "In any event, I just thought the part about the coffee was funny, but unfortunately, my twenty minutes are up."

There was a pause from both. Becky looked down and took another sip of her coffee, thinking.

This was her first real date in a while. It was the first one that was ending well in even longer than that. Becky was not sure she wanted it to end now, regardless of her words earlier.

She had been on a few dates, only in the last few months. Nothing stuck. None of these men knew what it felt like to be a parent or to lose a child. She usually felt annoyed by their questions, like they were not being genuine with their intentions but rather checking to see just how damaged she really was.

These were the things that made her think that men might be a thing of her past, at least long-term relationships. They were just too much work, and a casual hook up was much easier to find and didn't come with the baggage.

But this was nice. No pressure. All Troy wanted was to catch up, and it felt good. She had missed him in some weird way. That familiarity. Those shared memories.

Troy was still the love of her life—today had proved as much. She had no intention of ever remarrying, especially not her divorcee. This was good, though—she didn't want it to end. There was just so much history.

Here and now, just the two of them, something felt right, and she missed that. That feeling of warmth he gave her, his joking jabs that always seemed to make her crack a smile. No one else had given her this same feeling. This was her Troy, and she missed him.

She twirled her coffee around in her cup. "And how are you...*managing*?" Becky asked.

"...managing. He had an episode the other day. That was hard. Never seen anything like it. And I am in my parents' house. That is not...easy. Really, if I am honest, nothing about being in this place is easy. Memories everywhere. My dad, Mitch, you, Grace," Troy said softly. "But I'm managing. I needed to come back home. I would have regretted it for the rest of my life. Thanks for asking." In almost a whisper, Troy asked, "What about you? How are you getting along?"

"I'm...good," she lied.

"That's good, Becky. I'm glad."

The sound of his hushed voice was what broke her.

In that moment, she did not see the man that abandoned her in grief or the husband she had fought with day and night for months. She saw the boy she loved, that had turned into the man she loved even more. She saw the father of their daughter, the one who would tuck Grace in at night and read her books. The man that was always there to listen to Grace and herself, who always understood the irrationality of emotion and sadness with gentleness and care, but had the strength to push forward. In front of her was someone she truly missed dearly, not the broken mess she had needed to leave to survive herself.

"When do you leave?" she asked.

"A few weeks before the end of summer is the plan," Troy replied.

Another pause came and went.

"Maybe I'll call you, and we'll go out to dinner before then," Becky said in a statement as if to herself and not to who was sitting across from her.

"Maybe you will," Troy said. "It was great seeing you again, Becky." He stood up and pushed his chair in. "I'll keep my phone handy in case that's what you want. If not...like I said, I got my twenty minutes."

Becky nodded, not leaving her chair, staring off into the outside world through the closest window.

"See you, Troy," she said, softly.

"I hope so. Bye, Beck." And then he left.

***

When he arrived home, his parents were watching television, and he felt no need to tell them what had happened at Bruegger's. He doubted very much that she would call him—she was just being nice—but those twenty minutes were a secret just for him to relive until the day he left town.

CHAPTER 16

Troy rubbed the tiredness from his eyes with his knuckles as he headed into the kitchen. How long had he slept? He wasn't sure. He figured he had probably gone to bed somewhere around nine or so, fallen asleep by nine-thirty. Judging by the look of outside, it was somewhere around nine in the morning.

Twelve hours of sleep, and he was still beat. And it was not the kind of beat from a slumber hangover. No, he was still thoroughly exhausted all the way to his bones. He had been since his first night back in Black Lake.

He yawned and looked out of the front window.

Of course, both his parents were gone, his mother at the library, his father having gone with her. He did not mind that, though. He was happy to have the alone time, to dissect everything he had anticipated he would feel as he felt it.

Troy rubbed his eye with his knuckle again and headed out to the kitchen. He poured himself a glass of OJ, thinking that maybe breakfast was not quite the hassle this time around, as the memories of yesterday morning came bounding into his brain.

Becky.

He had run into her, and somehow it turned into more than he expected. He had gotten the twenty minutes, had gone over it, and had the possibility of another before he left town. He had played the scenario in his head every day for the last handful of years, and not once had he pictured it going that well.

Troy sighed a breath of relief and took a sip of his juice. He glanced up at the window that looked out into the backyard. A wave of anxiety washed over him, his mind darting back to only twenty-four hours ago when he could have sworn he had seen a yellow jacket...and a body floating in the water. The memory was so vivid and clear, and so was the body, that he swore even now he could see it there from the kitchen table.

The odd feeling in his chest, the one he had felt yesterday morning, crept its way back into him and through his entire body. The body, or whatever he'd seen — or thought he had — was gone when he had gotten to the lake. There was no trace of anything, even when he looked around later that evening when he had gotten home. There was nothing to be found. Nothing.

But it looked so real. It all felt so real.

He had not been dreaming, nor had he been daydreaming. Troy could remember the sand on his feet, the gentle breeze kissing his cheeks. The labored breathing he had after he had run out to greet...nothing. But God, that jacket, that yellow jacket and the body, it had all looked so real.

Real enough for him to gasp. Real enough for his chest to hurt from that anxious feeling you get in your heart when you know something terrible is happening.

But it wasn't, he said to himself. *It was not real. You had just had a weird play of the mind the morning before, nothing more, and you do not need to fear the window for it. That is something a child does after watching a scary movie, not a grown adult who has stared death right in the face. Twice you have stared at that face of death. Once two years ago with your daughter and even your own mortality twelve years ago.*

He scoffed at himself, but kept his distance from the window, instead opting to go sit at the kitchen table with his drink.

He thumbed through the stack of mail that had been left out, tossing addressed envelopes and mail ads to the side until he finally found a newspaper to distract himself.

This will do to keep these creeping thoughts at bay.

He wasn't sure why his old man had insisted on keeping his newspaper subscription—it was tedious, expensive, and totally unnecessary with the use of modern technology. Though Troy knew why. Louis Kender, the same man who wouldn't get rid of his truck, the man of old habits, would not cancel his subscription of paper mail either.

In this moment, though, Troy was happy he had something to idly do. To take his mind off it. In that different light, Troy had supposed this was just the reason his father had kept the newspaper around. An idle distraction from his slow demise.

But even when he flipped through the pages, he still felt a chill from that fucking window. That chill reminded him that he knew something was wrong in this town. He still was not sure what, but that chill reminded him it was there.

Troy thumbed through the newspaper faster, searching for a story that was exciting enough to work its intended purpose. It was a local one, specific to the happenings of Black Lake Township. There was a lot of misfortune in this town. That was something everybody knew, something everybody here lived with. "Bad things happen around Black Lake" was what people said since he was a kid.

They sure said it a lot more after Mitch drowned, now that Troy had thought about it. And the more he thought about it, the more he realized that things did get darker in the town after that winter. Like, the series of missing teens who had shown up dead on the outskirts of town, not far from the start of the same lake Mitch had gone missing at. They had found those bodies; however, the faces were so mangled from whatever had happened they were unrecognizable. They had looked like they had been melted by acid. No definitive cause of death was ever given.

There was one survivor of that group of friends. She had been taken into custody, but she never said another word after the events — or another tangible word at all. She was eventually moved to a custody behavioral institution as the leading suspect in a homicide. After no evidence could prove she was guilty of anything, she was released and transferred to a non-prison emotional behavioral hospital.

To Troy's knowledge, she was still there. No one talked about it openly. There were stories, but that was all. Troy avoided hearing them when he could, and given his mental breakdowns after Mitch's immediate death, people avoided telling him.

There was also Troy's senior year. Another student, an actual friend of Troy's, Brandon Vega, had set his own home ablaze with his family inside. He had been diagnosed with a similar disease as Troy's father, and it had weathered his mental state in a more extreme way. The cancer had spread and spread, and the best the doctors could say was how the sickness, coupled with his sister's untimely death two years prior (she had died in an accident when he had been driving), had led to a complete psychotic break in undiagnosed psychosis.

And then, of course, there was the case of Mitch's dad, who went AWOL suddenly and murdered his own family. Blamed on PTSD.

None of it quite added up to Troy, but then again, who was he to question anything? He himself had swallowed whatever the doctors gave him for years to battle his own psychosis and diagnosed schizophrenia disorder. But still, how many mentally ill people were in this town? And how many were so mentally ill they would, even with outside trauma, attack and kill their own loved ones? The amount this town had seen seemed like more than a rational number to Troy.

The idea only made his feelings about what happened yesterday, what happened to Mitch and himself over a decade ago — even what had happened with Grace — feel even stronger. There was a malevolent force at hand. He did see a body in that lake, didn't he?

Maybe something happened that winter..., his mind played. *Or maybe I just heard it more. Wasn't like we awakened something. Mitch drowned, for fucks sake.*

In that moment, Troy could have sworn he felt whatever he had thought was in this town was burning a hole in him through that window. His eyelid twitched twice.

Troy glanced up at the window, giving in to his frustrations.

You know what? I might just go march over there and see for myself that there is nothing! There is nothing there, nothing malevolent or evil about this town. This isn't some horror novel about a small town in Maine where a demon eats fuckin' kids! This is the real world!

He bolted himself up from his chair and took three large steps over to the start of the kitchen. When he was taking his last step, he stopped short, that feeling of paranoia becoming a feeling of dread and fear.

Something had caught his eye out of the sliding door into the backyard. He took a step back and spun to the door, peering out and squinting so he could see. He blinked twice to assure himself that it had not been another trick played on him by his subconscious mind. The figure of a little girl on the edge of the dock, her feet in the water, her back turned to him, remained in his line of vision.

Troy's eyes widened as the chilling wave of fear and anxiety rising in his chest grew into a mountain of horror. He felt himself wanting to look away, to pretend he did not see it. It had to be some form of hallucination, some evil trick on his psyche!

But instead of looking away and going back to his juice and paper, he found his footsteps propelling him, with a morbid, insane curiosity, closer to the door.

He was in a state of terrified shock as he felt himself put his hand on the latch and pull it open, his bare foot then touching the earth. The blades of grass moving beneath his feet sent a shiver up his spine as he stepped out into the backyard.

Troy squinted his eyes, still wanting to believe his mind was playing a memory, something not real. But the girl at the end of the dock remained.

He broke out into a light jog across the yard and eventually onto the beach, feeling as if his feet that were just tickled by the blades of grass were now sinking into the sand. Losing his balance, slipping and clumsily catching himself just before he fell, Troy realized how scared he was. His heart was pounding.

What the hell is a little girl doing out here on my parents' dock by herself?

It was not until he was ten feet away from the dock, twenty feet from the girl, that he recognized her. He came to a halt.

The beating in his chest, already thumping loudly, thumped harder. The chill trickle of fear was turned into a free-flowing cataract waterfall of terror and confusion.

"Grace?" he called out. "Grace, is that you?" He knew how absurd the question was, but he could not deny what he was seeing right in front of him.

"Hi, Daddy," she said in a soft, sweet voice. Grace still faced the water, her face out of view.

Troy could not believe it. But he had seen and heard it. There was no denying it now. He could be hallucinating. Certainly, he could be, but there was no denying that he was seeing his seven-year-old daughter. She was sitting at the end of the dock, her toes splish-splashing up water as she dangled them in the lake, kicking them around gingerly.

"Gracie baby, what are you doing out here?" Troy felt himself ask, almost as if he was out of body.

"Waiting for you, Daddy."

"What do you mean? Waiting? For me?"

"Yes, Daddy. I was waiting for you."

"Why?" Troy could feel a lump in his throat drop, and he took another step toward his daughter. "Why were you waiting for me?" he asked again, taking another step to the dock, standing at the start of it. His feet felt the jagged parts of wood that needed to be replaced, cementing in his mind that this was real. He was not dreaming. He really was seeing his daughter in some way. Talking to her, even.

"You said we could go fishing, Daddy. Remember? You said you would take me fishing later." Her voice was small, pretty, and playful. He loved her voice. He missed it. He missed *her*. Troy felt tears welling in his eyes.

"I know I did, baby. I know I did. I'm sorry," he choked out.

He took his first step onto the wood of the dock. Troy was not sure what was happening if what he was seeing was a vivid hallucination, a spirit sent from God, or a ghost sent to haunt him. All Troy knew in that moment was that he saw his daughter.

For the first time in two years, he could see her. He was ten feet from her now. He could almost touch her, brush her golden hair away from her face. Kiss her cheek. In that moment, Troy lost himself in the sick feeling of sadness and regret he had felt every day for two years as he stepped closer to the dock.

"Why are you sorry? Is it because I died?" she asked.

Troy sniffled twice. "Yes, sweetheart. Yes. It's because you d-di-died," Troy replied, croaking out the words.

"I'm sorry I died, Daddy. I just wanted to go fishing. I loved it when we went fishing," she replied.

Her voice was so...real. So soft and innocent. The Grace he loved and remembered.

"Come on, Daddy. Maybe we can still go fishing."

"I don't think we can, baby. You died. And I am still here.
I'm so sorry," Troy said again. But he had taken another step.

He knew he must be hallucinating now, but still, he did
not want it to end. There were so many things he had left to
say, so many unsaid "I love yous," so many hugs and kisses left
unshared. To many unsaid jokes that only he and Grace would
get.

Troy wondered then if Grace had been watching him since
she died. If she had seen the mess he left with her mother. He
wanted to tell her, "It's going to be okay, sweetheart. I saw your
mother yesterday. We went out for coffee. You should come see
us. Come see your mother. We can make this right." But he didn't.
He just wiped the tears from his eyes and sniffled the running
snot into his nose.

"But I *want* to go fishing," his Grace whined.

"I know, baby. And I want to go fishing with you, but we
can't."

Wiping the tears away, Troy found some tired resolve.
The reality was, she was dead. And there was nothing he could
do to change that.

Still, he was so close to her. Maybe five feet away. Troy
could practically touch her if he reached out far enough. He took
another step and another. He just wanted to feel his daughter
again. To hold her like he did every time she scraped her knee or
had a bad day at school. He could recall so many times he had
held her or when she had told Becky, "I just really need my Dad."
In those moments, he would hold her. And she would feel better,
and they would go for ice cream or watch some princess cartoon
movies. All Troy wanted was one more of those moments. He
desperately wanted it. Needed it even. And he took another step.

"I want to go fishing, Dad. You promised. Why did you
have to let me die?" she asked. "Why did you let him take me,
Dad? Why weren't you watching?"

"What? Sweetheart, I didn't—" Troy began, but his daughter cut him off.

"Why did you let me die, Daddy? Why weren't you paying attention? Why did you let me drown, Dad? I was so cold. I was so scared. I couldn't see anything. I could not breathe. I wanted my Daddy, but he wasn't there." She paused. "I called for you, Dad. My mouth just filled up with water. It's your fault. You let me die." The words were sharp, ice cold and resentful. Hateful.

"It was. I am sorry, Gray. I'm so sorry," Troy said. He was bawling now and doing everything he could to keep his tears from clouding his vision, to keep them from blurring the sight of his seven-year-old completely because it was true. It was his fault. Everything had been his fault, and Troy Kender knew it.

"It's your fault. It's your fault," Grace was beginning to chant. "You did it. You did it. It is your fault. Why did you let me die, Daddy? It is your fault. It is your FAULT. IT'S YOUR FAULT!" she screamed. "YOUR FAULT! YOUR FAULT! YOUR FAULT!"

She chanted this repeatedly, but the voice was changing. It was not Grace's voice anymore—it was deeper, much deeper. It was something Troy had never heard come from a human being in his life. He heard the voice scream again and again.

"I DROWNED, AND IT'S YOUR FAULT. I'M DEAD, AND IT'S YOUR FAULT. YOUR FAULT, YOU GUILTY LITTLE FUCK. YOUR FAULT! I ATE YOUR DAUGHTER'S SOUL, AND IT'S YOUR FAULT!"

She turned to face him. The face he saw was not the beautifully intact and perfect face of his baby girl. It was blue and puffy, swollen and bloated from water. From drowning. Most of her face was already beginning to decompose. He could see on the corner of her forehead where the skin had rotted to the bone. The places where her red and pink rosy cheeks now housed death and decay. Her nose was only half intact, the other half having completely petrified away, leaving only an open hole with folded flesh where Troy imagined the cavity of her button nose once lived.

His daughter stood up and was standing directly in front of him. Her clothes were soaked and sticking to her little bloated seven-year-old body. And she stunk. Troy had not smelled it earlier, but he could smell it now. She reeked of rot. Of sewage. Of death. The smell was so strong it brought on a feeling in his throat that left him dry heaving twice.

Grace's head jolted forward on her neck as she started choking. Troy could hear it; it was coming from her belly and up through her lungs and throat as she gagged and gagged. Finally, she opened her mouth and let the dark liquid fall from it. The sound of it made Troy heave a third time, expelling his own stomach contents.

A waterfall mixture of lake water, stomach bile, and something black came oozing from her lips, streaking down the front of her shirt. She gagged again, and more came out. And again, with more and more that poured out her mouth and down her little girl dress and onto the wood of the dock.

Finally, it stopped, having a bucket's worth lying on the ground in front of her. When the vomiting display was finally over, Grace looked down at the liquid and dipped her foot in it, twirling it around and around. Then she looked up at him.

"You did this to me, Daddy. Now I have to make it right," she said, and took a step toward him.

They were within reaching distance of each other now, and Troy backpedaled, his eyes wide and his heart thumping loudly. She took another step to match his. She reached her arm out, her fingertips just touching the fabric of his shirt. He screamed and swatted at the arm out of reflex.

The arm went flying as he contacted it, the meat of the thing disconnecting at the shoulder, going through the air some five feet before hitting the cold, hard sand to the side of them. She only grinned and took another step toward him.

He screamed again as he looked at where her arm used to hang from. It was rotten and jagged, having detached roughly from the joint and exposing tendons, ligaments, and bone through a film of partially coagulated blood. And he saw something crawling out of her flesh, poking out of bits of skin from where the arm had been launched.

Maggots. There were maggots crawling out of her... crawling towards him. There were hundreds of them, thousands even—no, there had to be tens of thousands of the things, and they were crawling their way steadily toward Troy with a furious and hungry pace. It was as if they, too, wanted Troy to pay, to be their new host.

Troy screamed for the third time before he took off in a full-blown sprint to the house. He turned and looked behind him only once to see that his daughter was still marching her way toward him, one armed and dead, smiling that once toothy grin from ear to ear.

Feeling a surge of pain in his shin right before he left the ground and became airborne, he landed with a loud and painful crash onto the grass. He had tripped over the barrier from the beach to the backyard. The same one he had so carefully avoided on his way to the dock.

Troy hoisted himself upright, digging his hands into the dirt and pulling himself up to his feet. He took another look behind him. To his bewilderment, she was gone. The bloated and rotting girl was gone.

He took three heavy breaths.

Had he imagined her? Had he imagined all of it? No, he could not have. It was too real. Too vivid. Too long, even, to be another hallucination. It had been, at least to some extent, real.

He scanned the backyard and the beach. Where was she?

Was she gone? Where *had* she gone? He was desperately combing everywhere in view, sweeping from left to right and back again, but he saw no trace of her. No trace of his daughter anywhere.

"Hi, Daddy," the voice of Grace whispered.

His one-armed daughter was standing to his right, staring at him, merely feet away. She still carried that awful, evil grin, though this time it had been cut into her face with a clumsy instrument. The lines were jagged and rough. The skin was wasting away, and the maggots—dear god, the maggots—were coming from her jagged wasting smile now.

Then it began to morph and change. The skin along his daughter's face began to peel away, revealing the bright maroon musculature underneath.

Grace's body raised its arm up and extended her index finger, pointing.

"Look, Daddy! Look! He wants to see you! He wants you to see him! Look!" Grace said.

Troy turned around, afraid to see what she was directing him to.

Mimicking Grace's position on the opposite side stood a tall figure, a creature of some kind that he had never seen before, human-like, with a face, though it had empty eyes. Where its eyes should have been were holes that seemed endless. It had a mouth of sorts, though it was more of an open sore. There was a nose, but Troy was sure it was not anything of this human world. It was...something else. The closest thing Troy could think of was a demon, like the pictures they drew in those Bibles in hotel rooms. He was sure there was evil within it. If nothing else, he was sure of that.

Now, as it was staring at him, into his eyes with its own dark black pools, was when he felt the shooting pain in his chest, his head, his heart. It was everywhere, but Troy couldn't put a finger on any of it. It felt like his insides were being pulled from beneath his skin, beneath his body. His best description was the feeling of his soul leaving his body. Like this *thing* was taking it from him, sucking it from his very bosom.

Grace began to laugh behind him, the sound erupting throughout the yard. Her voice began to change again, from the pure and honest Grace that he had known, loved, and raised. It began to shift to that deep voice, mocking and malevolent. The one that made him sure there was nothing left of his daughter.

He felt the chill in him rise to an icy freeze.

It, the thing Grace had pointed to, made a clicking sound. It was the most hideous sound Troy had ever heard...and that was when Troy turned and ran for his life.

He was only feet away from the door now. He was about to make it inside when he felt something grab at the back of his shirt, soft child fingers pulling at him. He dared himself to look one more time. He had to see it. He had to make it into the house.

She was lunging for him. About to take him in her cold, dead grasp.

He turned toward the door and tried to slow himself down in time, but it was too late. His face landed hard against the siding of his parents' home, knocking him unconscious.

CHAPTER 17

Troy shot up from his bed. The sheets were soaked in sweat. Looking around, he found that he was in his room, and aside from the sweat-soaked blankets, everything appeared as it did every morning.

He had been dreaming. That was clear to him now. It had been so lucid and striking that Troy could've sworn he still felt the damp sand between his toes and the knob on his shin from where he had hit it, yet he had awoken in his bed.

It had been a hideous nightmare. That was all it had been. Another trick his mind had played on him ever since he had come back to his hometown. This place was really starting to get the better of him.

He threw the sheets off himself and rolled them into a ball, figuring it would be best to wash them. They were soaked, like he had pissed himself in the middle of the night. If he washed them now, he could probably get it all done and taken care of before his folks got home and avoid another weird conversation of lying and excuses. He had lied to his father on this trip more than he had his entire life, and he did not care for it much. Especially given his father's circumstances.

He walked out of his room into the hallway and down to

the small laundry closet that sat at the end of the hall before the living room. The sheets were heavy in his hands, and he was still surprised by how much he had sweated in his sleep. He figured he should be severely dehydrated from it all, but he felt fine.

As he made it to the end of the hallway, to the laundry room that sat on the left-hand side, he turned himself into it, but something caught his eye.

The sliding back door that led into the yard was open. It wasn't cracked open like someone had forgotten to close it or had slammed it too hard on the way in. No, it was wide open.

Troy squinted and looked, believing his eyes to be deceiving him. They were not.

Throwing the sheets onto the tile floor of the laundry room, he took a step closer.

Who would have opened the door? Dad? Maybe, especially if he went out to have a drink or smoke a cigar. But he is always sure to close it. He has always been, ever since I was a kid. And didn't Dad say he avoided the dock anyhow?

Could it have been his mother? Maybe. She *was* losing touch with some smaller aspects of memory in her older age. It seemed perfectly normal to assume she had gone outside for some reason in the middle of the night and had walked in, forgetting to close the door. But that did not make sense. She was always paranoid of the family cat getting out, so that did not seem to add up either.

Could it have been...me? was the thought Troy had as he stepped onto the cold tile that laid in front of the sliding glass. When his skin touched it, though, it was not just the feeling of cold tile touching his bare skin—it was wet.

Troy looked down. His eyes could barely register what he witnessed as a sudden flash of memory came to his mind. His brain began to leap voluntarily, making the connection, his subconscious connecting the dots from what he thought was a dream to the evidence it was less a dream and more an event.

There, on the tile, laid a muddy track of a footprint. His footprint.

"Oh my God," he whispered to himself in horrified realization.

"Daddy?"

Fear struck Troy like a freight train. His chest seized up, and his throat swelled to the point where he could not breathe. A panic desperate breath tried to release itself from his chest, but it would not come up.

He wanted to turn around, but his body would not let him.

"Daddy? Can you hear me?" he heard again. The voice of his daughter. The fear engulfed the last little piece of him that was trying to remain rational.

He turned his body to face what he feared he would see — what he knew he would see. Turning so slowly he could feel his weight shift around on his foot, he faced the direction of Grace's voice.

But there he stood, staring down the hallway he had come from to nothing.

Grace was not there calling him. No rotting, haunted spirit of his dead daughter was there to greet him, puking sludge and being devoured by a horde of hungry maggots. In fact, there was no one there, nothing there either. It was empty.

A wave of mixed relief passed by him. Relief that his daughter was not there, not calling his name from another dimension. But fear still lingered, though it was a different fear.

He had probably been sleepwalking last night. That explained the track marks and the door. But that did not explain the hallucination. He had been getting them for days now — they were growing and leading to sleepwalking. He had not sleepwalked since his last meltdown, his psychotic break where they made him take all the pills and the therapy. And here he was — dreams, hallucinations, visions, and sleepwalking. Again. There was something going on here, something beyond the normal world.

He needed to get the hell out of this town.

But hold on, wait a minute. Get yourself together. This was what you wanted. To put the past behind you and move on with your life. To say goodbye to your father.

He couldn't leave. Not with his father so ill. He was in and out of hospitals now, or at least it seemed that way. Troy calmed himself.

And you are doing it despite the road bumps and despite finding Beck.

Becky! How could he forget? He could not leave, no matter the circumstance. Not with how last evening had gone. There was still hope and a chance in his heart that she would call him again. He did not know what that call would mean, but he needed to find out. That could very well solve the very issue he was facing. To come to terms with his ex-wife and him passing in one single summer. Then and only then could he rid himself of this mental and emotional rut he had been dragged through. He could move on.

Besides, whatever was going on in this town, he needed to find out. Whatever it was that was triggering this vision, whatever was causing that unnerving feeling, he needed to know. That was the only way now he was going to prove to himself that he was right. Something was wrong here. Something was wrong, and it wasn't him.

So, he brushed the thoughts of leaving from his mind yet again, partially for his father, partially for Becky, and partially for his own sake. But no less, he resolved himself to stay and see these things through.

As if to emphasize the very battle going on within his head, Troy was brought back to life by the chirp of his cell phone from within his bedroom. He made his way to it and checked for the message.

Are you busy tonight? It was from Becky.

He replied*: No. Why?*

Troy waited a minute for the reply.

Dinner? She sent back.

Troy held his breath and released it slowly to contain his excitement. Dinner? That was more than he had hoped. He looked at the clock on his phone. He waited exactly two minutes before responding, trying to avoid sounding like a giddy school kid awaiting his first chance at a prom date.

When and where?

My vote is Bruegger's, of course.

Troy would have guessed as much. They were primarily a coffee house and barely served any real dinner food. It would not have been his choice, but given the circumstances, he did not have any complaints either.

Fine with me. Just no black coffee. What time?

Five?

See you then.

Troy looked up at the clock. It was already twelve-thirty. He had slept way longer than he had planned, but this was good. He could pass the idle time by slowly getting himself ready for his date. And that was what he did, but even so, he could not quite rid himself of his dream.

CHAPTER 18

On his way over to meet Becky for dinner, his mother called him. After she asked him where he was, and he told her, she offered him luck before getting to the meat of why she was calling.

"Troy, I've got some...good, I guess, news. The hospital called me. The one in Marquette putting on those clinical trials."

"What did they say?" He replied.

"We got through the initial screening. They want us to go down there to do the final tests to make sure your dad can go through the trials, but they sounded pretty hopeful."

"Really! That is good news. How's Dad feeling about it?" His father had been staunchly against it when he first arrived home. That had not changed, and given how he behaved at the hospital just a night prior, Troy had his rightful concerns.

"He wants to go, believe it or not. I think after the last time, with you being there and seeing him like that, he wants to at least give it a try."

"Well, that is great news then. When do you guys leave?" Troy asked.

"That's why I called. So, they want us there as soon as possible. The spots are not reserved — once they hit their testing limit for these rounds of tests, that's it. We wanted to know what you thought before we did anything. You know he doesn't have much time left, but these clinical trials might help with his episodes in the meantime. We'd only be gone through the weekend, but we know you don't have much time here either. We want your honest thoughts," Tracy said. Her voice was plain, trying not to affect Troy's opinion.

"Go. Go right now. If Dad wants to go, you need to go. And you need to go before he changes his mind."

Tracy whispered, "That's what I was thinking."

Troy laughed. "Are you guys all packed? Do you need help?" he asked.

"No, we've got things at the apartment up there. Enough for this, anyways. With you agreeing we should go, we're going to leave now. Louis can't drive this close after an episode, and my eyes aren't what they used to be in the dark." In emphasis of their haste, he heard the turn of the ignition to their car.

"Okay. Well, keep in touch. Tell Dad I love him, and I am proud of his choice," Troy said.

"Will do, honey. He says thank you, and we both say good luck."

"Thanks. I'll do my best." And with that, Troy ended the call.

***

Troy arrived at Bruegger's in his normal time, fifteen minutes early. He was surprised to see Becky was already seated at the same table she had been yesterday, twiddling her thumbs impatiently.

"You're here early," Troy said as he walked over to her.

"Yeah. Figured you would be too. This time I beat you here for a change," Beck said with a smile.

After a few minutes of ordering and light small talk, the two spent the rest of the hour talking and joking. Falling back into a comfortable rhythm that neither of them had felt since the accident, not with each other and not with anyone else, made them both upbeat and talkative.

The conversation landed on Becky's promotion, which Troy took upon himself to say was long overdue. She deserved that promotion years ago.

She asked him about what he had been up to, and Troy gave a lengthy answer about his new school district. He explained that the principal, who played a large role in hiring him, had taken a chance, given him the opportunity to really get his life back in order, and that he had no intention of letting her down.

To this, Becky gave a warming smile. "It's good to see you be yourself again."

"Well, doing what I can anyway," he replied.

Becky changed the subject and asked how Louis was doing. Troy explained the phone call he had gotten earlier. He was genuinely glad his father had gotten in — if not for his sake, for his mother's, to give her that peace of mind that she had done all she could have.

Troy asked about her family. She kept it brief, knowing that at this point, Troy was not their favorite character. She quickly switched the subject to how his photography was going, which Troy was infinitely grateful for. He, too, hated her family for the way they had handled pretty much everything after Grace had died, fueling the fires of blame and guilt. It had taken everything Troy had not to fight his father-in-law at the funeral.

Though Derek Gordon had made more than a few shitty remarks in Troy's direction before, during, and after the service, Troy had kept his cool. At least until they had gotten home, and the shouting match occurred. That was when Becky's father blamed him for Grace's death outright, saying what a terrible mistake Becky had made. A terrible, awful mistake, and had offered for Becky to come live with them while they signed the divorce papers, though, at that time, no divorce had been mentioned to

Troy. Becky had remained silent, much to Troy's later contempt.

"It's going well," he said, bringing his mind back to the question at hand. "It's actually paying some of the bills now, though there isn't much left over after that. But it suits me, and I am fine with it. I just have a small one-bedroom place now. I don't need too much."

"What is that you do exactly?" Becky asked. She remembered how desperately Troy had wanted his photography side gig to take off back when they were dating. When they were teenagers, he had actually done quite well at it and was able to put himself through the first few semesters of college, more or less, on nothing other than his small-town neighborhood photo shoots and her waitressing job she had right out of high school.

"Well, I do teach an elective class at the high school. Outside of that, I do a lot of freelance stuff. I still do the client work I used to do that you probably remember. Weddings, birthdays, engagements, family photos, all that good stuff. But I also sell pictures freelance now. Things for book covers and movies, photos that end up in pretentious people's homes. That kind of thing. It is not super glamorous like I said. I am not living the high life or anything, but it supplements my salary with the Free Pine School District. There's a lot of luck involved, but it's happened to me a few times. The district keeps a roof over my head, and the photography puts a few extra bucks in my pocket." Not living the high life was a nice way to put just barely making ends meet.

Even with his side gig, his new apartment was outrageously expensive. He was barely making it through, sometimes with only a few dollars leftover in his wallet to pay for gas. But he neglected that half of the story for his own sake.

"Really? Seems like you are enjoying it, though. I'm happy for you, Troy," Becky said sincerely. "Have you had a chance to take any good ones while you've been back home?"

The question brought back his memory from the other day. The first vision he had when he was out in the woods by himself, trying to take some shots for his current project. The recollection of his youth and of him and her.

He remembered that odd tree that seemed so much like a person, dressed in those mismatched clothes. The flashing image of something in the lake...and that horrible sleepwalking dream from the night before. The memory of it jolted back that feeling of unease that he had felt since he had come back into town. He wanted to tell her about it, try and get her opinion. He felt so alone trying to figure out exactly what was going on. He wanted to share it with her, for her to be with him.

"Yeah. A few. Out in the woods by our old place," he said. "A few might turn out right for the project I'm working on, but you never really know until you blow them up and start playing around with them. Probably won't know until I get back."

"Our old place," she said. "I still own it, actually."

"Really?" Troy asked. He had loved that little house. It was small, but it was a good enough home for his once family of three. He had not expected her to keep it after they split. He gave it to her in the papers, but he figured she would sell it and run far, far away from it. From those memories.

He was happy she had not.

"Oh, yeah. I just could not stand to leave when it was all said and done. There were bad times there, lots of bad times. But there were good times, too. And I just could not get myself to get rid of it. It's like a little time stamp for happier days, I guess."

"I know what you mean," Troy replied. He paused a second, thinking. "Did you ever get rid of anything in the crawl space?"

***

"Actually, no. I haven't touched anything you put in there since you left. Why?" she asked, her voice not unkind. She was curious.

"Oh. I just had some old equipment in there. Some of it is probably vintage by now. I guess the hoarder in me just could not let it go. In a few years, it will probably end up being a collectible, with the way technology is going now. I think I left some of my early photo albums in there, too."

"Oh, okay. Yeah, I have not touched any of it. I am sure it is all still in there. You can have it back if you want — it is yours after all," she said, and gave a quick smile.

"Yeah! That would be great. You could drop it off at my parents, or I could meet you somewhere to pick it up later this week if that works," he said.

"I could do that." She paused. "You know, you can come on over and look through it if you want. Saves me time, and you can go through it all and make sure you get everything. If you want, I mean. That way, I do not have to touch your stuff. If you want." Troy could tell the worlds were falling out clumsily. She was blushing, and Troy took this as a good sign, hoping she was cracking the door open to let him in, to give him his chance. But he knew Becky well enough, even after all these years. She was opening the door but was still standing in the doorway, not quite allowing him through.

Becky was careful. Guarded. Troy was okay with that.

Troy wasn't sure why she was inviting him over anyways; this was supposed to be a one time thing. Two old lovers catching up. But it felt so much like home. Like nothing that had ruined them had happened. They fit perfectly together, and he desperately wanted to keep that feeling. He chose his next words carefully to allow her to remain guarded but allowing himself the opportunity, too.

"Yeah. If you are okay with that, I would love to. It'd only take a minute," Troy replied. He was trying hard not to blush, but he figured he was not doing a very good job of it by the look of relief on Becky's face.

"Well, let's pay then. It's getting kind of crowded in here," she answered.

Troy looked around. It was not crowded at all. In fact, they were one of maybe eight patrons in the entire establishment. He made no mention of it as he walked up to the register, handed the receipt to the hostess, and threw it all on his card, even at Becky's protest...he only hoped it wasn't declined.

Troy counted his lucky stars and said a silent prayer to the God — the one he didn't believe in but was admittedly starting to grow more and more fond of — when it didn't.

CHAPTER 19

"I didn't see it in there," Troy called back into the living room from the crawl space.

"You sure? I promise I didn't touch any of it," Becky said. She was in the living room making herself a cup of herbal tea in her Keurig. Becky always loved her fancy coffees and teas.

Damn near addicted to those things she is, Troy had thought when she started her Keurig after Bruegger's. *Almost went broke when we lived here, paying for that habit! But that was one of her quirks. Always had to be sipping on something herbal or coffee.*

"I haven't looked in there since before you left, so I don't know where it would've gone."

"That's all right. Like I said, it was years ago, and you know my memory is worse than a goldfish. Probably threw it out or something. But check this out!" Troy said, his voice growing as he walked into the living room and slapped three manila envelopes onto the coffee table.

"Just a second. Do you want anything to drink? I was brewing up some tea, but I've got pop in the fridge and some wine in the cabinet," she said.

"No, that's all right. I should probably get out of your hair soon anyway, but I wanted to check some of these pictures out with you if that's okay."

"Yeah, of course. Like I said, I have nothing better to do. If you're sure you don't want anything?" Becky replied, now emerging from the kitchen.

"I'm all right, but thank you," he answered. "God, Beck. Still living in this house. Hasn't changed at all!" Troy finished, looking around. It was true, too. The place looked almost the exact same as when he had left, though the marriage photos had been taken down.

There were still pictures of her and Grace. There were pictures of just Grace, and there was one picture of the three of them on the centerpiece of the entertainment stand — the three of them at Grace's seventh birthday party. Troy remembered the day well. He'd examined the photo when she first went to get herself something to drink from the kitchen but put it down quickly, not wanting Becky to see him hung up on it.

"Like I said, I found it kind of hard to leave," she replied.

Troy turned his attention back to the three envelopes on the table in front of him and grabbed the first one. He grabbed a stack of colored photographs and began thumbing through them. There had to be at least a few dozen in the pile in his hand, mostly pictures of himself and Mitch, capitalizing each memory they had together over their decade long friendship.

**

"God, I miss him, Beck. Here, check this one out. This one was on that hill...our hill. The one we took Grace sledding on her fourth Christmas break, you remember? Mitch and I had found it when we were kids. Right before you and I met."

"Yeah, of course, I remember!" Becky said, grabbing the picture and smiling.

It was a picture of a much younger version of her ex-husband, maybe sixteen at best, and his lifelong best friend Mitch Hampway standing at the base of a large, snow-covered hill.

They were dressed to the nines in snow gear, their arms wrapped around one another in a brotherly way. They were grinning from ear to ear, their snowboards in the bank a few feet behind them.

Becky saw the glimmer in their eyes — the glimmer of two teenage boys before responsibility hit. Two teenage boys who spent their winter break out snowboarding across the hills in town and played endless hours of videogames to wash the nights away.

"I miss him, too. I am sorry, Troy. I should have called when his parents.... When his dad.... You know," she said, unable to finish the thought.

"It's all right. My dad did not really have it in him to tell me either. Just found out since I've been back," he said with a sigh, and set the picture to his right.

"Oh. I didn't know. I thought maybe you knew. I guess I just figured since it was Mitch, it was like you had to know," she said, the words once again forming clumsily. Troy only shrugged in return. There was a moment of silence as the two looked at the picture of Troy and Mitch.

"Anyways. Glad I found these. Some of the last things I have. I should've taken them." He slid the stack back into the envelope and pushed them away, exchanging it for the center one. "These ones should have pictures of you and me, I think," he said as he opened it.

Becky took a sip of her tea, watching over Troy's shoulder as he began looking through this stack, the mood lightening significantly.

"Oh, God," Becky said, her voice pained with embarrassment. There were several dozens of pictures in this stack as well, ranging from when they had just met at the ripe and ready age of sixteen and seventeen, all the way through their fifth marital anniversary.

There were only a few pictures of the couple after Grace

had died, and when Troy had thumbed through to the back and looked at them, their smiles were pained and forced...a couple who was clearly struggling to hang on to the bits and pieces of their marriage after their daughter had died. After the third picture of its kind, he quickly went back to the front of the pile.

Becky was glad when he did. She liked the front of the stack—the happy pictures. There were pictures of Troy kissing her on the cheek on the day they reached six months of dating. She had a big smile on her face, and she was pretty, not aged by the sadness the last years had brought her.

About halfway through the stack were copies of their engagement pictures. Troy took his time as he went through them one by one, and Becky was grateful that he did. They were so happy then. The fall after they graduated, they had gotten married. Troy had proposed that summer.

Troy was not one to make a big deal of things, and he had not with their engagement, at least not in any cliché way. But still, when he had proposed to her at the creek, it was all she had ever wanted. They had a few pictures taken by one of his photography friends and a few taken by themselves.

They were so happy then, and it showed. Becky had long flowing hair and was built slender and beautiful, the blood rushing through her cheeks as her hands covered her mouth. Her eyes were filled with happy tears, and Troy had the biggest smile on his face she had ever seen. Becky reminisced about those times. She missed those times. That was before everything had gone...rotten.

***

"Look at us," Becky said. "We were so...happy."

"Yeah. I remember that day well. I was so nervous. God, we were a pair of dumb kids in love, huh?"

"That's the honest way of putting it. Though I think the only dumb one was you," she said with a smirk. "Remember, it started raining ten minutes after this? You didn't check the weather report," she jabbed.

"Ah. I do remember! I also remember you shoving me into the creek before we went back to my car if my memory is still correct."

"You deserved it! I wasn't ready for these pictures, and you *know* I hate getting my picture taken."

"Eh, deserved is very subjective. I thought you were the most beautiful woman I had ever seen. I don't think any amount of prep time would have made a difference," Troy answered, staring down at the picture. He put the stack back on the table lightly and went for the last pile. But before he could do so, he was grabbed gently by his forearm.

He looked up the arm to see his ex-wife looking back at him on the couch. Her eyes were that same deep shade they had been so many years ago. This was the woman he had fallen in love with all those years ago, and his heart yearned for her.

They sat there, gazing into one another for what felt like an hour. But still, when she pulled his arm away from the table and shifted her weight, slowly pressing her body onto his and meeting his lips with hers, Troy was still taken by surprise.

"Beck...are you—?" Troy started.

"Shh," she replied, and kissed him again.

Troy was in some shock, but he reciprocated, running his fingers through her hair, feeling it through his fingers and cupping her face. After some time, they wandered down her back and her body, landing on her waist. Troy could feel his heart beating hard and fast in his chest, and when she reached down and fumbled in his jeans, he felt it skip twice. He reached up and removed her shirt and threw it to the floor.

Before Troy had fully registered what had happened, Becky was pulling him by the hand from the couch and into the bedroom, the same bedroom he had shared moments like these with Becky hundreds of times over. The very same bedroom Grace had been conceived in.

The thought crossed his mind again.

The dreams...if they were even dreams at all. The occurrence in the woods. His father's words in the hospital. They flashed through his mind in detail, derailing him from his current surroundings momentarily.

Should I tell her? She has a right to know, doesn't she? Or is this you not wanting to be alone? But he threw the thoughts from his mind. *You're not alone now.*

He wanted this moment; He needed this moment. As much as Troy had spent the last two years attempting to convince himself otherwise, he was still fully in love with her, with every curve and divot of her skin. Troy bit his tongue and pushed the thoughts back as far as he could. He would deal with them later. Or never. He had not quite decided as he laid down with Becky.

CHAPTER 20

Troy felt Becky snuggle her body against his, laying her head on his chest. He laid there motionless for a second before wrapping an arm around her. He was still lost in thought over everything that had happened to him since he had come back home. He wanted to tell her, but he was not sure how. He wasn't sure why either. Maybe it was because, truly, the only person who knew exactly what he had gone through, had shared much of that pain with, was the woman lying next to him. He was also sure she was the only other person who would see what was going on around them, to make those connections.

"Is everything okay?" Becky asked.

"Yeah. Yeah, everything is fine. Good even," he replied. But Becky knew him too well and knew that stare at the ceiling just as much.

Troy could tell she didn't believe him. He wasn't hiding his anxiety well, not here and not now, alone with her and vulnerable. Troy's mind started racing to where her mind was going, and it didn't look or feel good. He could tell by the long pause she was giving, the way her body shifted away from his, that she was starting to pull away from him emotionally too, that she felt she had made a mistake.

Troy turned and looked at her.

"I'm sorry," she said.

"For what?" Troy asked, alarmed and confused.

"I shouldn't have. I just...I am sorry. It was wrong of me to do this," she said, motioning to them naked in the same bed he had laid in so many years ago.

"Oh, Becky. Oh, God. It is *not* that. Trust me, it does not have anything to do with this or you and me. I am fine. Really. More than fine, actually," he replied, and nudged her.

"I don't believe you."

"Why not?"

"You have that look again. The one that says there is something you want to tell me but feel like you can't. I shouldn't have done this."

"Beck, could you please stop saying that?"

"Saying what?"

"That you shouldn't have. Done this, whatever 'this' means."

"Then tell me what it is."

Troy sighed. He looked defeated like he had nowhere to go. He sat there for a moment, continuing his look at the ceiling, thinking of the best course of action.

He could keep it from her, tell a lie in its place. It would be the safe way, the way to ensure he had another night or two like this before he left. Maybe they would keep in contact after he left town. Maybe she would visit. Maybe in his wildest dreams, she would come to find herself wanting to be with him again for more than a night or two.

But he wanted to tell her the truth. No, he needed to tell her the truth. He had not told anybody about what had been going on, what he had seen. After the last two episodes, the last one even involving Grace, whatever they were, he needed to tell someone, have someone help him figure out what was going on.

She was the only one he could really think of. She was the only one who would get it.

"Okay. Fine. Becky, this sounds...crazy. Insane, and I know it. But ever since I came back to town, things have been... not right," he said, his voice lowering to barely above a whisper.

"What do you mean?"

"I've been having these weird things keep happening to me. Like, episodes. Flashbacks, and then something else. One of them happened this morning. And I was out in the kitchen, and I saw someone on the dock, a kid. A girl. So, I went to go see."

"So? Kids are always going on other people's docks, you know that," she replied.

"It was Grace, Beck. I saw Grace on the dock," Troy replied. "But it wasn't Grace. It looked like Grace, and it talked like Grace, but it was not her, Beck. It was something else. It was a dead thing. And it talked to me. And then it came to me like it chased me. It wanted to hurt me or to kill me or...something."

Troy paused a moment and looked away from her. After a moment that seemed to drag on and on, he spoke again. "I sound like I'm losing my mind. Like my brain is malfunctioning. I thought they were just dreams or visions or episodes or *something* that could explain it. But I just can't shake this feeling—this feeling that there's something more going on in this town."

Becky only stared at him, her face a puzzled blanket of confusion and pain from the mention of her dead daughter.

"Becky, I know it sounds crazy. But a few days ago, I was going to the hill to take some pictures and relive some memories, I guess. Our hill where we took her sledding—you remember, right?" he asked. Becky only gave a slight nod of her head in return, the look on her face unchanged. "I thought I saw someone up there. And then in the hospital.... When my dad went in, he had an episode. Like he wasn't himself. Like someone else was speaking through him." He paused to see if she was following.

She seemed to be, so he continued.

"He grabbed me, and he said, 'It is not over. He is still searching for you.' And then it was over like it never happened, and he had no recollection," Troy finished

"Things happen, Troy. Your dad has a brain tumor, so that is not really that odd...and accidents happen, and people die. There is nothing about this town that is any different than anywhere else. You of all people should know that," she replied, her voice stiff like she was not sure of her words.

No. No, it is not that. It is her voice she uses when she doesn't trust me, Troy thought. He knew the voice well. The months before their divorce, when he had hit rock bottom, he had learned that tone and what it meant.

Troy knew the conversation was going south and fast. He could see it on her face, he could hear it in her voice, and he could read it in her body expression, the way she detached herself from him, shifted her body away from his.

He had seen this, had lived this before. That way, she physically shielded herself from him, even though he had never laid a hand on her in anger. But still, it was like she was physically guarding her emotions from him.

The stiff words always came next. The short, to the point, emotionless phrasing that left Troy feeling like he was talking to a schoolteacher in grade school who had just had enough of it, not a wife or a woman he loved.

Of course, it was the looks she gave him that hurt most of all. That resentful, reproachful, "I don't want to hate you, but I do, oh God Troy, do I fucking hate you" look she had on her face. He had seen it every day from the time Grace died until he left this fucking town. And dear God, did he wish he could leave this place now. Forget what had happened — the coffee, the dinner — because whatever progress he had made over these last few days had been not only undone but completely backfired and made much, much worse.

There was no hope for them now, no hope at all. Troy knew that as he saw the signs and gestures unfold. But Troy, being the man he was, could not hold his tongue from the words that forced their way out.

"Becky, I know what I saw...and I saw her," Troy stated, this time surer of himself. He touched her softly on the shoulders and pleaded, hoping even if just for that moment that she would listen, that she would see what he was saying was the truth. "Becky, I swear to God I know what I saw. I've been debating telling you this. I know it sounds like I'm losing my mind, having another break or playing a sick joke or something. But Becky, I'm telling you the truth."

He let go of her and pulled away, alarmed by his own sense of belief in it all. Saying it all out loud had done what he had feared. It had confirmed what he knew. And what he knew was that it was real.

They sat there in silence for a moment, the building tension leading Troy to feel like his head and chest might just explode from it.

"Becks, say something. Please," he begged, his voice barely above a whisper.

It took a few moments for Becky's face to change expression, and when it did, it was not what Troy had been hoping for, though it was what he had expected. Her face changed from shock, confusion, and bewilderment to anger.

"Get out," she said.

"Beck, listen, I know it's crazy. I do. But just hear me out."

"Get out," she said again. "God, I knew this was a mistake. Just leave, Troy. Get your shit and leave," she said, throwing herself out of the bed.

"Becky —" he started.

"Goddammit, Troy. Get out, I said!" she yelled. "I can't

believe you! First, you coddle your way in here and sneak yourself back into my life when I made it clear that I wanted nothing to do with you. Then you come into my home and schmooze your way into my bed with that sick charm of yours. And then you have the nerve to fuck me, not just physically — no, that would not be enough for you! No, you decide to come in here, and right before you leave, you pull this shit and fuck *with* me over our dead daughter!" She was screaming now, her voice cutting through her lungs, tears flowing down her cheeks. "Just get your shit and leave. Do not ever contact me again, Troy. You sick asshole." Sobbing, she closed herself in the master bathroom, locking the door behind her.

Troy tried to say something else, but he was only met with a loud bang of a fist against the bathroom door and a ring of sobbing.

"I'm sorry, Beck. I'm sorry," he whispered as he threw his clothes back on and walked out of the room.

He stopped only once to thumb through the glass in the picture frame on the entertainment stand. It was the one picture of himself, Becky, and Grace at her final birthday party. He held it in his hands before bringing it to his chest. He let out a sob of his own and then walked out, tears now free flowing down his own cheeks.

CHAPTER 21

Becky had come out of the bathroom only after she was certain Troy had left. She was furious. More than that, though, she was heartbroken.

How could he? How could he march into her home, into her bed even, and play such a nasty joke on her? What was he trying to do? Was this his sick attempt at getting back at her? His try to reopen the wounds she'd spent two years trying to repair? Becky knew she had not always handled everything that had happened to the two of them perfectly. In her most honest moments, she often wondered, if she had handled Troy's and her own grief differently, how different would things be now? But she had never done anything to Troy to deserve this, had she? In that moment, Becky was not as sure as she told herself she was. She sniffled her nose and wiped away her tears as she exited the bathroom and went to her bed.

Maybe she had deserved it. Maybe Troy had a right to be furious with her as well. She had left him at a time when he was vulnerable, and it was for a good reason.

Who does that? she thought. *Leaves their husband during his spiral downward because...because...his daughter had died.*

It made her feel guilty. Depressed. It always had. Even

after the divorce, there were as many nights she regretted asking for it as there were nights she felt her decision was right.

But you needed to heal, she said to herself. *And Troy wasn't how you were going to do it.*

That was true too, and she knew that. Becky knew that had she not left Troy when she did, there was a good chance she would have fallen down the same slippery road. She'd had to move on, for herself, for Grace, and even in a weird way, she told herself, *I'm doing this for Troy, too.*

She felt a little better. She still felt guilty, but she felt a little better. But Becky supposed that was fair. It wasn't like there was a guidebook out there for saving your marriage after your daughter drowns in your in-law's backyard.

Becky sat there for a while, still shaken up. She had not thought of Grace, at least not verbally or even consciously, in months. Not since Christmas. These were memories she did not want to remember. And what was the nonsense about seeing things? Like he had seen...a ghost? A demon? They had never been particularly religious, and although Becky did have her superstitions about the paranormal, she doubted very much that they just up and happened to small town folk.

Wiping the tears from her eyes and the running snot that was pouring from her nose, she marched herself, still angry enough, into the living room.

The pile of photos was still sitting on the coffee table — the memories she and Troy had shared, as well as her daughter Grace. This thought brought her heart to the breaking point.

She had kept the pictures. She had even lied when she said she had not ever touched them. She had gone through them on every family holiday for the last two years in tears and could never bring herself to get rid of them. But now, fueled by the emotion of the night's events, the unexpected turn they had taken, she thought she ought to burn the bunch, or at the very least throw them in the shredder.

Becky walked over to them and grabbed one of the manila envelopes from the table, clutching it in her hands so hard they started to cramp. The feeling of the pictures bending and creasing brought her a sick satisfaction.

These were nothing but the memories of a life she had no interest in ever reliving, not after tonight. Every picture of him would go in its rightful place, the garbage. She would keep the ones of Grace, sure, but any trace of Troy needed to be erased from her life.

Becky was about to toss them in her kitchen trash can when it happened. The resolve in her hand faltered, and the death grip she had on the pictures within the envelope slipped and sent the lot of them falling to the floor.

"Dammit!" she cried to herself, bringing on another burst of sobs. She lowered herself to the floor, clutching her knees to her chest, and started to cry. No matter how angry she was, she knew she could never throw these pictures away. She loved him. She still did — the boy who had asked her to marry him, nervous and afraid, anyways.

With a defeated cry, she reached for the scattered stack across the floor. This had been one of the envelopes they had not gone through. She had not seen these pictures in years.

Carefully, she thumbed through them one by one, stifling her cries and holding back the tears. She slowed down, even more, when she got to the part of the stack that contained the photos of Troy and his best friend, Mitch.

Becky had known Mitch from the neighborhood for a few years, but it was only once she and Troy had started dating that they had even spoke. They did not know each other well for long. Maybe a couple of months, but he had been such a good friend to Troy. And frankly, he had been a good friend to her as well.

Becky recalled one summer when she and Troy had turned

sixteen, they had gotten into a big argument, and Becky was at her wits' end. She figured this might be the end of their teenage relationship and was festering in her anger the way a teenager tends to do.

Remembering it now was so easy for her; sitting on the porch, contemplating what she should do, how she should end things when she heard the roar of Mitch's Mustang. Becky figured Mitch had heard about the argument and took it upon himself to come over and explain things, explain the stress Troy was under and that he would talk to him. This only furthered her anger towards the situation, and then and there, she had made up her mind.

I am going to break it off tonight. What kind of guy can't even come to his own girlfriend's house? she remembered thinking. *What kind of guy sends their friend over like a halfhearted chicken shit?*

But when the roaring of the V8 stopped and slowly pulled into her driveway, she saw that, yes, Mitch was in the driver's seat, but it was Troy who occupied the passenger side.

After a brief encounter of the "What are you doing here? How did you get here?" set of questioning, they talked it out for two hours. And Mitch sat in the road in front of her parents' house, in the driver's seat, the entire time. Flicking through his phone, flicking through the radio for the entire two-hour stretch.

That was the last argument she and Troy had gotten into until their early days as parents. Becky damn well guessed that was what had kept them together. With the help of Mitch, they had patched things up.

If it had not been for Mitch, it was likely she never would have become Mrs. Kender a short twenty-four months later. She owed her whole marriage, even the birth of her daughter, to that rebellious and even sometimes obnoxious boy named Mitch Hampway.

Becky pushed the memories out of her mind. She was

already mad and sad. She did not want to remember Mitch right now, and she did not think she really wanted to remember the reasons why Troy was the way he was either—what Mitch's passing had cracked in his mind. It would be so much easier to hate him if she didn't see it plain and clear. He was falling apart, and he had good reason to be. He blamed himself for both the death of his best friend and the death of his daughter. Becky knew the latter was, at least in part, because of her.

She never said it, at least not openly, but she did and had blamed him for Grace's death. What she didn't say she let her father say at the funeral, and every time he saw him again. She knew those were her words coming from him, the dark, twisted thoughts in her mind. Troy knew it, too.

But even without her help, he would have blamed himself—that's just who Troy was, the man with constant guilt on his conscience. Becky had only added fuel to that fire after Grace died. But now, as she thought about it more and in this light, in her own objective view, she may have well dumped a gallon of kerosene on that fire every day until she left. Maybe even after, too.

It was an accident. It could have happened to anyone. It just shouldn't have happened to us.

The picture she was looking at now was the two of them together, Mitch and the younger version of her ex-husband. The pair of boys could not have been older than twelve years old and had their arms wrapped around each other's shoulders, smiling. They were so young here, so innocent.

She slid to the next one. They were standing together in front of the prized possession of Mitch—his Mustang he had gotten when he was sixteen, right before he died, the one he had driven Troy in when Troy did not have his own car. Mitch had a satisfied look on his face.

Becky remembered it was his pride and joy, and he would

spend hours and hours working on it, replacing and upgrading, tuning to his heart's content. Troy never cared much for cars, but he was there almost every day as a teen with him, drinking Coke and pretending to know the slightest thing about cars.

A sad, teary smile slid across her face as she shuffled to the next photo in line. It was the pair of boys, this time standing in front of a snow-covered hill, *the* snow-covered hill as fact would have it, dressed head to toe in snowboarding gear. They were standing side by side, their boards laying on the ground at their feet. This had become quite the spot in their little family over the years. Troy and Mitch had found it one day while they were out searching for places in the local woods to go boarding.

It was a good spot, too, being what was likely the biggest hill in the city. In the summer, it had also been their fishing spot, and Becky remembered the very first time Troy had taken her there with Mitch and the subsequent times after, just the two of them. It was beautiful regardless of the season and had become *their* spot.

Many years later, they had taken Grace there for sledding. They had waited until she was just barely big enough to go down the hill, and Troy would stack her up on his lap and have Beck push them. Grace would scream and cry the whole way down, with a death grip on her father that would cut his skin even through his hoodie. But when they reached the bottom, she would yell, "Again! Again!" every time without fail.

That little spot out in the country woods of Black Lake Township had become a bit of a staple in her life. She looked back on it fondly, even if she felt a jolt of pain in her heart as she looked at it. This town was tragic and depressing. Troy *was* right. There sure was a hell of a lot of misfortune in Black Lake Township.

Becky looked at the picture closely, eyeing the younger version of her once true love. He was so young here and so happy, with a big smile decorating his face, and his eyes squinted from the bright reflection of the sun on the winter snow. He had always been handsome, and there was something special about the youthful glow that he had back then before all the trauma his life had come to.

She supposed maybe she was being too harsh—maybe he was losing it. He had lost so much. His best friend, his daughter, and then her, too. He had lost his job, his family, his life.

Maybe he really was losing his mind. Maybe the tragic story of it all really was catching up to him. She felt a small pang of guilt fill her stomach. It was possible he was in the beginnings of a lifelong psychotic break, one that would not be healed or repaired from a therapist and psychiatrist, probably not even medication. Looking back, she highly doubted that he would ever do anything like throw their daughter's death in her face as a cruel ploy or joke.

But what he said does not make any sense! she said to herself. *What Troy had been saying was impossible. Like something out of a novel or a movie. It couldn't have been real.*

So, what does that leave? A hallucination, perhaps. Brought on by illicit drug use or alcohol abuse. If that were the case, should I really have involved myself? No, probably not. If that were the case, Troy would need help, professional help, not from his ex-wife.

She looked away from the picture again, the feeling of worry creeping into her head. Maybe she should call him, apologize, and tell him what she thought. That he needed help, serious, interventive help. Surely he would attempt to dismiss it, saying he didn't want a shrink again or to end up in the looney bin—probably permanently this time. However, if there was one person he'd listen to, Becky figured it would be her...wouldn't it? She thought so, but she was not entirely sure. She had just kicked him out of her house in a screaming fit the morning after impulsively sleeping with him.

Becky looked back to the picture. It was a sad thing to see her once strong, and able husband go from a well-respected and loved teacher in a small town to the shackled mess he was now. He said he was doing well enough, that he had gotten another teaching job, and he probably had—he was always good at it. He said he had been enjoying photography, too. Troy had said he was doing all right, but in that moment, Becky could not lie to herself. Troy was anything but fine. His life was a walking wreck. A ticking time bomb with no secret defuse wire to cut. He was a fully-loaded car stuck on the train tracks with a locomotive steaming right ahead, blaring its horn, the engineer screaming, "Move out of the way! Move out of the way!" But he could not. He would be doomed by that train coming on the tracks, smashing him and his life into tiny, fractured pieces—and frankly, so would she.

Life was not always fair, and it certainly had not been fair to either of them.

It was at that moment Becky made up her mind. He was her ex, but he was still the father of their deceased child, and she owed him that much. She would call him and speak her piece... maybe even call his parents and let them know what she thought and what he had said he had seen. From what she remembered of the Kendlers, which given the amount of time she had spent with them was a lot, she had made the reasonable assumption they would favor her thoughts. The more support, the better.

She was about to put the picture away, back in the manila envelope, and return it to its rightful place in the crawl and storage space in the back corner of her little home when it caught her eye.

The shadow. The odd shadowy thing in the picture standing in the background of the trees behind Mitch and Troy. At first glance, it did not look like anything but a weird smudge mark, a malfunction of the camera, but it had caught her eye, and she looked again. This time with intent.

What the hell? she thought. She blinked twice, assuring herself it was not just a weird occurrence, given her exhaustion and frantic emotional state.

It was blurry, but it was there. Through the faded lines and shadow, she could just make it out. It was shaped like a man, but it was not anyone she recognized. He was standing just behind the pair of boy's lines of vision, out of sight for most people, in the tree line.

It is just some person who was out for a stroll....

But the man in the picture was staring right at the pair of boys, grinning. The more she saw the figure, fixated on it, the more she realized it was less of a man and more of a monster. It was too tall, too thin, to be anything that resembled a healthy human, and although the picture was blurry so she couldn't make out the face exactly, she could tell there was something wrong, something eerily wrong, with this person in the photograph.

Becky squinted closer, and then saw the worst part.

The eyes, blurred as they had been, were now pointed in her direction. She had the feeling that those bottomless pits were staring at her now. She knew that was impossible, but it gave her a wave of anxiety, her heart dropping into her stomach at the very thought of it.

Becky tossed the photograph back on the table, her heart pounding. She still was not convinced, but she wasn't entirely unconvinced either, and she could not shake the feeling of unease that had come over her from looking at that face.

A simple camera malfunctions. Maybe, but a person had certainly been standing there. A bad shade of lighting or a bad flash could maybe explain the odd features of a man, but either way, a man had been standing, just out of sight of the boys, watching them from the trees.

People take walks, she thought. *We used to take walks. People take walks on those trails in the woods. Just some person getting a laugh at their expense. It was creepy, but it was an old photo, and it was some guy just getting a laugh,* she repeated to herself. *If he could see us now, he would say, "Hahaha! Don't you see! That was a funny old spook I had on the two of you!"*

She picked up another photo, putting the thoughts back into the corner of her mind and grabbing one from the stack of Grace's pictures.

Her daughter had always been a spitting image of her, even as a baby, with the light brown hair, little baby nose, and a smile that charmed almost anyone. There were, of course, pieces of Troy in there, too.

In most pictures and times, Grace was almost a replica of herself, but in others, she could see the staunch resemblance or her husband in her facial expressions. That happy grin, the sad puppy dog face Troy would always get, half-joking and half not, and of course, the funny faces he would make.

Becky smiled. Remembering her daughter like this was hard, and she did not do it often, but from time to time, she did, and right now, she needed it. She reached out and touched the picture, caressing the plastic face of her daughter, outlining Grace's smile with her fingertips.

Grace was always so...happy. God, how she wished she had only a minute, a second even, to relive time with her again. Her heart ached for her deceased daughter. She thought of her cold and alone, buried in the ground, slowly rotting away into nothing more than bone and stiffly aged hair. Even with modern preservation, it had been two years. Becky could not imagine her daughter would look anything like herself before she died. She imagined her skin was probably peeling away, revealing a layer of rotting musculature underneath.

Becky wasn't sure exactly what dead bodies in caskets looked like, but the image she had conjured up in her head made her stomach twist in a knot that worked its way up her throat until she gagged. She looked away from the picture, trying to forget what she had just imagined, but looked back to it when she realized it was fruitless.

And when she did, the twisted knot in her stomach dropped at what she saw. Behind Grace, maybe forty or fifty yards stood the man. No, not the man, the *thing*. The same thing that had been in the photograph of Mitch, and he was looking straight at her.

Becky squinted, believing her eyes to have deceived her not once but twice. She could not believe it. No, it was impossible that this figure would be in both pictures. But it was, and it was staring at her daughter.

She looked back at it in true disbelief, and it was then that the figure tilted its head. Becky screamed and threw the picture, believing it not to be true, to be a lie, from her unconscious brain. But when she picked up another picture of Grace, it was there again, this time closer, maybe only thirty yards away, its eyeless sockets dead set on Grace's body.

Becky screamed for the second time, throwing this picture to the floor in the same fashion and picking up the entire stack. She thumbed through them as one might thumb through an animation of sticky notes to find that the man-thing was there in every single picture, inching his way nearer and nearer to Grace. With each flip, she could see this demonic presence coming closer and closer, clearer and clearer in resolution. The face that had been blurry and hard to see was now coming into view.

It had long, jet black hair that hung down on either side of its face like lengths of twine. And the face—oh God, the face! Becky barely held in another scream as she looked at it. It was a purply white, much like the color of her daughter as Troy had drug her from the water, and it was rotting in places, all the way down to the bone.

Becky could just make out its mouth, which seemed to be stitched together or held by some thin web-like skin that covered its teeth...and the eyes.

By God, the eyes were the worst part. They were huge things that took up almost half the space of its face, with pointed eyebrows that contoured themselves into a triangle like structure. But there were no eyes in those sockets. No, there were holes where eyes were supposed to be, but those holes...they were nothing but deep, dark pools of a black abyss. They were empty. Empty and sinister. Devoid of all semblance of life.

And he was heading for Grace with a smile on that mouth, the mouth that was webbed over by bits and pieces of rotting skin and bone. As she flipped through the pictures again, Becky could see that the man, the creature, was reaching his long arm out to her, extending it more and more with every flip of the stack of photos.

When she had landed on the last few, she saw the thing's arm was fully extended now, and its hand, with its long and ugly skeleton fingers, which were all contorted like they had been smashed with a sledgehammer over a cinder block. He was only inches from touching the shoulder of her daughter.

Becky reached the last photograph in the pile she had grabbed, which was the last picture before her beautiful daughter Grace had drowned. It was from that very morning, Grace in her bathing suit out on the dock, somewhere around eleven, four hours before she would be pronounced dead on site. The creature was standing directly behind her daughter with his hand on her shoulder, digging its long-pointed fingers into her flesh. It was staring ahead, straight at the camera in the same way Grace was.

Becky let out another scream, this one so loud she would not have been surprised if her glass cup from earlier shattered. Becky watched in horror as she saw the head of the thing, whatever it was in the photograph, turn its head to her, tilt it slightly, and point.

CHAPTER 22

Troy loosened his foot from the accelerator as he glanced back and forth between the road and his photograph. The tears that had been welling in his eyes were now falling freely down his cheeks. He blinked them away, already barely able to see in the night.

He had left the house, the house he had lived in with his family, for the last time. He was not going back. In fact, he was not sure where he was going, but he was almost certain it would be the end of the line for him.

He was not sure exactly what he was going to do, but he knew where he was headed. He was going to the hill. That special hill where some of his best memories laid, where his life had been intact...and where he had lost his best friend. He figured he could drown himself out there easily enough. He had heard that drowning, once you accept the fate, was one of the easier ways to go...and he was not much of a swimmer. All he would have to do was go out to the middle of the lake, which was not far from the hill—not far at all—tread water till exhaustion seized his body, and then let the water free him.

That would be sentimental, wouldn't it? The lake, the town that took his life from him figuratively, would take him physically now as he gasped for air. *It would be so much like it was twelve years ago,* Troy thought. *No, this isn't sentimental or even ironic. It's tragic. But that's what my life is, isn't it? Tragic.*

He would die, but he would die with some part of his sanity still there. He could make that choice, give himself some kind of...what he did not know, but he did not love the idea of being locked in a cell for his entire life. Or worse, cause someone harm due to his failing psyche. Plus, maybe this had been a long time coming. It had been over two years since he had felt a single ounce of happiness. Every waking moment of his life had been a deep wallow of despair and tragedy.

He peeled his eyes away from the picture of his family, glanced at the road, and then looked at himself in the rearview mirror.

How would Grace see him now anyways? He was no father that she would recognize. No success stories. In fact, he was just the opposite. He was alone—her mother too. His marriage had slipped right through his fingers, and he blamed himself for that, too.

Now he realized why he had truly come back to Black Lake. He wanted to see if he could fix something, anything that he had fucked up. If he could have fixed things with Beck, done something even—even if it wasn't romantic—but if he had just been able to rekindle a single spark of their previous lives, his life could have some kind of meaning, purpose or silver lining. But he had not. He had done just the opposite and had pushed her away further.

He could have done something, anything for his father and mother. But no, since he had gotten back into town, his father had only fallen deeper and deeper into his illness. He was dying, he didn't have much time left, and Troy could hardly bear it.

And what about Mitch? What kind of honor could he have done Mitch? He came home to find out Mitch's entire family had been killed — by Dan, no less. Something he partly blamed himself for, too, like he blamed himself for Mitch's death. How could he have not even known it happened? He found out far after the fact from his sick, dying father, and it was because he had run out of town like a coward.

Was there anything he could have done? he wondered. Anything that he could do now?

No, everything he'd tried to do had backfired. And Troy knew what his next move was. He hated life, and he hated himself, and he would do well to end it. Besides, there was some poetry in it all, wasn't there? A passage of morbid poetry as he took his own life at that lake. That lake that had taken so much from him.

Eventually, Troy was brought from his daydream. After realizing he was swerving from his lane to the oncoming traffic lane more than once, he convinced himself to pull over. He stared at his picture for a good long moment before allowing his body to bend him over in his seat with sobs.

The heartache was even causing him physical pain now — in his chest, his head, his hands even. He was not sure what was happening exactly, but he assumed this was it. He had finally lost it and would do better to not get anyone else killed on his behalf.

How many times had somebody died at his hands? Directly, of course, there were none. But indirectly...well, in his mind, he could count several unsolved cases that had mounted over the years...his best friend, and lastly, his daughter. His beautiful, sweet, and loving daughter had drowned. He had spent the better part of the last two years trying to pretend to himself that he did not place the entire blame squarely and heavily on his own shoulders. Sometimes accidents happened, after all, but without the blurriness of thought that came from a bottle or an endless slew of antidepressants, antipsychotics, or a cocktail of all three, with his plans with Becky falling completely flat, he realized it was all a lie. He did blame himself. And he hated himself for it.

Troy was lost in his emotion, sobbing incoherent sentences of a man who was not sure if he was seeing things from another dimension, hauntings of a great and terrible evil, or losing his mind. He was so lost, in fact, that the first soft, gentle touch along his forearm almost went unnoticed.

Almost.

Troy turned in the direction of the feeling, his eyes locking onto what was in the passenger seat. Though it was dark on the back road of the small town of Black Lake, Troy could just make out the shadow that sat next to him, staring directly back at him.

It was Grace.

The knee-jolt reaction of seeing his dead daughter again — with the rotting flesh and the maggots, the sickening smell and that voice…oh god, that horrible, evil voice — almost made Troy jump out of the car.

Troy did everything he could to hold back the terrified scream emerging from his throat. He was just able to hold himself still long enough to keep himself from cowering away from the thing, to realize that it was not the Grace he had seen before. No, it was his Grace. His beautiful child with no trace or stench of death on her.

"Grace?" he whispered. "Is that really you?"

"Hi, Daddy," Grace replied, her voice just as quiet.

"Is it you? Is it really you? The real you?" Troy asked, his voice trembling.

"Yes, Daddy. I am here," Grace replied, her voice still as soft.

"How? Where? Why?" Troy stuttered out. "What is going on?"

Grace's shadowy figure blinked, tears swelling in her eyes. "I came to warn you, Dad. I came to warn you."

"Warn me? Grace, what do you mean?" Troy said, wiping

the tears from his red and itchy eyes.

"It saw Mommy, Dad. It saw her, and now it can get her." Her voice was a terrified whisper.

"What?" Troy replied, confused. "Who saw your mom? What's happening?"

"He did, Daddy," she said. "Maromoth."

"What? Grace, what are you talking about?"

"Maromoth, Daddy."

"Who is Maromoth?"

"It's not a he, but a what. It is who killed them, Daddy. It is what got them. Uncle Mitch and his dad. All of them. And it wants Grandpa, too. And it got me. And now it wants you, Daddy. It wants you and Mommy. He wants to hurt you for what you did to him," she said, her eyes now full of tears. Her voice was barely audible over the nighttime noises. "It wants to hurt you for what you did to him in the lake. For when you stabbed him, Daddy. He wants to hurt you now."

There was a pause, and then she continued.

"Maromoth wanted you, Daddy, before I was born. It tried to get you. He said he almost had you, but you got away. So, he got Uncle Mitch instead. But Maromoth didn't want Uncle Mitch. He wanted you, Dad. That's why he got me. That's why he made Mitch's dad do the bad thing. That's why he made Grandpa sick. To get you here. Get you here, so he could get you."

Troy cleared his head. "Grace, I don't understand."

"Maromoth, Dad. He normally just wants kids. He likes kids. He likes sad kids and kids that have seen him because they almost died already. If you die and come back to life, sometimes you see him. That's how he got Uncle Mitch's daddy. He did a sad thing…."

Troy read between the lines. She was talking about his suicide attempt.

"So, he saw him and made him do the bad thing." Troy

connected the dots to the murder of his family. "But he doesn't want Mitch, or Mitch's dad, or Grandpa, or even me, Daddy. He never wanted us. He wanted you. He wanted to get you back home so he could make you pay for what you did to him with that knife. That's what he told me. He hates you, Daddy. That's what he told me."

There was another pause before Grace finished with a cry. "You have to stop him, Daddy. You have to."

"Grace, no one can get me and Mommy. And you drowned, baby. You are not real. I wish you were. I wish you were here, but you aren't," Troy said. He reached out to touch her face, to confirm to himself his suspicion that he had lost his mind.

"Oh, my sweet baby, I am so sor—" Troy stopped, his stomach lurching hard in a twisted knot as the skin of his fingertips touched...flesh. He held them there on her cheek as the warmth and feel was on his fingers, and he cupped his whole hand around her face doing everything he could to not cry out.

"Grace?" he asked.

"I'm real, Daddy. And I am here, but I must go soon... before it finds me. Listen, you must help Mommy. You have to stop it before it gets you, too," she said, her voice rising to a strong and stern command. "It won't stop. It wants you too badly, Daddy. It won't stop. Not until you stop it. Not until you kill it."

"Who, Grace? Who is coming? I don't understand," Troy replied, dumbfounded. "Who, Grace? Who is coming? I don't understand," Troy repeated.

"Maromoth. He is coming, and I do not have much more time. Dad, you must stop this. You must stop it before it gets Mommy. You hurt it before. Now you have to make it go away forever," she said. She was starting to grow impatient at his lack of understanding, or rather his refusal to accept that this was real.

Then it hit Troy.

At first, the mention of the name had held no significance. He had heard it in one ear, but it had gone through the other. But at the second mention, something had clicked. Troy's heart sank further, and he felt his voice tremble as he asked the question.

"Did you say Maromoth?" he asked, the thought of when he had just crossed into the city limit flashing through his mind.

Officer Moth.

Grace said nothing, staring off into the world outside her windshield.

"Moth, Grace? Did you say Moth?" Troy asked, his voice breaking into a panicked yell. This thing, whatever Grace was warning him about, had been there all this time since he first entered town, and he had gone right past it so unexpectedly. He wanted to scream, to cry, to hold Grace, to do anything other than accept the unthinkable. Accept the unbelievable.

"He saw you, Daddy. He saw you. He knows you are here again. He knows he can hurt you," she said. "You've got to stop him, Daddy, before he gets you and Mommy."

"How?" Troy asked, disbelief crossing his face. He pressed his palm against her cheek harder, confirming that she was as real as he could let himself believe.

Just as Grace was opening her mouth to continue, they heard the purr of an approaching engine.

"He's here. I love you, Daddy. Goodbye."

"No! No! No!" Troy screamed as he felt the warmth of his daughter's cheek leave the skin of his hand. He cried and felt for her, pawing at the leather in the seat next to him, but there was nothing but coldness greeting him.

"Grace! Gracie baby," he said through the tears. He needed to see her. He was confused and scared. He was sure it had happened, and he was sure now that he wasn't going crazy.

There *was* something malevolent in this town. He could feel it clawing at him day and night. He had chalked it up to his mind slowly deteriorating, but it had all clicked with what his daughter told him. He supposed somewhere down deep, he had always known it but had refused to believe it. And that force had taken his daughter and his friend, and probably more deaths in this town than Troy dared to think of.

"Gracie, come back," he cried. "Please."

He was met with no answer. He looked down at his photograph of Gracie smiling at him.

"I love you. I am so sorry," he choked out.

The tap on his driver's side window broke his attention, causing a flight of anxiety to rush through his veins like an especially strong drug as one single thought ran through his head....

He is here. I love you, Daddy. Goodbye.

Maromoth. He is here.

CHAPTER 23

It took over an hour for Becky to finally calm herself to an even remotely reasonable state, and even then, reasonable was a subjective term.

"What the fuck is going on?" she audibly said to herself as she paced back and forth in her living room, not daring to look at the scattered stacks of photographs, all of which she had come to discover were met with that wretched, ghostly figure that was haunting her family.

At first, she thought she had lost her mind, that somehow the insanity her ex-husband was now facing had wiggled its way into her brain like some kind of contagious virus. But the night had led her to believe it wasn't so.

Unless we are sharing a delusion, she thought. She had heard of that before. The phenomenon where people share horrible, horrible delusions. Becky supposed she might be sharing a schizophrenic episode with her husband. If that were the case, she too might end up in an emotional hospital, released under the condition of severe mind-altering medication.

It was either that or Troy had been right. There was something malevolent here. Something that had been stalking her family, killing her family and friends for years now.

When regarding whether she preferred vomit or shit, the mental imbalance being vomit and the paranormal being shit, she would have gladly picked vomit, taken the mental institution, and been clinically off the rails.

In her heart of hearts, Becky knew the truth.

What she had seen was real, and it was confirmed when, only once, she picked up the picture to see that the figure was still there. And when she had touched it, her blood had turned icy cold, a cold that chilled her thoroughly, going to the bone.

No, Becky knew she was not going crazy, though she had much preferred that be the answer and accept whatever easier fate that would have given her. She did not know what was happening, she did not have the means to put into words what she had seen, but she knew one thing.

The alternative, the thing she knew to be true, was far more sinister.

She paced all around her home, unsure of her next course of action. Should she call the police? No, they would not do much of anything except maybe put her on a watchlist, at the very least.

Becky supposed she could call any number of people — her parents, Troy's parents, a few of her friends — but she knew it was fruitless. She would get the same reaction from them all — after two years, she, too, was finally beginning to crack, the yolk of her sanity falling and spilling like a dropped egg on a tile floor.

The thought came to her mind then. The only person who would believe her was the person who had told her, the same person she had shoved away. She needed to call Troy and tell him what she had seen... what they would do then, she did not know. But every second she did not act was another second wasted.

She made herself walk to her bedroom in search of her phone, which she had misplaced sometime before or after she had threatened Troy. Or was it before they had sex? She couldn't remember, though if it had been the latter, there was no way her phone would even have a charge.

Oh, God, she thought. He had been seeing that man, that thing, for days now. It had been manifesting itself to him, and she had pushed him away, thinking she was the victim of some cruel joke. Now he was all alone, left to himself to deal with it. A pang of guilt strong enough to buckle her gut hit her in the side as she let out another sob.

She rushed into her bedroom, throwing herself at the door and barely catching her feet as it swung open. The stumble almost kept her from noticing it, almost kept her eyes from seeing, but she had seen it.

Grace's elephant sat on the nightstand next to her bed, its torn and weathered ear facing her.

Her heart jumped twice. The last time she had seen it was when it was buried with Grace. She was sure of it because she was the one who wanted it buried, against Troy's pleading wishes. There was no logical, rational, earthly way for it to be here in front of her now...but here it was, staring her right in the face.

"Grace...," she whispered, stepping toward it.

As she touched its soft cotton head, she wondered for the last time if she was suffering the fate of a cracked psyche. But it was finally put to rest by the voice of her daughter behind her.

"Mommy," Grace called.

Becky flipped around as fast as she could manage, now facing the door that led to the living room and her baby girl, standing in the doorway, dressed in her nightly pajamas. A thought jolted her away, and she let out a scream as she stammered backwards. Troy had said he had seen Grace, too. That he had seen her on the dock, rotting away, with maggots and death. That Grace had come to attack him with that...that thing.

But this was not at all what Troy had described. This was their daughter, their beautiful daughter that she remembered on her saddest and happiest days.

Becky could see that in every way she looked just as she had the day she had passed, before the accident. Her hair was flowing down around her shoulders the way it had a handful of years ago. Her eyes were full of light, not darkness. Her skin carried a soft olive glow, not the blotchy blue and purple and gray that Troy had reported.

Becky took a careful and deliberate step forward. She flared her nostrils and took in a big breath of air. There was no smell of death like Troy said he had experienced.

It was Grace, their Grace, her Grace standing in front of her now. Whatever Troy had seen, it had not been their daughter.

Becky cried a mixture of sadness, relief, and fear before Grace cut her off.

"There isn't much more time, Mommy. It saw you, Mommy, just like he saw me and Uncle Mitch. And he saw Daddy, too. And now he wants you, and he wants Daddy. And it is killing Grandpa. Every day it is killing him. It is what made him so sick. It's why Grandpa hears voices and says things because he's almost got him. It will not stop, Mommy, not until it has all of you. And now it can get you because it saw you. You must help him, Mommy. You have to help Daddy before it's too late," she said in a hurried breath.

"Gray, I don't understand? What is *it*? What are you talking about?"

"You do. You always have. It is him, Mommy. It is Maromoth. He has lived here a long time, longer than any of us. You know it. You always knew it. Now you have to hurry."

Becky took a step toward her, not in disbelief but in wonder. She reached out and touched the cheek of her deceased child, who had not aged a day since she had passed so many years ago.

"Gracie," she said, cupping her face in her right hand.

"I love you, Mom," Grace whispered.

"I love you, too, baby," Becky whispered back.

"You're running out of time."

"But how?"

Grace replied, "Daddy will know."

"Where is he?" Becky asked.

Her question was never answered. As quickly as Grace had stood before her, warning her of Maromoth, which was certainly the name of whatever she had seen and had seen her, she was gone. There was nothing left but the draft of wind that came through the bedroom window and fluttered the drapes that stood in front of it.

"Grace?" she called, not once, not twice, but three times, and three times she went unanswered. She choked back a sob, unsure if it was from what she had seen or what she knew lay ahead of her.

Becky allowed herself a moment to digest what she had seen, but no more. If what she saw was true, and she believed it was, she needed to act fast.

When the time had passed, and Becky had collected herself, she searched for her phone, which had fallen somewhere on the floor during her and Troy's cluster of embraces. She bent down and picked it up, pushing for Troy's number as she did so.

Seconds after she pushed the call button, her heart sank. It had gone straight to voicemail.

CHAPTER 24

Troy sat, planted in his chair, his vision still on the passenger seat where the vision of his daughter had been just moments before.

He is here, Daddy.

Who?

Maromoth.

The words ran wild through his mind. Maromoth. Could it be the man he had met on his first day in town? Officer Moth, that was what he had said his name was. Troy was almost sure of it.

Troy shuddered. That would mean that this thing, whatever it was, had been with him, stalking him, toying with him, since day one, since he had gotten into town. This thing had been waiting—no, not waiting, luring him—for two years to come home, to come back to Black Lake, and here he was all alone.

This thing, this entity, had taken his best friend, was killing his father, had taken his sweet daughter, and was coming to finish its work with him now. It was only a matter of time. Troy was sure of that.

There was another tap against the driver's side window, and Troy did everything he could not to fling himself from his seat, duck out the passenger door, and run. Run as far away from this town as he possibly could. To run and forget.

But he knew he would not. He needed to stay. The words of his seven-year-old rang through his ears like they had just been spoken.

He saw Mommy, and now he can get her too.

He was not going anywhere. He had to stay and end this thing, end this cycle that had plagued this town for as long as he could remember. Troy Kender would stay and fight Maromoth, or he would be swallowed whole by it. He would stay and defeat it or die for his wife's sake. As much as she had pained him, he felt no ill will towards her now and knew it was his duty to save her. Troy Kender was not going anywhere.

Tap. Tap.

This third tap against the glass was harder now, impatient. Troy felt his throat drop down into his groin as the fear and realization of the decision he had just made struck him. He swallowed hard, and his body shuddered as his testicles retracted inside him from fear. A trail of sweat forming against his brow glistened in the moonlight.

He cleared his throat and slowly turned his head to the window, ready to face whatever was there waiting for him.

But when he turned his head, it was nothing that he recognized.

In fact, it was not anything out of the normal at all. An officer stood there, but it was not the officer he would have expected. It wasn't Officer Moth there, or the rotting form of his daughter, or that appearance of Maromoth that had come after him when his daughter had appeared.

It was a regular police officer, an older gentleman, standing there impatiently as he raised his eyebrows in a confused and annoyed look.

Troy, still unsure of himself and this situation, reached his trembling arm over to the switch and rolled the window down a little more than halfway, having to try twice before he finally found his index finger on the window control lever.

"Evening, Officer," he said, his voice shaky and afraid even with his best attempt to conceal it.

"What in the good lord's name are you doing? I tapped on this window three times before you answered," the officer replied. The man had a resonating and wet voice to him that sent a wave of odd relief through Troy. He spoke with more concern than anger, and though there was some amount of irritation there, it was not overwhelming.

"Sorry. It has been a rough night, Officer. Guess I wasn't thinking straight. I thought you might be someone else," Troy replied, his voice only slightly stronger than before.

"What are you talking about?" the office replied. Though his tone was authoritative and no-nonsense, his voice wasn't as unkind as Troy would have guessed it to be.

"It's a long story. My wife and I—well, ex-wife—we lost our daughter two summers ago. She had invited me over—this is my first time back home in years—and it didn't go so well—"

Troy was cut off.

"I've heard enough. You been drinking?" the officer asked.

"Not a drop."

The officer eyed him suspiciously. Troy was sure that the man had half a mind to go back and call in for a breathalyzer and maybe a backup unit, but he seemed to think better of it. There was nothing to smell, and although Troy's voice was nervous or shaken up, it did not slur.

"You know, I could go and test you on that account, but I don't think I will. Tell me why you pulled over."

"I guess I just…." Troy was at a loss for words. "This is a little embarrassing, but I was looking at this picture of me, my wife, and my daughter, and I…." Troy paused and lightly handed him the picture. Troy was feeling the tear fall down his cheek and felt the officer looking at him. He couldn't say the words, but Troy was sure the man knew what he was feeling. "I just didn't feel safe to drive anymore, so I pulled over. I'm staying with my parents; they are not too far up the road here."

The man handed the picture back to him. "What's your name, son?"

"Troy. Troy Kender."

"Kender, hmm? Sounds familiar."

"I used to work in the high school here before my daughter passed. I left town after that."

"Really? When was that?" the officer replied, cocking his head as he searched through his memory bank.

"About two years ago," Troy stated.

"Kender. You say you worked at Black Lake High, right?"

"That's right."

"I can't put the memory to it, but it rings a bell." The officer sat there a second, still waiting for the memory to strike him, and come to think of it, Troy felt he looked familiar, too. There had been quite a few transfers that came in two months due to the increase in suspected homicides, suicides, freak accidents, and all. It took its toll. Officers left town often and came in even faster. He hadn't gotten around to meeting them all before his departure, but that's where he had figured he saw the man. He did not mention it, though, and waited for him to reply.

"Either way, I see no problem here and don't need to be bothering a grieving man either. I'm sorry about your daughter. She sure was a beautiful little girl."

"Thanks. Yeah, she was. Am I free to go then?"

"Free as a bird unless you need something from me."

Troy thought on that a second. "Officer, there actually is something if it isn't too much."

"Well, shoot, then."

"Do you know a Black Lake officer by the name of Moth?"

"Moth? No, that doesn't seem to ring...." He thought a second, putting a hand to his chin. "Nope. That name does not ring any bells. Sorry."

"That's quite all right," Troy answered.

"Well, if that'll be all, then I'll see you around. Enjoy your stay, and do not find yourself any trouble. And like I said, I'm sorry about Grace," the officer said.

Troy nodded in return, and with that, the man was off back to his car. He had jumped in his cruiser and sped off, Troy about to put his own car in drive and go back home, when the terrifying thought struck him.

Grace. He had not said her name.

It didn't take long, not long at all, for Troy to get a grip on himself and accept what he had seen. Deep down, somewhere in his chest, he knew that he had known it all along. This town, this place, the deaths, and the misery...there had always been something about it that had not sat right with him. He was not going crazy; it was not mental illness or trauma-induced psychosis. It was the presence here that had been with him since he was a kid, and he had just come face to face, yet again, with its perpetrator.

Troy took one last look at the empty passenger seat on his right and knew what he had to do. With as much speed as he could, he turned his car around, heading back to his ex-wife's home. The tires squealed against the pavement as he took off, and he didn't dare look behind him to see if that officer was behind him waiting to pull him over—no, that wasn't right. That was no officer of the law...it was no human at all. Whatever it was that had pulled him over, confronted him, spoken to him, it was what Grace had warned him about.

The horror struck Troy hard. This thing could be anything, anyone, and anywhere.

The word rang through his head again like a gunshot. Maromoth.

Whatever it was had killed his friend. Had killed his daughter. Had tried to kill him...and was going to kill Becky if he did not get to her. Fast.

Troy pushed the pedal to the floor, almost redlining the little thing, causing its chassis to vibrate back and forth as he flipped a U-turn and headed to Becky as fast as he could.

CHAPTER 25

In half the time it had taken for Troy to leave the house, he was there in its driveway in the same spot he had been the night before. The little home that had once been his that housed all his memories stood without a trace of malevolence. Whatever may be going on inside, whatever Grace had warned him about only minutes before, was completely concealed within its brick walls.

Troy bounded up the steps, contemplated knocking on the front door, but thought better of it. Knowing his ex-wife the way he did, Troy knew there was no reason to kick it in, that it would be unlocked and inviting in the apparently safe town that was Black Lake. He turned the doorknob and walked in, just as he had expected. If, by chance, he was wrong, at which point there would be far greater problems for him to contend with, such as losing his grip on reality, he would have the law to answer to. Probably locked up and a restraining order. These concerns were well worth the risk, Troy thought as he stepped inside.

"Beck?" Troy called out. He waited a moment for an answer. "Becky?" he tried again, moving his way swiftly but warily through the entrance, the kitchen, and into the living room.

The pictures he two had been looking at together earlier

were still out—in fact, most were lying in disarray across the floor, and now that it caught his attention and he looked around some, Troy could see they were spread out all the way into the kitchen.

"Becky?" Troy cried again, his voice growing louder. There was still no answer.

Troy took careful steps around, searching for his ex-wife, wondering where she could have gone.

Her car was still parked in the driveway when I pulled up, so she could not have gone far, he thought. Panic started to settle and grow in him. She could be anywhere...doing anything.

He's coming for Mommy, Dad, Grace's voice rang in his ears again,

Taking another quick look around before resolving to...what? He did not know, but in the swift search, he found something that caught his eye. The lone photograph on the coffee table that was sitting only a handful of feet away from him.

He started toward it, a strange feeling that he could not quite explain, somewhere between curiosity and fear, overtaking him. His pace slow and careful, he headed for the table. In the silence that he walked in, he heard nothing but the slight hum of the air conditioner and the subtle drip-drip from the bathroom, which was muffled by the door.

Troy lifted the picture to his face. It was of Grace on the day she had passed—the last picture they had of her. It was her in her little one-piece bathing suit, the one Becky had picked out the week before, simple with polka dots lining it. Grace was on the dock, a big smile on her face and squinting because the bright late morning sun was flashing itself in her eyes. Just like Troy, Grace hated the sun being in her eyes.

Then, before his very eyes—which was the only reason Troy believed it was happening—Grace's face began to change. The crooked smile of his little daughter opened wide in what looked like a scream. The squinting eyes, which were almost entirely closed shut, opened wide in fear. Her body began to hunch and shrivel away from her right side, and that was when Troy saw it. The thing that was digging its long hook-like, skeleton hands, with its rotting flesh and their contorted and broken shape, into Grace's shoulder. The same thing he had seen in his dream, which he now knew was no dream. It was the thing the haunted version of his decaying daughter had told him to look at, the same thing her innocent spirit had warned him about only ten minutes ago in the passenger seat of his car.

It was that thing whose name he now knew, now understood, as Maromoth. And it was sucking the soul from his daughter. Some form of weird light that would otherwise look like a defect was flowing from Grace's body, from her eyes, into the wide gaping mouth and eyes of Maromoth. And then, in a flash of a second, both disappeared.

Troy stared at the picture in horror, the room around him disappearing. This was what had happened to his daughter, his baby girl, his sweet seven-year-old. She had the life and soul sucked right out of her on the back dock of his parents' home. It had killed her, and worse. While his father had....

His father. The thoughts leaped out to him in the silence. His father. His father had some form of cancer like illness that was not explainable in any way through modern medicine. Louis Kender, who was always so smooth with words and smooth with action, like everything in his life was a precise Kodak moment, was now having slips of his mind and hearing voices. Voices Troy now presumed were of Maromoth himself.

"It is not over. He is still searching for you," was what his father had said.

That was when the final piece clicked. Louis Kender did not have an illness of this world. He was slowly being sucked dry of his soul by Maromoth. And it was coming for him. And his ex-wife.

You have got to save Mommy, Dad, he heard in his head. And that brought him back to life.

"Becky?" Troy screamed. "Beck, where are you?"

Troy stopped and listened, but the only thing that answered was that same low hum and that same drip-drip.

Drip-drip-drip.

"Becky!" Troy yelled once more as he headed for the bathroom door, putting the pieces together. "Beck!" he cried as he twisted his hand around the doorknob.

It was locked, as he figured. He attempted to twist the door handle again, seeing if he could somehow budge it. He couldn't. He knocked on the door and called her name again, but there was no answer.

More panic set in, and without thinking of any normal world consequence, Troy took one big step back, braced himself, raised his right foot waist high, and sent it flying into the spot he learned could break in a door back in high school when he had locked himself out. He hit it twice, and it flew open on its hinges with a bang.

The sight of what lay in front of him took a second for his mind to register, to overcome the shock of it all. Becky was lying in the bathtub, submerged in water, her skin a faint blue color.

In an instant, Troy was at the side of the tub, grabbing his ex-wife and pulling her out. Running on autopilot, he did the only thing that came to mind. The same thing he had done to his daughter's lifeless body so many years ago to no avail. He could still feel the warmth radiate off her, even though the water she had drowned in had been cool. A light bulb rang off in his head. If her body was warm, that meant he had gotten here just after she lost consciousness.

I might have time, his panicked thoughts cried. *I have time. Dear God, please give me the time!*

He pushed his palms into her chest with a rhythmic motion.

One, two, three, four, breath, one, two, three, fourth, breath, again and again. Troy could not tell if it was seconds or minutes that had passed, but based on the soreness overcoming his upper limbs, he assumed it was closing in on the latter.

"C'mon, Beck. C'mon," Troy yelled, tears streaming down his cheeks, the rhythmic pulsing of his arms into her body beginning to wane and mistime itself as his arms were giving out. He gave Becky a final breath and round of CPR before his body gave its final cry of effort.

As the last pulse of energy went through him and into Becky's body, her eyes fluttered open violently, and she took in a sweep of air that quickly turned into a choking fit. It went on and on, releasing her lungs from the liquid that had resided in them.

After a drawn-out round of coughing and attempted breathing, the water came out and splattered, with bile and other contents of her body, into a heap on the floor. Becky took long gulps of oxygen as if she had never had the stuff before. As if her life depended on it. And, of course, it did.

After a few moments, the color returned to Becky's face. They looked at one another, both sitting on the tiled, wet floor of the bathroom, without saying a word. Troy stood up slowly and grabbed her towel. Becky wrapped it around herself gratefully.

Minutes passed before either of them spoke. It was Becky who broke the silence, though her voice was barely above a faint whisper.

"Troy." She paused, attempting to calm the trembling in her voice. "I saw it. I saw him." And with a trembling hand, she opened her fist to reveal a clump of wet, jet-black hair. "It's his."

CHAPTER 26

"Beck," Troy said for the third time, taking her hands in his to direct her attention to him. "What did you see?"

Her face was pale, a shade of white that Troy was unsure he had ever seen someone wear before. She was trembling, violently shivering as she sat on the couch, even though she had on a robe and was engulfed in blankets.

"I saw him, Troy. I told you, I saw *him*. That thing." She paused and swallowed hard as if the words she was about to speak were poison, and the very utterance of them would make them real, make the impossible possible. But Becky knew now that it had been the truth, that her ex-husband had been right all this time. "You were right. He killed her. He killed Grace. And Mitch. And it's what's killing Louis."

Troy took a long deep breath, seating himself on the couch as much as he could, hoping he could just disappear into it, to cease to exist.

"What are we going to do?" he whispered.

"What *can* we do?" Becky said in equal reply.

Troy thought of Dan's makeshift basement workshop. Had he known all along? Those pictures, the evidence, the quotes on the wall. Grace had mentioned something about that. Something about how Dan knew about Maromoth, about how they had seen each other.

Grace's voice came to his head, crystal clear from when she was in the car. "If you died and come back to life, sometimes you see him." That must have been his seven-year-old's way of saying Dan was close to death or died even. That was the access to the world Maromoth lived in.

Grace's words came again. "That's how he got Uncle Mitch's daddy. He did a sad thing...." No doubt the sad thing had been his attempted suicide. "So, he saw him and made him do the bad thing." There was no question there—the bad thing was the successful murder of his own family.

He had lost his son, so his grief had been great.

After his attempt, Dan must have seen Maromoth—he must have known then what it was. He had visions. He probably heard voices. He and Troy probably shared much of this new reality together without even knowing it.

But he had figured it out. Dan had figured all of it out. What had been plaguing this town, what had taken his son. While Troy had run, Dan had figured it out and lost his life to the soul-sucking demon.

Troy clenched his fist, furious with himself. A new resolve was forming.

Troy remembered now the last thing he had looked at before he left Mitch's house. The picture of the knife. Dan had figured out how to stop it.

The townsfolk thought he had gone crazy, but that is not what happened at all, Troy thought. He had figured out how to defeat Maromoth. Through an obsessive depression, Mitch's father had thought it all through and come up with an answer. While the townsfolk thought he had gone crazy, become depressed, lost his job, become a drunk, went off the rails and killed his whole family, and attempted and eventually committed suicide, he had figured it all out.

He was knocking on death's door, Troy's mind yelled. *Knocking on death's door. On death's door.*

In a furious second, Troy had gotten up from his seat and walked over to the bathroom, investigating the bathroom where the clump of hair had fallen from Becky's hand and remained.

It had been too much at that moment for either of them to process it, but now as time had passed, Troy had begun to put the pieces together in his mind. As he analyzed the coarse strands, the thoughts and memories churned in his brain repeatedly.

Becky had almost died. In fact, she basically had died. She had been hanging in the terrible balance between life and death, but Troy had shown up just in time, and she had brought back with her a clump of the ghoul's hair.

Louis, who was having the life drained from him day by day, had been having visions, thoughts, and now had even been possessed for a moment in the hospital as his life hung in the balance.

Grace was so close to it the day she had died. So close that Maromoth, the demon, had been standing there right next to her, closer and closer until he had finally taken her.

And Troy himself, on that fateful night he and Mitch had driven the snowmobile...Mammoth had shown itself only when they were both submerged underwater. That was when he grabbed Troy. And Mitch. When they were on death's doorstep.

The key to beating this thing was being at death's door.

"Troy?" Becky said. "Troy, what is that?"

In the heat of his discovery, Troy had not heard Becky's soft footsteps that led her only a few feet from him. In another moment, it may have frightened him, but in this one, it did not.

He also had not noticed how the clump of hair sitting in his palm had been liquefying. The strands were now beginning to fall into droplets of a blood-like fluid as dark and black as ink.

They hit the floor with an icy drip, drip, drip until there was no more solid left in his hand. There was nothing left but the blood-like, watery substance.

Then came the smell. It was so strong Troy felt his gag reflex kick him in the gut so hard he almost did not hear Becky run to the sink, lean over it, and empty the contents of her own stomach beside him.

It was putrid, like rotten meat, but stronger. The only thing he could relate it to was....

"Oh my god," he said through gags, and false vomits. "Becky, that smell."

She answered with a hurl.

"I remember it," he said, exiting the bathroom, escaping the immediateness of the stench. But it clung in his nostrils, so much so that when Beck gave her final heave, he had to swallow hard to keep himself from doing the same.

Becky left the bathroom and met him where he stood. They were quiet for a while, but Troy broke the silence.

"I remember that smell, Becky. I remember it. It was there when I saw Grace. When she was at the dock and asking me why I couldn't take her fishing."

She did not say anything. She only grabbed his loose hand. He turned to her.

"It was her, Beck. It was Grace. That smell was her. When her arm...when her arm came off, and the maggots, and that... that...oh, dear god," he choked out, the tears beginning to well in his eyes.

"It wasn't her, Troy. It was not her. It is this thing. This evil thing. It was him, Troy. It wasn't her. It was Maromoth."

Troy took a big calming breath through his nostrils, the smell hitting him again. But this time, he did not feel fear or sadness. He felt rage.

"It must be stopped," Troy said.

"What are you going to do?" Becky whispered, afraid of the answer.

He replied with an angry boldness. "I'm going to kill it," Troy paused. "I'm going to kill Maromoth."

CHAPTER 27

Troy knew what he had to do and where he would have to start. Becky knew, too, even as she pleaded for him to find another way, another option. In the end, she was the one who drove him to the old Hampway house to get the knife he had left there days before.

Becky sat still and had not spoken a word while Troy explained exactly how he was going to go about killing Maromoth.

Troy's plan and logic were simple. And risky.

He had wounded Maromoth with Mitch's knife twelve years ago. He had weakened the ghost, and that was why it had sought such horrible revenge. In Troy's mind, that must mean it was vulnerable to it now. So Troy would kill this demon with the knife.

Becky objected, saying he could not be sure it would work. But Troy mentioned Dan and his basement, the picture of the knife glued to the walls. Becky was still not convinced. That was when Troy reluctantly told her of Grace visiting him in the car and how Maromoth wanted revenge for what Troy had done to him with the blade.

"What other option is there, Becky?" he asked her.

She didn't say anything in return.

Right or wrong, Becky knew this was the best lead they had. If her daughter told Troy in a vision — a vision that sounded similar to what she herself had experienced, strengthening her belief that Grace *had* come to Troy — that was why Maromoth was so obsessed with killing Troy now, as a sick form of revenge, then she would have to accept that it was, as Troy insinuated, their best option.

"Besides, that is not the risky part, or at least not the riskiest," Troy said. This didn't bring comfort, but it did seem to end the discussion on the knife.

The truly risky part was in how they would gain the upper hand. Maromoth was a demon and seemed to only be vulnerable during an attack that was abruptly interrupted. Troy in the lake when he stabbed it, or more recently, Becky, who had almost died and met Maromoth. She had taken a fistful of his hair in a struggle and was only seconds away from her death when Troy had come and revived her.

Maromoth came to them when they were near death. Mitch and Troy had been drowning. Grace had been lured by Maromoth to the same fate. Mitch's father was suicidal. Louis had cancer. And Becky had succumbed to drowning.

The key to defeating Maromoth was through death. And that, beyond all else in the plan, was what scared Becky the most.

Like Troy had said, the plan was simple, really.

Troy was going to drown himself in the very lake that had taken Grace with a weight tied around his ankle at the edge of the dock, where the water was just deep enough. After exactly sixty seconds of submersion, Becky was to cut the weight from Troy with Mitch's knife, pull him to shore, and revive him with CPR.

"When you revive me, I will bring Maromoth with me, like you did with the clump of hair," he said. Becky did not say anything. "And then I will kill him with the knife."

After a long moment of silence, Becky finally spoke.

"Troy…." She was sitting on the floor against the wall in her living room, still trembling from the events of the previous hour. "We don't know that it will work." She watched him as he said nothing in return. "And even if we did know Troy, what if…what if you can't beat it? What if he kills you, too?"

"Becky, "Troy said. "He has taken everything from me. He took my best friend. He is killing my dad. He took my daughter. He took my marriage." Troy swallowed hard as the tears gathered in his eyes. "He took my life from me, Becky. I have to do this."

"But I just got you back. After two years, we found one another back in each other's lives. I just got you back. I cannot lose you, not again," Becky nearly whimpered.

Troy bent down on one knee to sit with his ex-wife. He reached out his hand, and she accepted it. "Becky, it won't stop. It won't stop until it's dead."

A voice spoke from the corner of the room, the soft but steady voice of their seven-year-old daughter.

"Daddy's right. He must stop it, Mommy. Daddy has to stop it," Grace said.

Becky and Troy jumped at the sound of her voice. Turning and running to her, they tried to hug her but felt nothing.

"Grace," Troy said. "You're here again."

"You have to stop him, Dad. Mommy, he has to stop Maromoth before he gets anyone else."

"I know, Gracie. I know." Troy whispered.

"Grace…It's not that simple." Becky said, grabbing where her hand would be but only feeling chilled air. "What if you can't, Troy? Or, what if I…," she paused, and when she spoke again, her voice was barely audible, "I can't bring you back?"

"He took everything. *Everything* from me. If I can't…." Troy's eyes left hers and went to the floor. "If I can't stop him…." Troy looked back at Becky with an intensity Becky had not seen since he had tried to save his daughter all those years ago. "Even if I die, Beck, it's worth the risk."

Becky swallowed hard, and through the shaking and trembling voice, finding Troy's eyes, she knew he was sincere. There was no stopping him now. The best she could do was help him in any way she could. For him. For Grace. For herself.

"What do you need me to do?"

CHAPTER 28

It was pouring down rain. There was no conversation between Becky and Troy in his sedan as they drove down the road, but the rain was so loud as it hit Troy's car, he wasn't sure if he could've heard anything anyway.

He could barely see, even with his windshield wipers turned all the way up, wiping away water viciously. This was not anything new to Troy or Becky or Black Lake, of course. It was always raining here, but today, considering everything he'd found and everything he'd learned, something was different. There was an eerie tension in the air that clung to everyone, to everything.

Grace had vanished almost as quickly as she had appeared, and he had not seen her since she spoke to Becky, but Troy could still feel her presence with them. He could not see her, but she was there silently guiding them. Protecting them.

Troy reached for Becky's hand. She closed her fingers in his with a nervous squeeze. They had hardly spoken at all since they left her living room, but they were in it together now. All three of them were going to finish this once and for all.

Troy closed his car door in sync with Becky. They had not split up again since he had gone to her house a few hours ago. Everything felt like a dream as they stood in front of the old Hampway house. She found his hand again as he pushed the front door open and walked inside.

The knife was still on the floor where Troy had dropped it, which in some way surprised him. But then again, nothing really surprised him anymore.

He grabbed it, sheathed it, and walked back to his car, still holding Becky's hand.

***

It was still pouring rain when they arrived at Troy's childhood home. It was still pouring as he gathered the supplies he needed from the shed, the rain pummeling the roof, making that noise that sounded like a hundred pounding feet running after him or an audience laughing at his plan and his ultimate demise. He was not sure which he would have preferred, but he closed his eyes and exhaled. *There is no turning back*, he told himself as he checked to make sure the knife was still in his jacket pocket.

He ran through the plan in his mind repeatedly. He would tie the rope to his ankle and the weight to the rope. He would go just a few steps past the dock...that was where the little drop-off was that would put the water just above his head. The knife would be waiting with Becky, ready but secure. Becky would be waiting at the edge of the dock with a timer to cut the rope and the dumbbell from his ankle, releasing him.

Getting to that point was easy. The hard part was after the rope was cut. He reminded himself of how strong-willed a woman she was as he told himself that, yes, Becky would be able to grab him and drag him to shore. Once she brought him to land, she would then, through the miracle of CPR, bring him back to life.

And although Troy did not know exactly how, he would have Maromoth in his arms. He would bring him back with him as he was resurrected. And then he would kill him with the knife.

Troy could feel his heart begin pounding in his ears like an army marching with battle drums as he envisioned stabbing the son of a bitch right through the throat. The spray of that putrid black matter would paint the beach of his parents' home like a canvas. And it would be over. It would all be over. Tonight.

That was what he told himself again and again as he walked to the dock and to Becky with the dumbbell in his hand.

She looked away from him as he approached her. She had given one final attempt at reason in the car on the drive over, begging to use a different plan or a different day, or anything that wouldn't leave her with her husband—ex-husband, as he had reminded her—dead in the water.

Troy's mind was made up. This was the way, he knew, to beat Maromoth. With his father and mother back in the hospital, his condition only growing worse, awaiting transfer to a longer care facility, it had to be tonight. More than that, he wanted to end this tonight. No, he *would* end this tonight.

When he reached the dock, he dropped the items on the ground. Embracing his ex-wife in his arms, he bent down and gave her a soft kiss on her rain wet forehead and tear wet cheek.

"I will be fine. This *will* work. It'll be over soon." He paused to give her a reassuring squeeze and hardened his voice just enough. "You remember what to do?"

Becky nodded without resistance. There was no use in the argument now. She would trust this plan the best she could because if it failed, she knew she would have nothing left.

CHAPTER 29

Becky could barely stand the sight as her ex-husband tied his ankle to the weight with the short piece of rope, knowing what was to happen next. He sat at the edge of the dock with the weight in his lap. She joined him for what may have been the last time.

"You remember, it's two breaths then thirty compressions?" Troy asked. Troy remembered, that was for sure. After Grace's death he.... He shook the thoughts from his brain—now was not the time to think of the past. Now was the time to think of each second in sync, what he must do, how he must make sure everything went according to his plan.

"Yeah," Becky croaked. "Yeah, I remember."

"It'll be fine. It's only sixty seconds. Just remember to cut the rope and set the knife right next to me," Troy said, pulling the blade from his pocket and handing it to her. "Then, just get the *fuck* out of here. I don't want you anywhere near here when I bring that thing back."

"Okay," she said, but she had no intention of leaving. And they both knew it.

"Beck, I mean it. Find somewhere far away from here. Your house, your friend's house, anywhere but here, please."

"Yeah. Yeah, somewhere far away. Are you sure you can

do this, Troy?" Becky asked.

After a long pause, all Troy said in reply was, "I'm sure I have to try." With that, he gave her a final peck on the forehead, a soft embrace, and whispered, "Here goes...everything," as he and the weight slid into the water.

Becky watched as he took a step forward, and then another, and a third. She had hoped he would turn to her, run back and tell her to forget this whole thing, that they could just pick up where they had left off now that they were back in each other's arms. She would move to Chicago; they could start over and never speak of this again.

But she knew her husband. And she was not surprised when he didn't look back at her as he took the step at the drop-off and vanished out of sight. Troy had set his mind to this, and all she could do was pray to whatever god was on the other side that he would come back to her now.

She watched, gut wrenching, as he took step after step, the waiting game seeming endless. Then in a second, he was gone, submerged under the water. The ripples of his disappearance bounced throughout the surrounding surface of the otherwise cool lake. His head had just gone underwater.

Troy was now about to drown, and it was her job to rescue him.

Becky set the timer. Sixty seconds.

She could see the air pockets bubbling on the water's surface where Troy had last been seen. She made a mental note of that to be sure she knew where he would be when the timer went off.

Fifty-eight. Fifty-seven. There were still bubbles. He was still breathing or trying to. Becky imagined him choking, the cool water filling his lungs as he sucked for air. She imagined that lightheaded feeling, the same one she had just experienced, as his vision faded to black.

The bubbles were still forming...that meant there was time! Becky's mind danced around the thoughts again. She could dive in and cut the rope and free him now.

But she knew her husband. This was his choice, and there was no stopping Troy. Maybe once she could, but he would find a way to do this again and again if she stopped him then, too. He would not rest until the mission was accomplished.

Eleven. Ten. Nine. That was when she saw the bubbles stop forming. He was no longer attempting to breathe under the water.

Even though her timer had not reached the limit yet, Becky secured her grip on the knife and dove off the dock. It would take a few seconds to find him, a few seconds to get him free of the rope, and even more time to get him out of the water.

That counts, right? she thought to herself. Then she realized she really didn't give a shit if it counted or not. If she grabbed him and he was still somewhat conscious, this would be the way she would get him to end this. They would move to Chicago hand in hand even if she had to guilt him one last time, even if it took more guilt than she had placed on him for Grace. It may be selfish, but Troy would be alive.

She waddled through, submerged to her chest, gunning for the spot she thought she had lost sight of him. She splashed around as she made her way there, searching with her arms, her feet, everything she had. The water felt so abnormally heavy against her limbs. It was almost as if, almost, the force of Maromoth was even weighing the water, keeping her from effectively searching. Becky asked herself if that was even possible. She supposed she didn't know, so she assumed it was.

Maromoth must be trying to keep me from finding him, she thought, so she paddled around harder. When she was at the spot she could have sworn he was at, she took a big gulp, closed her eyes, and went under, searching again with everything she had.

When she had to come up for air, she came up empty handed. It was then that panic truly set in.

"Oh, God. Oh, God. Oh, God," she whimpered to herself.

Becky took another breath, filling herself with as much air as she could, and dove down again, this time thrashing around as she looked for any sign of Troy. She opened her eyes, but she couldn't see anything but black and the smallest reflection of the moon above her.

Her head spun as the panic consumed even more oxygen, and she again resigned herself to come up for air.

"Oh, God," she cried again, the warmth of her new tears contrasting with the cold water on her face. She closed her eyes. "Oh, God. What have I done?" she whispered.

"Mommy?" a little voice said—the little voice of her daughter.

Becky stopped, unable to believe it. Until she heard the voice again.

"Mommy. Daddy did it. He's got Maromoth," the little voice whispered.

Becky opened her eyes to see her daughter treading water in front of her. She was glowing, a lighthouse on a stormy night, the water reflecting her rays.

"Grace?" Becky breathed. "Is that you?"

"Yes, Mommy. It's time to go get Dad."

"I can't. I can't find him. I tried, and I can't find him," Becky cried. "Oh, God. Oh, God. I killed him."

Grace reached out her hand, grabbing Becky's. Becky felt the warmth of her daughter radiate through her like the sun on a summer's day. It was at this moment that Becky knew, with Grace's divine help, together they would find her ex-husband and Grace's father. Together they could do this.

"I can find him. Are you ready?" Grace asked.

Becky nodded.

Together they took a deep breath of air and dove below the water's surface.

Grace, in all her spiritual glory, illuminated the otherwise dark lake. Becky could feel the gentle tug of her daughter guiding her. In a moment, she saw Troy bobbing from the rope attached to the weight. His eyes were closed, and there were no more air pockets coming from his mouth. He bounced up and down, the rope catching him as he tried floating on the surface.

Becky inched toward him, knife in hand.

Am I in time? Do I have time to save him? These questions, she realized, were irrelevant. Either way, she was going to try like all fucking hell.

With the knife in her hand, she sawed at the rope back and forth until it was cut free. With the strength of her daughter's spirit, she brought Troy to shore.

CHAPTER 30

Troy felt his last breath escape him, and the water filled his lungs as his body involuntarily gasped for more.

This is it, he thought. *There is no turning back now.*

Just like twelve years ago, he felt his vision fade away to black, but this time there was no saving himself from his fate. This time he didn't accept it. He longed for it. This was the moment he would bring this all to its end. This was when he would bring Maromoth to his end.

In a flash of blinding light, he was standing in the dark, the light reflecting off the snow around him. His feet were freezing, and when he looked down, he saw that he was barefoot. In fact, he noticed he was entirely naked, standing in the snow.

Troy looked around, confused.

Where am I?

He couldn't make sense of any of it. Then he heard the crack.

His head spun around to meet the sound. He was standing on a lake, and the ice had cracked. But it wasn't just any lake. This was Black Lake.

Troy saw Mitch. He saw himself, too, on the back of a snowmobile, desperately trying to stay above the water that was rising up the sides of it. He heard Mitch scream, and he heard himself, his sixteen-year-old self, scream as they fell through the ice.

What felt like an hour passed before he saw each of them both surface and grab ahold of the ice. He heard Mitch yell again, "Kick and pull! Remember, kick and pull!" He watched as they did it, pushing themselves up onto the ice.

Troy heard his own voice again. "There's something down there, Mitch!"

Troy knew what happened next. That terrible noise that came from his best friend was somewhere between a terrified shriek and a shout as he was yanked underneath the water. It was followed by his own cries of his name.

"Mitch!" he cried. "Mitch!" But there was never an answer.

Troy watched himself walk around a while, then fall to a crawl, and finally roll over onto his back as he remembered his sixteen-year-old self giving in to his fate.

Troy watched his own lifeless body lay there for an eternity before the phone that ultimately saved his life rang. He watched the younger version of himself crawl again, almost dead, to it and make the call.

"The lake. At Benson Pine Avenue," he said before hanging up.

Then there was silence. Troy watched his own almost lifeless body lay there.

Then the voice entered his head. The sinister, malevolent voice. It sounded so hungry, bloodthirsty. Like it couldn't wait another moment to devour him.

I never wanted him. I never wanted Grace. Or your father. I wanted you.

The voice was cold. Dead. Heinous. The voice of Maromoth was the embodiment of evil.

Troy turned to face it. It was every bit as depraved as Troy could imagine. Now standing only feet away from him, Troy could see the rotting flesh of its face revealing its bone. Its long skeleton fingers that were deformed and broken twisted and twitched as he stood in front of Troy like they just could not wait to dig themselves into him. He saw the jagged hole that Troy had made by stabbing the knife into it a decade ago.

Maromoth looked more like a monster than a human. The jet-black hair trailed down to its waist in those familiar locks of twine-like strands. But it was the eyes, those soulless holes for eyes, that made Troy shudder once again.

I knew from the moment I had you. You were mine for the taking.

Troy only blinked.

It took so long. I had your friend. I had your daughter. Your father. Even your friends' mother and father — even their little girl. Then I got yours. Oh, how I devoured Grace's saddened soul. She cried for you; did you know that? She asked for you when I sucked her soul from her defiled body. But I never wanted her. I wanted you. After all this time, you are finally mine.

Troy stepped forward. Maromoth cocked his head, his dreadful bottomless pits of eyes locked onto him. Troy continued walking, his plan in mind until he was right at Maromoth's feet.

Maromoth cocked the hint of a smile with its peeling face. He grabbed Troy with both hands around the sides of his skull, picking him off the ground as he did so. Partly in pain and partly in fear, Troy closed his eyes, but before he did, he saw the demon open its mouth demonically wide and point it right at him.

Troy could feel a part of him leaving, though he could not exactly describe the sensation.

He let out a cry of agony. The pain he was feeling was excruciating as he felt parts of him, parts of his spirit and soul, being fiercely separated from his body, being sucked into the mouth of Maromoth.

He grabbed at Maromoth's hands that were still firmly

gripped around the base of his head. He felt something—he assumed it was blood but couldn't be exactly sure—leaving his ears and dripping down, covering him and Maromoth.

Troy was dying—he was almost dead. Becky wouldn't make it in time. The plan had failed. He had been so close, but his plan had failed.

Troy took a breath of acceptance. Just as he was about to give up, just as he was about to resign himself to his fate, he heard Grace's voice.

"Daddy?" she called.

He could not speak through the tormenting pain he felt through every inch of his body, but he could think. He could say the thoughts in his mind, and he assumed—no, he hoped—that this would be enough, that in this other world, Grace would hear his thoughts.

Grace, he thought.

"I'm here to help you, Daddy. Mom is about to bring you home," she said, answering Troy's question. "Are you ready?"

I'm ready.

He saw, through his closed eyes, a vision of Becky nodding her head. That was the last thing he saw before the burst of light.

It was all Troy could muster to grab at anything of the demon that he could. What his fingers found was a familiar feeling of a clump of hair.

And then it was all gone.

CHAPTER 31

One breath. Two breaths. Thirty compressions, Becky said to herself again and again as she did them.

One. Two. Compress, compress....

Troy's eyes were staring back at her, but there was no life in them as she gave her rescue breaths and thirty compressions.

"C'mon, Troy! C'mon!" she yelled, giving another round of compressions. Two more breaths. She checked his pulse.

Nothing. Shit!

"Troy, please," she pleaded as she pressed into his sternum with all her might. "Please, don't leave me."

Becky could feel the warm tears streaming down her face, tickling her cheeks as she counted and repeated: *One. Two. Three... twenty-nine...thirty. One breath, two.*

After another set of rounds, Becky lost count. Her arms were starting to give out, and she didn't know how much longer she could keep going. The blood pooling inside them was starting to burn like fire, and the energy was being zapped from her with every round of compressions.

She didn't know how much force she was putting into Troy, but she knew there was no way it would be enough. She could barely move her arms from compressing his chest. She could hardly move her hands to his face to give him the rescue breaths, they were so heavy.

But she remembered Grace guiding her to Troy.

He made a promise, she had said. *He made a promise that he would end Maromoth forever. Daddy always keeps his promises.*

And Becky knew Grace was right. She knew she couldn't give up. Not yet.

Becky gave another unsuccessful round of compressions. She tilted his head and blew all her air into him, watching his chest rise and then fall, but there was, again, nothing.

Grabbing him by the shoulders, shaking him in a cry, she screamed, "Troy! Don't leave me! Troy!" She blew her final breath of air into his body.

Troy's eyes fluttered. An enormous cough followed, launching water from his system. Becky rolled him to his side as he hacked and blew out another spout of lake water.

"Troy!" Becky sighed in exhaustion, grabbing his face. "Oh, my god. Is it you? Oh, God. It's you. You're alive. You're alive!" she yelled, sobbing. "I thought you were dead. Oh, I thought you were dead."

"I was," Troy coughed up. They laid there together, hand in hand, as Becky sobbed tears of relief.

She felt the words flow out clumsily. She hated this part. This awkward moment where she cracked the door open for more but stood in the doorway, not allowing him through.

***

In a moment, Troy remembered everything that had happened in Black Lake and Grace coming to his aid and rescue. He remembered that burning feeling of his soul being taken from him and Grace reaching out just in time to save him. Troy remembered searching for something of Maromoth to grab onto, to bring him here.

That realization hit him as Troy regained himself, taking

in deep breaths and coming back to life, his body carrying the sensation that whatever had happened, whatever it was he had just gone through with Maromoth, had been reversed by the hand of Grace when she brought him home.

Troy finally spoke again. "He's here, Becky." There was another pause as Troy expelled the last of the water from his lungs in a violent cough and vomiting display. "I got him. He's here." He held up his hand, his fingers locked onto a large clump of black, twine-like hair.

He threw the hair to the ground. Adrenaline must have gotten ahold of him, or at least that was Becky's thought, as he pushed himself to his feet, spinning around.

"Where are you, you bastard!" he screamed. "Where are you hiding? Come out, you son of a bitch! Come out!" He was screaming into the lake, into the woods, and his parents' home. Nothing had shown itself to greet him.

Troy bent down and picked up the knife. "I will kill you; you are a fucking bastard! I will find you, and I will kill you! For Mitch. For Grace. I WILL KILL YOU!" His voice was so strong it burned his vocal cords and threatened to empty the contents of his stomach again.

And so did the smell. As he picked up the knife from the ground, that now-familiar decaying, corrupted, rancid smell filled his nostrils. Troy scanned the area in front of him. There was nothing. He turned around to face his childhood home, and again his vision saw only Becky to his immediate right.

It wasn't what he saw but what he heard that made Troy's blood turn cold.

"Daddy?" It was Grace.

"Daddy?" It said again. "Daddy? Where are you?" Her voice was clear, ringing even, through the beach and yard.

"Where are you, Daddy? I'm scared. Maromoth, he's here, Daddy. He's going to get me. He's going to get *you*. And Mommy, too." She paused. "Help me, Daddy. You want to help me, right? You don't want me to die again, do you? Help me, Dad, please. Give yourself to him, Daddy, so he'll let me go. He said if he could have you, he would let me go."

And that was when Troy saw it—the image of his dead seven-year-old was there again, the version of Grace from the lake, with its rotted, bloated, purple skin. She had no eyes this time, only deep, empty, decomposed eye sockets, just like Maromoth.

Her arm was missing. The maggots were crawling all around the open wound that was leaking that vile liquid blood substance of Maromoth.

Grace's face grinned as she walked toward him, dragging her limp, dead legs. "Do you think I'm pretty?" she asked. "You did this to me, Daddy. Remember?"

Becky shrieked, gagged, and heaved.

Troy stared down the body, the terror gripping him, but he had been here before. He had seen this vision of his daughter. This would be the last time, one way or another.

Becky was whimpering at the sight of Grace. Troy didn't look at her, but he could hear it.

She needs to get out of here, he thought. *She can't see what is about to happen.*

"Becky, get out of here," Troy said calmly, gripping his fingers hard around the knife. "Becky, I need you to run now. As far and fast as you can."

"Troy...." Her voice trailed off.

"Becky, go. Now!" he said forcefully.

In answer, he heard her footsteps. He wasn't sure how many she had taken or where she had gone—he hoped it would be enough. No, it *had* to be enough.

Flipping the knife in his hand, Troy walked toward Grace's decomposed body, and she walked toward him. He gave a battle cry scream as his walk turned into a jog and then into a run.

She smiled at him as he came.

He barely registered what had happened as he brought his hand up, only feet from her. With as much force as he could, he jammed the blade into the top of her skull.

The putrid liquid came shooting out the top of her head, spraying his clothes, the now familiar stench filling the air. The maggots followed the black blood, crawling from out of her head, coming by what appeared to be hundreds at a time.

She laughed. Grace's body erupted that terrible, deep demonic laugh so loud that it filled the woodlands surrounding the home and the lake.

Grace's possessed body grabbed him by the arm and threw Troy to the ground hard enough to take his air out of him. He thought he heard Becky scream, but he couldn't tell over the ringing in his ears.

In an instant, Troy felt the weight of his daughter mounting atop of him, though for the forty pounds she weighed, he was pinned to the ground.

She grinned at Troy, the maggots still crawling from the gaping wound in her skull. They made their way onto Troy's body, trying to burrow themselves feverishly into his skin. Troy screamed. Grace's body gagged and gagged, appearing to choke. Then the flood of maggots came from her mouth by the thousands, pouring onto Troy, covering his face, landing in his mouth, landing on his eyes.

Troy, still clutching the knife in his hand, raised it and swung for the head of his daughter, plunging it into her cheek. The pressure let off him just slightly, and he tossed her body to his side.

Getting up as quickly as he could, he brushed the burrowing maggots away with the knife, cutting himself in the process. He was bleeding from the holes, but that paled to being rid of the ones that had managed to latch themselves on to him.

Grace rose to her feet, more putrid black liquid and maggots crawling from the wound in her cheek. She grabbed one that was free of the mass and had crawled to her eye. She flung it with her fingers, much like one might flick away a mosquito. It landed on Troy's shoulder. With a wave of Grace's hand, it began to grow and grow. First, it was the size of an inchworm, then a pencil, and finally the size of a snake.

Troy swung at it with the knife, cutting its head where its teeth were beginning to sink into his flesh. He screamed as the terrible pain of these razorblade teeth of the maggot sunk themselves into him. He stabbed it with the knife, and it made a squealing sound, so he did it again and again until it fell from his shoulder.

Troy raised the knife in the air, pointing it at Grace's body, knowing it was the only thing that could damage any of Maromoth or its minions.

"You cannot kill me!" it screamed. "You cannot kill me! No mere mortal can! I am the eater of souls! I will devour you like I devoured your friend. I will feast on your soul like I did your cunt daughter's!"

Grace's body began to split open at its invisible seams following her words. The purple rotted skin stretched to its breaking point and broke open, ripping the flesh and revealing the blood and the maggots underneath. Her body fell to the ground like a shell of an animal that no longer had an inhabitant, and what was left standing in its place was Maromoth himself.

Maromoth reached out his long, skeleton fingers, grabbed Troy by the throat, and with a simple flick of his arm, flung Troy to the ground.

There was a moment when time froze as Troy realized the events that had happened. His ears were ringing hard, and his vision had been blurred from falling on his head. He heard the icy snarl of Maromoth approaching, but there was nothing he could do. The sound got closer and closer, hungrier and hungrier, like a wild, rabid dog who had not eaten in days and now stood atop its prey.

Seconds later, he felt the presence of Maromoth over his face, the smell of death on his breath. It reached out to Troy, caressing his face like a low, dreadful breeze.

Troy was pinned to the ground, the weight of Maromoth's beastly strength holding him in place, making him unable to move.

The knife was only a few feet away, lying on the beach. Try as he might, Troy was unable to find his own strength to reach it.

He could feel Maromoth and his eyeless sockets searching for him now, drinking in his resentful, sorrowful soul through his own eyes. He felt the presence of them holding him there, gluing him to the spot and cementing his vision to the ghoul.

Is this it? Troy wondered. *Is this how it ends? Have I failed?*

It was as if the memories of his past were coming to life now. That night on the icy lake with Mitch, watching as his best friend was taken down into the lake's depths, never to be seen again. That feeling of acceptance, even longing, for death, crossed over him again.

Then it was gone, replaced by the vision of his daughter and his hands on her limp body, pushing up and down on her chest repeatedly. He felt that feeling of her ribs cracking underneath the pressure, the feeling he would never forget as it moved through his hands and up his arms.

Ten compressions and then a breath, or was it two? Or was it thirty breaths and a compression? That was what he had asked himself before the realization that, in the end, it didn't matter because his baby was gone. No amount of CPR classes would have saved Grace from this otherworldly fate. She was destined, as Troy realized now that he was, that Mitch had been, to the fate of Maromoth.

That was when he heard Becky scream.

Troy looked away, searching for her. She was supposed to have run away, but it was obvious to Troy now that she had not. His eyes danced everywhere but at the eyeless Maromoth. If he were to die here at his hand, would she be safe? Would Maromoth take his victory and leave? Or would he go for her, too?

He would fight it; he had to.

Maromoth grabbed his face with his rotting fingers. The foul metacarpals guided his head and eyes back, even as Troy shook with all his might, to his line of vision. Troy closed his eyes hard.

With a careful but forceful flick, Maromoth opened Troy's eyelids and once again peered into his soul.

There was the funeral where Troy could barely feel. The hospital when he had attempted to take his own life. Becky just sat in the chair and never said more than a handful of sentences to him at one time, and again he saw the disdain in her eyes. The pain, too. The pain he had caused. He saw the day she blinked it away, and it was all just muddled into hate.

And Troy packed his things without a word from Becky because all the words had been said already, and they never made a damn of a difference anyhow.

Troy felt that feeling again—that feeling of acceptance, even longing, for death. For his pain to end. His life had been a waste, hadn't it? It was filled with pain, sorrow, and loss. Guilt ate him alive day after day. For years on end, he had swallowed a handful of pills to level his own sadness, but everyone around him knew it was just a pack of gauze on the misery he felt every single day.

He deserved this. He wanted it. He locked eyes with the

demon, and as he rolled through his memories, through his life of anguish. Troy let him without a fight.

A fiendish gasp of pleasure and evil escaped the open mouth of Maromoth, and that was when Troy knew it was almost time for the end. He braced himself, but he didn't look away.

It is almost time. It will all be over soon. The hurt. The pain. The guilt. It will all be over....

"Troy." He remembered that voice, but Troy could not tell whose it was.

"Do not give up," it said.

Troy opened his eyes in disbelief to see someone he had not seen in over twelve years.

His childhood best friend Mitch was standing in front of him, dressed in the same clothes he had worn on that terrible night. But he looked different now, older. It was Mitch as he would have been had he not been claimed that night at the lake.

"Mitch? It can't be," Troy asked. "Is that really you?"

"Yes. Yes, it is me, Troy."

"H...H...How? How are you here?"

"It isn't important. Just know that I am."

There was a silent pause before Troy let out what he had been feeling for years. For a decade. "Mitch, I'm sorry." Troy began to cry. "I'm so sorry."

"I know. I know. It wasn't your fault. It was Maromoth, Troy. You know that now. That's why I'm here," he said patiently.

"What do you mean?" Troy asked.

"I'm here to make sure you fulfill your promise," Mitch said, softly but assuredly. "You promised you would kill Maromoth."

"I'm not sure I can, Mitch. I thought I could, but I can't. I'm sorry," Troy replied.

"You didn't promise me, Troy. You promised her." Mitch outstretched his hand as he helped Grace step into view.

"Hi, Daddy."

Troy stopped. Every thought in his mind went blank. "Grace?" Troy's voice trembled as he spoke.

"Daddy, you can't go. Not yet," Grace said softly. "You told me you would beat it, Daddy. You said you would kill it for me and Mommy and Uncle Mitch. Don't give up, Daddy. Please."

Troy threw his head to the side away from Maromoth, searching for the voice of his daughter.

Grace was standing only a few feet from him, just behind the knife. Her hair was back in a single braid, the way he and Becky both liked it. She was wearing the very dress she had picked out to surprise Becky with Mother's Day pictures so many years ago.

"You promised, Daddy," she whispered. "You promised."

"I know, Gray. I know. I'm just not strong enough. I'm sorry."

Reaching out for him, both Grace and Mitch touched his hand with their own. Troy felt the warmth and tingle of their fingers running through him like electricity.

"I...I can feel you!" Troy yelled, astounded. "Grace! Mitch! You're here! I can feel you!"

"We're here to help you, Daddy. Uncle Mitch and I are here to help you keep your promise," Grace said.

"You can do this, Troy. You beat it once. It's time to end this for good," Mitch followed.

Mitch and Grace stepped to Troy.

"You can do it, Dad," she said, her voice sure and full. She bent down and kissed him on his forehead. "I love you, Daddy."

"I love you, Grace."

Closing his eyes, Troy reached his arm forward for the knife, guided by the presence of his best friend and his daughter. With their strength, he inched his fingers forward and forward until they wrapped themselves around the weapon's handle.

With a war cry and the warmth of his daughter and Mitch's hands laced over his, he thrust the blade into the side of Maromoth's skull. He pulled it from the head and again launched it through the face of the thing. One time. Two times. The putrid black blood of the thing sprayed out of the open holes like a geyser, going in all directions and covering his face and chest in it.

The stink of the liquid leaving Maromoth was so foul it made his stomach turn, and it burned his skin on contact like some kind of acid, but Troy was not fazed. He flipped the body from him and proceeded to turn and pierce the demon again and again.

Troy was unsure how long he had been going at it, though it had been long enough for the entire right side of his body to ache and writhe with cramps, but he did not care. He would stab and stab and stab away, like a monster himself, if he needed to.

It was only the call of Becky who made him come out of his emotional frenzy.

"Troy," Becky whispered.

At the sound of her voice, he felt his body give out, leaving the knife in its mouth with his final blow. He then rolled back over and vomited twice before he came back to himself and stood up.

Becky and Troy were standing over the body of Maromoth.

It lay now on the ground, defeated. The puncture wounds from Troy's knife were leaking its liquid black blood, and also a smoke of the same kind from every hole Troy had dug into it. Laying there now, it was reminiscent of a burned-out fire, whose embers were smoking away the last of its heat and flame.

"Is this it?" Troy asked.

"It must be," Becky replied, nudging his shoulder.

Troy looked over to the direction she gestured to and saw, just a few yards from them, the thin, spiritual lines of his friend and his daughter. Mitch gave him the slightest nod of approval—the one he had given Troy so many times in their youth—and then disappeared into the air.

"You did it, Daddy," Grace said.

"We love you, Grace," Troy and Becky said in unison, tears streaming down their faces.

"I love you," Grace replied, then she was gone.

CHAPTER 32

1 Year Later

Becky bent down to place the flowers on Grace's grave, her baby bump underneath her dress nudging into her upper thighs. She was still getting used to the fact that she was pregnant, though she was glad the morning sickness was over with.

She took a big sigh, setting the flowers neatly against the headstone before standing back up and leaning into Troy. He wrapped his arms around her, cupping her pregnant belly.

Everyone was there.

Louis, who was now cancer-free (described by all doctors as a miracle, but somehow he had the inclination that indeed it was a miracle, even if he didn't believe in such things), stood next to his wife Tracy, just behind his son and daughter-in-law.

Becky's parents were there too, immediately to Troy's right. It had taken a little time for them to welcome Troy back into the family, but after a few short weeks together again and more than a handful of trips to Black Lake to stay with Becky, they had given their approval. Not that it mattered since Becky had made up her mind she was moving to Chicago as soon as the house sold — which, in fairness, did take some time. Black Lake was still not the place for newcomers.

Becky soaked it all in. This was a touch bittersweet, but for the first time in a long time, it was more sweet than bitter. This was such a different year than any of the others she remembered since Grace's death. For the first time in a long, long time, they were celebrating Grace and the short life she had lived.

Becky could feel Grace there too like she was standing over them all with a big smile on her face. She was sure Grace must have been watching Troy and Becky celebrating the rekindling of their family and the addition of another beautiful baby, this time a boy, in just eight more weeks. Mitchell Daniel Kender was what they had decided on in the single bedroom apartment in Chicago.

She felt the softest warm touch against her free dangling hand. She looked over to see the spirit of her daughter lace her little fingers in hers. Becky smiled.

"Hi, Mommy," she whispered.

Grace had stayed Troy and Becky's little secret, even after the haunting of Black Lake was over. Even if anyone would believe them, it was their secret to keep and keep it they did. To that end, Becky only responded with a small tilt of her head and the hint of a smile.

They would see her sometimes, Becky and Troy. Sometimes they would see Grace together, sometimes separately. It was never more than a second or two, maybe three at the most. But they would see her, and it would bring them the comfort they needed, knowing their baby was still in existence and her soul intact.

Troy saw Mitchell and the rest of the Hampway family, as well. But only one more time, a few days after the dark events came to an end. They were all outside of the old Hampway home when Troy went there one last time before leaving town to return for the school year in Chicago.

Becky wasn't there, but Troy told her. He told her they all gave a silent nod and waved. A job well done and a thank you. Becky knew it to be true. After that, everything started to feel right in the world.

After a minute, Grace spoke again. "I don't think the three of you are going to fit in that little bedroom."

Becky snorted the smallest of a laugh.

"What?" Troy asked.

"Just thinking, we're probably going to need a bigger place," she said, rubbing the top of her belly.

"Yeah. Yeah, I guess we will, huh?" Troy replied. A minute passed before Troy spoke again, this time his voice somber and curious, "Becky, do you think she would be happy? Grace, I mean. Do you think she *is* happy, wherever she is?"

"Yeah, I think she is," Becky said, peacefully. She nudged Troy, nodding to Grace. "See for yourself," she whispered so only he could hear. "I think she's pretty happy for us."

T.C. Breen, a Michigan native and author of *The Haunting of Black Lake*, has been a devout fan of horror entertainment from an early age. Using inspiration from his favorite authors, such as Stephen King, Anne Rice, John Saul and Peter Straub, Breen aims to strike emotions in readers by bringing imperfect and relatable characters with real-world struggles, relationships and problems. These characters are then thrust into a unique and often paranormal filled world that grips and terrifies you. Although a true horror fan at heart, T.C. Breen believes that consuming many genres from many authors is one of the best ways to hone the craft of your own work, and when not reading horror, Breen enjoys works in fantasy, young adult and the occasional romance novel.

T.C. Breen, a public-school teacher, now resides with his family in his new home state of Utah with his wife and daughter.

www.ingramcontent.com/pod-product-compliance
Lightning Source LLC
Chambersburg PA
CBHW030242200626
46816CB00002BA/473